RETRIBUTION

Time to Stop Running

Tania Park

National Library of Australia Cataloguing-in-Publication entry
Creator: Park, Tania, author.
Title: Retribution: time to stop running/ Tania Park.
ISBN: 9780994284723 (Paperback)
ISBN: 9780994284730 (Ebook)
Subjects: Suspense fiction. Love stories.
Dewey Number: A823.4
Book Cover Design: Pickawoowoo, Laila Savolainen
Interior Design: Pickawoowoo Publishing Group

Printed & Channel Distribution
Lightning Source | Ingram (USA/UK/EUROPE/AUS)

Dedication

This book is dedicated to John Harman, author and ghostwriter. It was during a short story workshop that John gave me the skills and inspiration to pen my first short story, for which I was awarded third prize in a competition. Amazed that the judge, a notable author, enjoyed my written words, I became determined to better my skills.

To this end, I attended all of John's workshops on novel writing at the University of Western Australia and wrote copious notes. Each time I returned home, I edited the three novel length manuscripts I had already written, according to the gospel of John Harman. Each time my work improved exponentially. I have read and studied those notes many times, putting into practice the skills learned into my later manuscripts, which haven't required any where near the same number of edits.

I can never express how much I appreciate John's expertise.

My heartfelt thanks also go to Ted Witham, a fellow writer's group member, for his excellent editorial advice. I never see an editor's comments as negative. There must be a reason for someone with such experience to pick out an area of concern. I give those suggestions a great deal of thought before making appropriate changes. In this instance the suggestions have made a much better story.

My final thank you is to Dr Alan Hancock, who gave me the first line to this book in yet another workshop. It was supposed to begin a paragraph as an exercise in creative thinking. My paragraph morphed into a chapter and the ideas just kept flowing. This book is the result.

Other titles;

Mistaken

A great read. Kept me up all night wondering till the end where you would take me.
Wendy Pleas – lover of books.

Hooked me on the second page. Perfectly balanced with intrigue, suspense, romance. Everything in the right measure. Jana Hardy – journalist.

A tale filled with suspense, a potential romance and a couple of twists and turns.
Lisa Berson – author and blogger.

Tania masterfully creates an intriguing book from page one and carries it through to the very end. Keeps the reader turning pages – wanting answers. Jodie How – writer.

The Only Way I Know – an inspirational true story about overcoming the roadblocks life throws at you.

Coming soon;

Yes, the next one is called '*Blind Justice.*' When pianist, Christine Mears meets detective Ben Somers, she becomes a victim of a drug smuggling gang.

Chapter One

Shoving with her shoulder to force a path through the throng, Amy fought for breath as she ran as fast as the crowd would allow. Sharp talons of terror gripped tight around her windpipe as she ignored the squeals and grunts from the workers she bumped into as they streamed from the Perth city buildings. All she could manage were a few mumbled apologies although by the time the words came out she was way past her victims. She didn't care if she caused any injuries as she ploughed through. She couldn't take the time to care.

He was here.

Somewhere.

How he'd found her she had no idea. But it was Rico. Of that she was certain. Even though she had been assured of her safety, his scent, the strong spicy aftershave he always used, had been the first hint that had sent her innards into a coil of fear and her nerves on instant alert. Then the touch, followed by harshly whispered words growled into her ear were all she needed to confirm his presence. Having been grabbed from behind she hadn't seen his face but she knew… just knew… he had found her.

Keeping her head down her eyes skittered from side-to-side as she tried to avoid the masses heading for home after a long day of work, but at the same time taking as much shelter as she could between bodies and shoulders. Mostly she saw dark smudges, blots of dried chewing gum and discarded flattened cigarette butts between waves of feet covered in shoes and sandals in every style and colour imaginable. She moved with the surge, knowing it would be useless to fight against it. For once she was thankful for the teeming stream of robotic humans, using them as shields. Normally she hated having to be a part of the city throng during rush hour but it had been impressed upon her that it was easier to be a nonentity in a crowded city than in the smaller regional towns she'd grown up in and much preferred.

'Watch it, lady!'

A shiver snaked down her spine as long fingers gripped into the flesh of her bare arms and a hot breath following the angry words licked against the side of her face. She tensed her body in defensive readiness as she felt herself being hoisted from her feet then thrust aside. With her arms held so tight her only weapon to attack were her legs. She could do legs but before she had a chance to bunch her muscles for a kick, she landed awkwardly with one sandal shod foot sliding off the edge of the kerb. She shot her arms out to maintain her balance, dislodging the hands gripping her, but the suddenness of the action caused her to waver precariously before gravity took over and she began tumbling onto the road.

A loud horn blasted then a squealing of brakes registered through the turmoil in her brain at the same time as a pair of arms grasped her around her waist and hauled her upright back onto the even ground of the pavement.

'Have you got some kind of a death wish?' The same voice from a few seconds ago ground out the words as she was jerked onto solid ground and slammed against a wall of muscle, the arms tightening around her upper body like a vice, squeezing the air from her already tortured lungs. Her mind registered only one lucid fact: the man holding her was not Rico. It was a different voice, a different strength and the masculine odour was not the same. This man wore a less invasive aftershave, something with a hint of spice and something sweeter. God, why was she even thinking about aftershave?

A gush of hot air hit as a heavy vehicle skidded to a halt mere centimetres from her still held body. She felt her chest heaving, sucking in mouthfuls of air that seemed to scorch the lining of her lungs. Then it registered how putridly hot the day was.

'Are you all right?' The tension around her chest eased as her saviour took one step back but he kept his hands in a firm hold on her upper arms, preventing her from moving. As if she could move even if she wanted to. An adrenaline surge seemed to have turned her legs into lead weights and nailed them to the ground.

With her mind whirling and having little comprehension about exactly what had just happened in a few split seconds, she glanced up into an ordinary looking face marred by angry frown lines. 'Yes, thank you.'

Then she remembered. Rico was here. Not daring to move from the security of the stranger's arms, Amy peered around each of the man's shoulders, searching the still surging crowd for any sign of Rico.

'What the hell did you think you were doing?'

Jerking in fright as another hand landed heavily on her shoulder, Amy spun her head. The skin across her shoulders tightened in a frisson of fear and her lungs took a holiday from breathing leaving her last breath lodged in a throat that had constricted. It took a moment to subdue her racing heart when it registered that this man wasn't Rico either.

Her eyes honed in on a logo sewn onto the pocket of a pale olive green shirt. The same image adorned the side of the bus that was shaking rhythmically as it idled right behind the uniformed man who was standing below the kerb. She slid her eyes closed as she waited for her heart to quit hammering and wondered if the day could get any worse.

'I'm sorry. I was knocked off my feet.' She turned her head slightly and glared at the man still holding her, sure it was the same person who had bumped her off balance.

His returning look was sardonic. 'Because you were barging through everyone without a care in the world,' he ground out.

'I was being chased!' At the glimpse of an ebony head of hair from the corner of her eye, Amy stiffened. 'Oh, God, I have to get away!' she gasped as she watched Rico, who was standing less than three metres away on the top of a set of four stone steps, lift one hand and form the shape of a gun. It didn't take a genius to figure out his mouthed words as he pulled the imaginary trigger twice. *Gotcha.*

'Who the hell is that?' asked the bus driver.

Twisting her head around Amy noticed both men next to her were staring in Rico's direction. When she glanced back, Rico was gone. Struggling free of the stranger's arms, she peered in all directions, searching the continual spilling crowd.

'Where did he go?'

'Into the building.' Amy winced when the man grasped her shoulder again. Any more jolts like that and her heart would probably give out altogether. 'Do you want to explain what is going on? You almost got yourself killed?'

Amy felt a hand cup under her chin forcing her to look up. This time the touch was far more gentle and warm. Even compared to her above average height for a woman, the man was very tall. Apart from that he was ordinary looking with features she supposed were classed as ruggedly handsome under a head of brown hair that was in need of a trim. The frowning wrinkles had gone but she could tell he was still irate. So she'd bumped him but that didn't mean he had a right to become so uppity.

'I have to go,' she said to the man then turned to the driver who was still standing just outside the front door of the bus, his arms akimbo. A line of curious eyes watched from the bus seats.

'Where are you headed?' she asked the driver.

'The hills, why?'

'I need to get as far away from here as I can.'

'That man threatened you. Shouldn't you call the police?'

A snort of derision escaped from Amy's mouth before she could hold it back. To prevent any unguarded words from slipping out she planted one hand over her lips. How much could she tell these two? Could she trust them? Then she remembered - Rico had found her and the only way that could have happened was by someone in authority telling him where she was. She could trust no one apart from her lawyer and her father and they were both dead.

'I can't go to the police and I can't involve anyone in this. It just isn't safe. The last person who tried to help me disappeared.'

'What do you mean disappeared?' asked the man, jolting Amy as he gripped her arms tighter and held her right in front of his body. Even though she felt desperate to get away, the firm hold this stranger had on her prevented any hope of escape but at the same time she felt safe. Safe with a man? Unbelievable but even with Rico so near he wouldn't dare grab her again when she was so close to others. For a brief moment she hoped this man would never let her go then reality struck. She didn't even know who or what this man was. He could even be one of Rico's cohorts.

'Disappeared as in she hasn't been found yet. There is no proof but he,' she pointed to the top of the steps, 'is responsible. I know that for sure.' An uncontrolled shiver wove down her spine as she dropped her head. 'I'm sure she is dead.'

'What the hell have you got yourself involved in? Are you wanted by the police?' asked the man as he shook her twice.

Amy couldn't hold back the gush of laughter that gurgled from her throat in a stuttering accompaniment to the shakes. Even though she knew it was ridiculous, she recalled a childhood memory of humming with her uncle patting her rapidly on the back with cupped hands. The resultant drumming sound was similar to her stammering laugh. 'Oh, no, the police don't want me. They arrested Rico and put him in jail. But they didn't tell me he was out.'

'I assume the man chasing you is Rico.'

Amy swung her head to look at the bus driver then wondered why he was still standing there. 'Shouldn't you be taking your passenger's home?'

'Oh, hell, yes.' Looking stunned he turned towards the door of the still idling bus. A wave of applause erupted from inside. He muttered something uncouth under his breath as he mounted the two steps.

'Wait!' Amy called. 'I'm coming with you.' She struggled free of strong hands, grasped the shoulder strap of her bag and heaved it higher then stepped onto the bus.

'Here, take this.' Amy turned back to the man. He was holding out a business card.

'Call me on the mobile number if you need any help. I have a brother who is a lawyer. He might be able to give you some assistance.'

Pausing, Amy studied the man's face more intensely. His silver blue eyes looked concerned and appeared to show real empathy. She wavered then reached out and slid the small oblong card from his fingers. 'Thank you for saving me, but I can't involve you.' She turned and hurried up the stairs then flopped into the nearest seat, ignoring the murmur of discontent amongst the passengers and the eyes she felt boring into the back of her head. Knowing she would never involve anyone else in her mess, she searched around for a rubbish bin in which to toss the card. Finding nothing and not being in the habit of littering, she unzipped the front pocket of her bag and dropped the card inside.

At the same time the bus doors hissed shut, the indicator clicked in a steady staccato then the driver eased the articulated tandem vehicle into the stream of peak-hour traffic. Amy dared a glance out of the side window without obviously turning her head. A feeling of dread engulfed her when she noticed the dark Italian features of Rico staring at her from inside the building. Standing directly behind the full-length pane of smoky glass, he was scribbling something in a notebook.

Far out, the bus number. He'll find out where the bus is headed and follow. She had to get off. Rising from her seat, she stumbled towards the driver, trying to maintain her balance as the bus swayed with each change of gears. She grabbed hold of a seat back as the bus ground to a halt and jolted her off balance. Peering through the front window as she steadied herself, she realised they were at traffic lights. Bending at the knees she searched the pavement for Rico. Would he follow and try to get on?

'I won't open the door to him.'

Swinging her head up, Amy caught the driver's eyes in the rear vision mirror above his head. She took the remaining few steps forward. 'How much do I owe you?' she asked as she reached for the zipper on her large leather bag containing her laptop computer as well as her everyday work essentials. The bag went almost everywhere with her to the extent she felt naked without the weight of the strap hugging her shoulder.

'This one is on me.' The man smiled into the mirror then turned his attention to the road as the light turned green. 'Where do you want to get off?'

'I think Rico wrote down this bus number so I need to get far enough away that he can't follow on foot but he'll soon find out which direction this bus is going and once he gets into his car he'll follow until I get off.' She didn't want to think about what would happen then but visions of their last meeting stabbed into her mind and she shuddered.

'In that case I have an idea,' she heard the man call. Amy silently thanked the man for cutting into gruesome memories as she glanced back at his eyes in the mirror.

'I'll be passing the nearby bus station as we leave the city. Why don't I drop you off there? Then you can go inside and find a bus going on a different route. What's your name?'

'Pardon?' Amy couldn't figure out why he needed her name but his idea sounded feasible and besides, her mind was too jumbled to come up with anything better. All she could think of was escaping. Where to, didn't matter.

'I find it hard to carry on a conversation with someone if I don't know their name. But if it is a problem I'll just call you Jane.'

'Oh, there's no problem. I'm Amy, Amy Mac…. Oh, far out, Amy Masters.'

'Sounds like you're not sure of your own name. Are you certain it's not you the police are looking for?' He caught her eye in the mirror again. This time he wasn't smiling, in fact he looked downright accusatory.

Amy could tell he was having second thoughts about the veracity of her story. 'I had to change my name to hide. It's Amy Masters now.' She sighed. 'I guess I'm going to have to change it again. God, what a mess! Why can't he just leave me alone?'

She gripped harder onto the smooth stainless steel pole delineating the driver's cabin as the bus pulled into a bus stop and slid to a standstill. Terrified Rico had followed them Amy scanned the sidewalk for any sign of his dark features. He wasn't tall for a man, which meant he could hide fairly well amongst the people just as she had done to escape him. Three passengers squeezed past her to alight before others surged up the steps. She pulled herself up tight against the pole as they milled at the ticket machine to have their weekly tickets electronically verified before hurrying down the aisle to find any spare seats in the already crowded bus. Suddenly realising there were passengers also entering via a second door in the rear section, Amy craned her neck as she swung her eyes from door to door, checking out each person as they entered.

The tension whooshed from her body when the doors swung shut again with a definitive clang but she in no way felt safe. It wasn't until after the bus was moving in the main stream of traffic down the terrace that she became aware of the driver talking into some sort of microphone. Even straining her ears she couldn't make out the words above the thrumming of traffic and rumble of the bus engine. Behind her the passengers had settled into silence; a silence that further unnerved her as thoughts of what to do next tumbled through her mind.

'You just need to give your name to the security officer at the door.'

The sound of the driver's voice jolted Amy into awareness. 'Thank you, but why give my name? Surely the bus station is an open public space. Err… what is your name?'

'Bill.' He smiled at her in the same mirror. 'And I just called ahead telling the security officer of your plight. Go to him if you suspect your pursuer is around and he'll guide you to any bus you think you need.'

'Thank you… Bill,' she mused. 'My father was called Bill and he was an amazing man. He would have appreciated a namesake giving me assistance as you have.'

'Would have?' Bill turned his attention to pulling into the next stop then glanced at her again as the door swung open.

'He died last year.' Amy drew herself up against the steel pole again, her eyes catching the features of every person clambering onto the bus. She noticed the sighs of relief and hands brushing sweat from brows then remembered how hot it still was outside. Only then did she recall co-workers complaining about the heat as they returned from tea and lunch breaks but having spent the entire day trying to get her layouts at least half finished for an upcoming presentation, she hadn't wasted precious minutes by going out for refreshment. Instead she had munched an apple for lunch while still working and taken mugs of tea and coffee back to her workstation whenever the need arose. As if she had willed it to happen, her stomach emitted an embarrassing rumble, telling her she was in need of substantial sustenance.

Her hand unconsciously patted the leather bag still attached to her hip by way of a wide shoulder strap. There were still a few hours work to complete overnight before she would be satisfied enough to show her boss the progress she had made. She felt more than confident Brendan would be pleased but she wanted to do a bit of tweaking and polishing to sharpen the designs so the customer could see exactly how they would work.

'Are you ready? This isn't a normal stop so you'll have to alight quickly.' Bill's words brought her mind back to the present predicament.

Steadying herself as she made the short way to the top of the steps, Amy grasped the silver handrail, the metal feeling blessedly cool. As the bus drew to a standstill she glanced around outside, taking in the entire length of the almost deserted concrete slabbed pavement shadowed by a row of shady Plane trees. The lack of pedestrians indicated the scarcity of general offices in this part of the city. But traffic was heavy. Vehicles whizzed past down the next lane while the bus held up the vehicles behind. Was Rico in one of those cars? The moment the doors hissed open, Amy moved down the steps. 'I will be eternally grateful,' she called as she stepped onto the kerb and ran for the opening bearing the bus company insignia.

After shooting across the narrow pavement she noticed the uniformed security guard standing against a wall. 'Amy Masters,' she called as she neared. Without waiting for a response she turned to inspect every vehicle as the lane of traffic began moving off. Half expecting Rico to step out of one of the taxis, she felt intense relief when no car stopped to eject an olive skinned Italian.

'Miss Masters.'

Straightening up, Amy spun around to find a tall lanky man standing behind her. His dark features and thick black hair caused a shudder to wind down her back.

'Joe Zurzolo.' He reached out one hand in greeting. 'Bill explained your circumstances. Where do you want to go?'

Italian was her only thought as Amy took a tentative hold of the proffered hand. She knew it was ridiculous to judge every person by the actions of one but Rico had taught her to never trust an Italian. Then Joe's question registered. Where did she want to go? The short answer was as far away from here as she could. The other side of the world was preferable or even some far off planet. She glanced at her watch. Was it less than twenty minutes since she had walked from her building? It felt like an eternity.

'Ma'am?'

The single word was a question as well as a demand, bringing Amy back to the current problem. Where did she want to go? She had no idea. 'I guess I need to get home. I usually catch the 107 from the city.'

'That bus leaves from here but it takes you back into the city first. I gathered from what Bill said that you needed to escape the city. You were being chased, I believe.'

'Yes.' Amy paused to think, her hand rubbing her brow as if it could clear away the turmoil. 'Rico took down the bus number I was on so I'm guessing he will follow that route once he finds out where it is going. He won't waste time hanging around in the city. He saw me get on so knows which way I've gone. Therefore, I feel certain he won't expect me to return.' She glanced towards the heavens. 'I pray he won't.'

'This way then.' Joe grasped her elbow and led the way past a maze of small walls, doors and openings. Even though working hours were over for the general public, there was still a hive of activity in the depot.

The heat slammed into her as Amy stepped onto a vast concrete concourse shimmering with heat haze. To one end was a line of buses in various stages of load and unload. Two stood empty, their doors shut. One had a queue of people staring anxiously at the door then eyes searched the concourse for the missing driver. It was obvious it wasn't time for the bus to leave but impatient passengers, desperate to get out of the heat or to get home, appeared to be willing the driver to appear despite the timetable.

When her elbow was jerked in the opposite direction, Amy turned and struggled to keep up with Joe's long strides as he headed towards the row of empty buses, all parked behind each other. They gleamed in the still fierce rays of the lowering sun.

'I can't believe how hot it is,' said Amy as she swiped at the band of perspiration already forming on her brow.

'The hottest day of the summer, which has caused chaos for us,' said Joe as they walked between two of the glinting green buses.

'How come?' asked Amy.

'Buses tend to overheat after idling so long on steaming roads. It reached forty-six Celsius today. All our spare buses are already out and the mobile mechanics have been on the go all day. Today has been a nightmare. Here we are.' Joe glanced at his watch. 'The driver should be…'

Before Joe could finish the sentence another man arrived. By his uniform, Amy guessed it was the driver. Her instant reaction on seeing the blond buzz cut was, thank goodness he isn't Italian. Within minutes she was headed back into the city. It took only two stops before the bus was jam packed with sweaty bodies seeking escape from the overheated city streets. She could feel tension emanating from silent, frowning commuters, all appearing to be lost in deep thoughts. Probably all just wanting to get home and drown under a cold shower, she thought as the bus travelled her familiar route. It was certainly what she was looking forward to. That and figuring out what the heck she was supposed to do now that Rico had found where she was working.

Landmarks she had seen so often they didn't register passed in a blur as Amy sat in a trance. She felt numb, unable to believe Rico was out of gaol let alone having had tracked her down. She'd moved across the country, changed her name, her appearance and her work. She hadn't contacted any of her old friends to ensure they had no idea where she now lived, or seen her family. In a deliberate and carefully calculated move, Amanda McPherson had disappeared from the face of the world in less than twenty-four hours. In her stead, Amy Masters had arrived in a city on the other side of the continent: a new person - a new life. So how had Rico found her? Why was he even out of gaol?

The *bling* of the bell brought Amy back from her troubled reverie. Realising she was one stop past hers, she shot from her seat and wove through the standing passengers. Once alighted, she headed back down the road. It took only ten metres before sweat was trickling down her spine and between her breasts. Seeking out as much shade as she could, she rounded the first corner and decided to take a zigzag route through the local streets to reach home instead of the more direct way down the main road. She kept close to the fence-line, scooting from tree to tree, lingering in the shade then hastening her steps between to shorten the time she was under the blazing sun. She wished she'd had the forethought to pack a hat when she'd left home in the cool of the morning but she'd had no idea the day was going to be so scorching hot. Maybe watching the weather report would be a good idea.

With only two more corners to go, she knew her face was glowing red from the heat and she was imagining how refreshing a glass of icy water from the fridge was going to be. She rounded the last corner then came to a grinding halt before scooting backwards until she was concealed behind a verge tree. Parked under the shade of a large eucalypt halfway along her street and directly opposite her house was an unfamiliar car. There were two shadows sitting in the front seat. Gut instinct told her that whoever was in that car would be waiting for her. Waiting to tell Rico where she was. Or maybe it was Rico and one of his father's cohorts.

Amy swore under her breath when it dawned on her that if Rico knew where she worked then he sure as hell would also know where she lived. Turning tail, she headed back the way she had come, sending up thanks to any deity listening that she had missed her regular bus-stop. If she had gotten off at the correct one, she would have walked head-on towards that car and been seen without a doubt.

Adrenaline surged when she heard a car engine rumble to life. She couldn't be sure it was the same car but the noise was certainly coming from that direction. Lord, had she been spotted? With panic setting in she began running, guessing she must have been seen in the rear vision mirror. She needed to hide. Glancing around, she spotted an open gate leading into a backyard. After a quick peek down both ways of the street to ensure nothing was coming, she raced across the melting bitumen then down the heat-hazed brick paved driveway. As she darted past the corner of the house, she spied a dark blue blur whiz past at the end of the road. The parked car was the same colour. A screech of brakes had her dive behind two large refuse bins, one dark green, the other a lighter shade but with a bright yellow lid, tucked into the corner of the house. Similar bins dotted the verge along the roadway since it was rubbish collection day.

***

Enrico Giovonnazzo held the mobile phone to his ear as he tailed the bus. 'Dad, I found her. She's now a blonde but it is definitely Amanda.'

'Did you get it?'

'I only saw her, Dad. There were too many people around for me to get at her. She's on a bus. I'm following it now. I'll grab her when she gets off.' Seeing the bus taillights flash red, Rico slowed, pulled to a halt and cursed. Being so close, he couldn't see the passengers alighting. He craned his neck over the passenger seat but still couldn't see.

'Twenty-four hours, son, that's all you've got.'

'I know, I know, don't sweat.' The bus pulled into the traffic but sitting in such an awkward position Rico got caught out. Two cars passed him before he was able to force his way into the lane, incurring the wrath of several drivers that had to pull up suddenly in a chain reaction. A blast from more than one horn followed him as he eyed the two passengers walking along the footpath then continued trailing the bus when he confirmed neither was Amanda.

'Verteramo and Lo Presti are watching her house,' his father ranted in his ear. 'I'll let them know you are on the way. Make sure you get it today. I didn't pay half a million bucks to get you out of gaol for you to make another stuff up.'

Rico swore under his breath, briefly shut his eyes then slammed the phone shut when his father's words hit home. Stuff up! According to his father, everything Rico had done all his life was a monumental stuff up. He could never do anything right even when he obeyed orders and deals ran as smooth as butter to end in the wanted result.

The only right royal stuff-up he'd made was in losing his grip on his sanity and hurting Amanda in the process. How could he have ever let it happen? And it was his father's fault to start with. Then it registered that this damned bus wasn't heading anywhere near Amanda's home. It was going in the opposite goddamned direction.

'Bitch,' he yelled as his fist hit the steering wheel. Then he frowned and his mouth turned up into a smile. 'No you're no bitch, sweetheart,' he said as he withdrew his favourite photo of Amanda from the pocket of his navy shirt and glanced at it. The photo was well worn, having never left his proximity for five long years. 'I was a fool. I did this all wrong, frightened you when all I wanted was to speak to you, apologise and beg your forgiveness.' But unable to hold back he had to go and reach out and touch her soft skin. It felt just the same as he'd remembered – smooth, silky and warm. He wasn't sure if it was his touch or the rasp in his voice when he said her name that frightened her and caused her to run off. He snorted. He'd been so choked up at seeing her again that his voice had come out hoarse and rough. But he knew, deep down, that Amanda would have been on the alert and wary and he didn't blame her. So what the hell was he supposed to do now?

The bus pulled into another stop where three business-suited men alighted. Even though this bus was heading east instead of west, she had to be on it – he'd seen her mount the steps. Maybe, since she now knew he was looking for her, she was leading him on a wild goose chase. Cursing, he decided that to not follow was insane and besides her house was being watched. Either way they had her.

Chapter Two

'Put your hands behind your head and come out!'

Startled by the loud demand, Amy lurched around so quickly she lost her balance, hitting her head against the brick wall as she toppled from her crunched up toes to her hip.

'Far out!' she mumbled under her breath as she scrambled to her feet while rubbing at the side of her head. 'You scared me half to death,' she shouted at the voice since she couldn't see to whom it belonged. But it certainly wasn't Rico.

'Hands!' The barked order brooked an immediate response. Amy hitched up the shoulder strap of her bag and gripped her fingers behind her head over the elastic scrunchie holding her ponytail in place.

By the way the man was yelling Amy felt sure he was one of the men from the car. Either that or an officer of the law, the way he was spitting out demands. But when she spied slippered feet poking from the edge of the corner, she wasn't so sure.

'I don't mean you any harm. I was hiding. There's a man after me.' She prayed her quivering voice sounded more definite to the owner of the slippers than it did to her.

'Come out slowly.'

She crept, edging her way behind the bins then stepping onto a patch of lush green lawn until she had a full view of the man. The imposing bear of a man was quite a shock since she'd expected an elderly person from the slippers. This man, she guessed, was only in his early forties, if that. The incongruity of well-pressed suit trousers over the shabby pale grey corduroy slippers brought a smile to her face. The well-worn slippers, frayed at the edges and with a tiny hole at one toe, were obviously favourites.

'You find this amusing?' He didn't sound amused but she couldn't suppress a gurgle of laughter.

'The slippers with the suit,' she gasped as she fought to regain her composure. 'The clothes tell me understated quality - an astute but fair-minded businessman. The slippers tell me an entirely different story.'

'And that would be?'

She wasn't sure but she thought she detected a twitch on the corner of his mouth. That slight movement eased her fear somewhat. When he dropped the broom he had been wielding as a weapon, Amy lost all control. The poor man looked so darn ridiculous. Giggles bubbled forth until she planted a hand over her own mouth then bit on the inside of her cheek to gain control. 'I'm sorry, but the slippers tell me you are a real softie and you look so…. so ludicrous. That broom is hardly a weapon.' But his size was and he looked to be very fit. Even with her defensive skills she wouldn't want to tackle the man and wouldn't want to try.

Her words were met with stunned silence. Amy could do nothing but stare until the sound of a car driving slowly down the street brought her back to the reason she was standing in a stranger's backyard with her hands clasped behind her head, grinning like some inane idiot. 'Oh, God! I need to hide.'

The man's demeanour altered in an instant. 'Do you mind telling what is going on?'

'Can we go inside? That car.' Amy waggled her fingers in the vague direction from whence the still running motor was coming. It sounded as though the car was cruising down the street searching for her.

'Who is in the car?'

'I'm not sure,' she lied, 'but I was almost accosted when I left work this evening. I was grabbed and threatened. I live just around the corner. Number thirty-seven. When I arrived home there was a car with two men sitting inside parked under a tree outside my home. Look, I can explain more but I really need to be out of sight.'

The sound of slamming doors followed by approaching footsteps echoing on the paving bricks had Amy duck back behind the rubbish bins. She must have looked terrified because the man grabbed her by the elbow then shoved her around a second corner towards the rear of the modern brick home then through an open sliding glass door. She felt the instant relief of cooling air as he slid the door closed then yanked an open-weave drape across the opening. Amy gasped when she spied through a side window two large human shapes emerge from the corner then begin searching the grounds. The first place one man looked was behind the bins where she had been only seconds ago. His shape through the barely opaque curtains showed a tall man with broad shoulders but nowhere near as big as the man hovering over her inside.

'Far out!' Amy whispered, her hands rising to her mouth.

'Come with me!' The man physically turned her around and pushed her ahead of him across smooth tiles, through an archway, down a tiled hallway then into a smaller room. A large modern desk in one corner containing a range of computer-ware, a wall of glass-enclosed bookshelves and two swivel chairs told her it was an office. Piles of books and files indicated the room was well used. Terrified of being seen, Amy glanced at the window, her shoulders slumping in relief when she saw tightly closed slats of varnished wooden Venetian blinds.

'Tell me why I shouldn't go outside to let those two men know you are in here.' The man indicated for Amy to sit before sinking into the other chair. Folding his arms across a substantial chest made him look very serious and forbidding.

Amy plonked down, finding the chair to be of the very best quality and extremely comfortable. The smell from the whoosh of air as she landed, told her that the dark green covering was leather. She unslung the shoulder strap and dropped her bag to the floor beside her. 'It's quite a long story but I had a man put in gaol five years ago?'

'Why, what did he do?'

Amy could feel the blood rush from her face. This was something she tried so hard to erase from her memory. Recalled vivid pictures flooded her mind. 'What didn't he do?' she murmured to herself then cleared her throat.

'He almost killed me.' Her voice came out stronger. 'Then while he was in gaol he harassed me with written threats and emails. When he was freed he was going to make me pay were the main gist of his threats. The authorities gave me a new identity. I moved interstate and changed my entire life. I thought I was safe. Today Rico was waiting for me as I stepped outside my place of work.' Amy shuddered then paused.

'Go on.' The man reached over and touched her hand, his gentleness belying his enormous size.

Feeling very uncomfortable about disclosing personal details to a virtual stranger, Amy glanced around the room. Soft green painted walls were clear of adornments except for one picture – an oil-painted landscape. It appealed to her. 'He grabbed me,' she said as she swung her gaze back to the man. Her eyes caught a single thread on the ground. 'Threatened me and tried to drag me along with him. I wriggled free and ran.' Then she gabbled as she related the story, her words running into each other as though she were still running.

'I see. I'm James Ward by the way.' He held out a hand in greeting and smiled. She wondered whether the smile was meant to ease her discomfort – if so, it failed. Her innards were still churning and her heart felt as though it had just completed a marathon.

'Amy. Amy Masters.' She shook the proffered fingers that literally swallowed her entire hand then dragged it free and sank back into the seat. His nearness was unnerving. 'I don't know what to do. I can't go home. Rico knows where I live,' she said to the same thread on the floor.

A loud banging at the door interrupted Amy. She shot from the chair causing it to spin around. 'Please don't answer that?' This time her eyes were planted firmly on James.

James rose far more sedately and steadied Amy's chair. 'I promise I won't let them know you are here,' he said as he made for the door. 'But with an open gate, it is fairly obvious someone is at home or at least that someone ran into my yard. I was probably seen driving in since I had only arrived minutes before you. I left the gate open after I dragged in the rubbish bins from the kerb. To not respond would make it apparent I have something to hide.'

He made sense but a sensation of dread felt like a lead mantle had fallen over her and weighted her into the ground as she watched him leave. Would he give her away? Not about to take any chances, she searched the room for a hiding place. Unable to find anything remotely large enough for her to hide behind, or in, she crept to the door then poked her head out before searching both ways up and down the passage. She heard a mumble of voices then a clearer, louder expression of shock from James.

'Police?'

The single word jarred in her mind. Why were the police looking for her? But she knew and the knowledge was more alarming than just having Rico on her tail. Not waiting a second longer, Amy leapt into the passage and headed for the nearest door. She turned the silver knob, shoved the door open then stepped inside, dragging the door closed as she glanced around. The king-sized bed with a solid base afforded no safe place to hide but a bank of painted wardrobes along one entire wall looked promising. Trying desperately to not make any noise, she crept rapidly on tiptoes and gingerly eased one door open only to find a row of drawers with a shelf across the top. The second door yielded a double row of hanging rails. Ignoring the top row containing a range of shirts all hanging according to colour, she dived into the lower row amongst neatly hanging trousers then crawled to the end and arranged the hangers as best she could to cover her concertinaed legs. The rattle of metal hooks swinging on a metal rail sounded ominously loud and caused her breath to hitch in her throat.

A definite musky masculine odour gave Amy the distinct impression James was a single man. There was no doubt she was in his room but there was not a single hint of feminine perfume in the air. Casting her mind back, she fought to clarify what she had glimpsed in the brief scan of the room. Dark bedcovers, no female fripperies scattered around and bare bedside tables apart from a lamp on one side only verified her first thoughts.

'You can come out now!'

Scared witless at the suddenness of the voice, Amy swore under her breath as the wardrobe door opened.

'Will you quit scaring me half to death?' she mumbled as she peered between two pairs of pressed jeans. Pressed? Who presses jeans, she thought to herself then uttered aloud, 'Did you let them in?'

'Ah! The police. You seemed to forget the bit about the police searching for you.'

She didn't like the way he said, ah, so figured now was definitely the time to act dumb. 'The police?' she squeaked. 'Why do the police want me?'

'Maybe you should come out of my wardrobe and begin telling me the truth. I can easily call them back.' He held up a small white rectangular card and waved it around in the air. It reminded her of her frantic race from work and the man who offered his help.

'I have the number right here.' His other hand patted the shirt pocket on one side of his chest. He'd removed his tie and unbuttoned the two top buttons of his shirt in the brief time he'd been away. 'And my mobile phone.'

'So you didn't tell them I was here?'

'I seem to recall making you a promise. Amongst other things, I am a man of my word. But I will have no hesitation in phoning them if I think you are jerking me around. Now come out.'

With his voice becoming demanding, Amy realised she couldn't stay curled up in a stranger's wardrobe forever. She crawled out on her knees then turned to align the row of clothes in some sort of neat order.

'Leave those.'

A hand descended onto her shoulder then unceremoniously spun her around. 'I don't mind entertaining beautiful young women in my bedroom but this particular woman has some explaining to do before I trust her verity, even remotely.' He frog-marched her back into the study then forced her back into the same chair. 'Talk. And it had better be good.' Just to make her feel even more uptight, he tugged his chair closer so they were almost knee-to-knee. Even though they weren't actually touching she could feel his nearness.

'Why are you hiding from the police?' he demanded.

'I'm not, well, not really.'

'It doesn't look that way to me.' James folded his arms as he leaned back, giving him that overbearing forbidding look again and giving her the feeling of claustrophobia and intimidation.

'Okay. Rico was a cop. Cops tend to stick together. They stand up for each other; defend each other. You have no idea how hard it was for me to get the authorities to believe me when Rico…' She paused and gulped down rising bile. Just the thought of that day made the sensation of terror return. 'It was only when I sought the services of a female lawyer that I was able to press charges.'

'What did he do to you?' James screwed his eyes as though thinking.

'Oh, God.' Amy felt herself shrivel up inside. 'He raped me,' she managed to force out in a harsh whisper. 'Beat me up and then left me for dead,' she managed to add before her throat closed over.

'Hell, I'm sorry.' James leant forwards and gently squeezed her forearm. He sounded sorry, which was almost Amy's undoing. She felt tears well but fought them back. She didn't do tears any more. No tears, no tears, she chanted in her mind.

'It was five years ago. I try not to let the memories surface but after today I'm fighting a losing battle.' Her unladylike sniff sent a rising heat to her cheeks. Feeling mortified, she covered her face with her hands.

'I still don't understand why the police are looking for you.' James eased her hands from her face to show her a look of deep concern.

'Nor do I but my guess is that Rico has spun them some story. He probably told them he was still with the force. If they find me, they'll tell Rico and he will come to get me. He vowed to make me pay. He'll kill me. I know that for sure.'

'That sounds a bit extreme. In fact this entire story sounds unbelievable. What proof do you have?'

'Proof? You want proof?' Her voice rose then realising she sounded like a wild banshee she paused and drew in a calming breath. It took a while before she felt able to speak again. 'You don't believe me do you?' She slumped back in her chair feeling totally dejected. What was she supposed to do now?

'Quite frankly, I don't know what to believe.'

'There is proof. I have proof. The records from Rico's trial must still be around. There are hospital records and there were a lot of photographs taken of my injuries.' Her voice faded. 'A lot of photos.' And she had copies of them all but they were in her house, the house she was too scared to enter. One tear escaped. She swiped it away with a clenched fist then gritted her facial muscles, daring any more to fall. She was over the tears. She was no longer a naïve trusting innocent too afraid to stand up for herself. She was strong and confident and could now defend herself or at least that was what she had been trying to convince herself over the past few years.

'Okay, I can check those but I need full names.'

'You can? How?'

'I'm a lawyer. A QC actually.'

'A lawyer?' Amy shuddered then wrapped her arms around her body to hold in the trembles. 'I can't do this. I can't be responsible for another death. I have to get out of here.' She made to rise from the seat.

'What in heaven's name do you mean?' James dropped from his chair onto his knees and grasped Amy's hands, pulling them away from her body at the same time as he eased her back into the seat.

'That female lawyer I told you about - the one that helped me. She was my lawyer at Rico's trial. She disappeared a week after Rico was sentenced. They never found her.'

***

A sinking sensation of dread had settled deep into Rico's gut. Somehow, he knew Amanda had eluded him. She must have alighted in the few minutes it had taken him to reach his car, get connected to the bus company through directory assistance and find out the route of the bus. Being unfamiliar with the city hadn't helped but he'd caught up with the bus as it crossed the Causeway over the Swan

River. No more than ten minutes had passed before he caught up. They were now rising up and snaking a way through the hills and the bus had emptied considerably. If he'd let her escape his father would be none too pleased. Rico cursed. His damned father was never pleased so what the hell difference did it make. The only positive about the situation was that his pig of a father was on the other side of the continent and besides, what he didn't know didn't matter and Rico sure wasn't going to tell him how Amanda had escaped his clutches.

Only sole passengers alighted at each stop and not one looked anything like Amanda. Pulling into the kerb opposite a large orange and black sign saying *terminus* after the bus drew to a halt, Rico studied the remaining passengers as they stepped from the bus, his dread deepening with each person. Just to be sure Amanda wasn't hiding on the bus he eased from his car and ran across the road then jumped to peer into the windows as he approached the door.

'I'm not leaving for half an hour,' the driver said as Rico stepped onto the bus.

'I'm looking for my wife. She was supposed to be on this bus.' The bus appeared to be empty but he strode down the aisle peering into every single seat.

'I have to check in but the next bus is fifteen minutes behind, she'll probably be on that,' the driver said as he stood, bag in hand and waited for Rico to alight.

'Thanks mate,' Rico said aloud as he stepped onto the ground. 'Not bloody likely,' he muttered to himself as he headed back to his car.

Chapter Three

There was a definite hiss as James sucked in a long slow breath. He rose then wheeled away, one hand brushing through his dark brown hair then resting on his nape where his fingers ran up and down. The silence was electric. Amy didn't dare breathe as she watched and waited.

'Sydney. I heard about that but didn't realise she hadn't been found. But that was years ago. Susie someone wasn't it?'

'Sally Bowers.' As she whispered the name, Amy kept her eyes fixed on James. He looked agitated with a range of emotions flittering across his face as he paced around the small room, his size making the space feel oppressive. 'So you know why I can't involve anyone else in my life. I still can't forgive myself for Sally's death. I wouldn't be able to cope with someone else dying because of me.'

'But you don't know she's dead.' James turned to face her then stilled.

A cross between a snort and a laugh slipped from Amy's mouth. 'Come on. Be realistic. She disappears from the face of the earth one week after Rico is sentenced. Her bank accounts haven't been touched and besides I know for sure.' Amy jumped in her seat when James leapt in front of her.

'How?' he demanded.

Amy trembled, wondering if any crook ever got the better of this formidable man. He must certainly maintain a strong presence in the courtroom. She felt certain she wouldn't want him representing her opponent. 'The day she disappeared I started receiving emails every day until I closed my email address. It was the same rhyme every single time. *Lawyer, lawyer gone for good. Who's the next one in the wood?* Then today, when I was grabbed, Rico threatened me, said we had things to discuss and told me I was going with him whether I liked it or not.'

'Who is this man? And why?' James plopped back into his seat then muttered something incomprehensible under his breath before pausing at length as though working out what the rhyme meant. 'Did you pass the message on?'

'I forwarded copies of all the emails to my lawyer's office before I cancelled my email account, my phone, my everything else, changed my name, my looks and almost everything else about me.' She sighed. 'I'm not who I used to be.'

'But he still found you.'

'Yes.'

'How?'

Amy sighed. 'Now that is the proverbial million dollar question.' She paused as she settled back into the chair then wriggled to get more comfortable. The wriggling didn't work. Despite the cushioned softness her muscles were tense and no amount of squirming was going to ease her tension. 'I wish I knew. But my guess is that the only way he could have found me is from the authorities who helped me change my identity.'

James leant forwards in his seat. 'Which authority are we talking about?'

'Federal Police.'

'Phew! The big boys! But that kind of information is supposed to be locked away. Even I can't access those records.' James glanced at his watch. 'Have you eaten? I was in court most of today and missed lunch.'

Mystified and cautious with the completely different line of thought, Amy checked the time on her plain gold watch. Her eyes widened in surprise. 'In one sense it's a lot later than I thought but it's only been an hour and a half since I walked out of my office building.' She lifted her eyes towards James. 'I'm actually starving. I missed breakfast so I could get to work early and only had an apple for lunch. I should go home but somehow I don't think it would be the wisest thing to do right now. I guess I need to find a hotel room.' She glanced down at her clothes. 'Stupid idea - I've got no clothes, not even a toothbrush.'

'Then stay for dinner so we can discuss your options. I was about to take a shower when I spied this beautiful young female lurking in my backyard and looking rather stealthy.' James grinned at her and waggled his eyebrows, an action that did nothing to ease her apprehension.

Suspicious about the sudden change in tack, Amy inspected her clothes then ran a hand across her head. The feel of loose tendrils that had escaped her tied back hair confirmed her suspicion that she looked a complete wreck. 'Hot, sweaty, crumpled and messy doesn't constitute beautiful but I'll accept your compliment in any case since it's not often I receive one.'

A lengthy silence was followed by a husky, 'I find that hard to believe.'

She was startled by the comment, especially by the warmth of his voice. 'I tend to shy away from forming deep friendships.' She sat back in the chair wondering which way to go. If she fled, would he call the police number on the card he had slipped into his pocket? 'I'll also accept your invitation to dinner since I don't have a clue what else I can do right now. I need time to think.' And to keep an eye on you, she added in her mind. Trusting any man was not easy, especially one she had only just met. After all she'd trusted Rico hadn't she, and where had that got her? Almost killed! No she couldn't trust this man despite him being a lawyer. Rico had been a cop and he was crooked as all get out and his father was way worse. Oh, wow! How crooked could members of the legal fraternity get?

James laughed as he headed for the door and she wondered what she'd said to cause such a reaction. 'You can watch TV while I shower then I'll find you a towel so you can freshen up. I suggest a cool shower will make you feel heaps better. This way.'

Just to ensure he didn't do anything sneaky, like ring the police, Amy picked up her bag and followed. 'I need to get some work done so if you have the end of a table where I can set up my computer I'll get started rather than watch TV.' And she could keep an eye on his whereabouts at the same time.

She'd only just opened up her file and began tweaking the first design when a towel dropped on the table in front of Amy. She squealed as she jumped in her seat, not having heard James approach. 'If you keep scaring me like that, Rico won't have to kill me. I'll have already died of heart failure.'

'Sorry. The bathroom is free and if you want to change into something more comfortable, I've left the door open to my daughter's room. Feel free to raid the cupboard.'

'Your daughter? You're married?' Amy was stunned.

'What makes you think I'm not married?' He held his left hand up in the air and waggled it around showing off a thick gold wedding band she'd not noticed before.

'I thought... gosh... there is no lingering aroma of feminine perfumes or... your bedroom.' She felt an uncomfortable heat rise up her face as her fingers wavered in the direction of his room. 'There is nothing feminine in there.' Digging a large hole and burying herself sounded like an excellent idea, she thought. It would solve all her immediate problems.

'I moved house after my wife passed away. I couldn't stand the emptiness. She died eighteen months ago. Breast cancer.'

Amy felt like a heel. 'I'm sorry, that must have been very difficult.' She placed a hand on his forearm as a gesture of understanding while wondering why he still wore his wedding ring.

'It was.' He glanced towards a small silver framed picture on a narrow side cupboard standing against the wall of the dining room she'd been shown into. 'I loved Glenda a great deal but quite honestly, I was glad when she passed away. She fought the disease for five years but cancer cells had spread and kept coming back with a vengeance. Three bouts of chemo took their toll on us all, especially Glenda. The last time the cancer reared its ugly head it was in her liver. She decided that enough was enough and refused the treatment, which, at times was nastier and more agonising than the disease.' Lifting the photograph, he stared at it in silence before replacing it and running a finger in a loving gesture down the picture.

Realising James still loved his wife, Amy felt not only saddened but also awkward. 'I'm really sorry. I understand how hard that must have been. My Dad died of undiagnosed stomach cancer. By the time they discovered the tumour it was too late for treatment. It's not easy watching someone you love go through such a debilitating disease.' Amy fought back tears as she searched the ceiling for strength, not daring to look at James lest she lose her very tenuous control. After what had happened, she hated showing any weakness. 'It was hard for me because I couldn't spend much time with Dad. Having altered my identity, I could only meet him in secret. I only saw him twice before he passed away and then I couldn't attend his funeral.' Fighting down overwhelming emotions she hugged her body tight then grabbed the towel and headed for the bathroom, forcing back her tears until she was under the stream of tepid water where the two sources of fluid melded into one steady flow. She knew she had been rude but hated allowing anyone to see the tears she thought she was over.

Amy emerged twenty minutes later with wet finger-combed hair tied back in a low ponytail and wearing her own clothes. She hadn't felt comfortable about rifling through a stranger's bedroom searching for something to wear and besides she doubted another girl's clothes would fit her since she was taller than average.

She followed the trail of rich cooking aromas until she found herself in a large open planned kitchen/dining area. James was stirring something in a pot at the stove. He had his back to her. Glancing around she noted modern appliances graced a chef's paradise. Places for two were set out on an elegant wooden table. Two places, so where was the daughter? A jug of orange juice stood next to two glasses. Beads of moisture forming on the outside of the crystal jug caused Amy's mouth to water. The delicious smell of whatever was being stirred in what she could now see was a large wok, caused her stomach to rumble.

'That smells wonderful. What is it?' Amy moved further into the room.

'A simple stir-fry. I call it my fridge-door dinner. I open the fridge door and toss in anything I can find.' James twisted his head around and stared at her with a look of concern etched across his face. 'Are you okay?' At her nod he grinned then added, 'How about pouring some juice? There's wine if you prefer but I need a clear head tonight. I have my closing statements to prepare for my current court case.'

'No wine for me, I also have to work. Juice is perfect.' To keep her mind focussed away from unpleasant thoughts, Amy moved to the side of the table and lifted the jug, pouring the juice into the two tumblers then handing one to James. 'I have no idea what to do. I can't even take the chance of returning home even to get a change of clothes. I should go to work tomorrow but can call in and work from wherever I'm staying. My computer is linked to the office. But I can't do that forever and I have a meeting with clients in the afternoon.' She sighed as James spooned thinly sliced meat strips and mixed vegetables coated in a rich brown sauce onto two dinner plates then handed her one.

'Sit and get some food into you. We can discuss options while we eat.' He pulled out a seat for her then moved to the other side of the table. They ate in contemplative silence for a few minutes: the silence unnerving to Amy.

'This is really good,' Amy said to break the pressing atmosphere. 'I need to book into a hotel but I'll need you to drive me or call a taxi.'

'I've been thinking about that. You can stay here tonight. I have to spend a few hours working. The trial finishes tomorrow so then I'll have a bit more free time to help you sort things out.'

Amy dropped her fork with a clatter. Stay the night! Help me! 'I told you already I can't involve anyone else. I need to contact the sergeant who helped me change my identity. But his number is in my house.'

'Do you own the house?'

Wondering where this was going, Amy retrieved her fork and began eating again, waiting until she had chewed and swallowed before answering. It gave her time to think but nowhere near enough time for nothing logical came to mind. 'I wish. No, I rent. It was easier in case I had to move quickly.'

James paused in his eating, his filled fork held in mid-air. Amy felt mesmerised watching the food waver and wondering if it would fall. 'As far as I can figure things out that is probably a good thing. It will be relatively easy to move out. Do you have a long term lease?' All the food fell from the fork and he frowned as he scooped it up again.

Amy's lips twitched as she attempted to hold back her grin. 'Three monthly, I'm due to renew in about four weeks.'

He swallowed his food. 'I can find you somewhere else to live.'

'But how am I supposed to pack my belongings?'

'Do you have much? Is the furniture yours?' Another forkful vanished behind sealed lips and his jaw worked.

'No, the house is furnished. There are only my clothes and a few personal knick-knacks.' She placed her fork on the plate and slid it to the centre, her hunger deserting her. 'I didn't accumulate much as I was always worried I'd have to move again at a moment's notice but I thought I had another four years before Rico would be released. They were supposed to let me know if a parole review came up.'

'And they didn't?' James slid his empty plate to one side then leant back in his chair, one arm resting on the table while the other toyed with his glass.

'No, which has me worried for I can't understand why he was released so early.' For something to do, Amy took a sip of her juice.

'Ten years is a long time for rape in this day and age. He probably received a good-behaviour bond and is out on parole.'

'Do you really think so?' She wasn't up to disclosing details about why Rico had received such a long term in gaol. 'But doesn't that mean he has a parole officer? Would they let him move interstate?' No way was she going to reveal that it wasn't just rape. As far as she was concerned, ten years wasn't anywhere near long enough. Life wasn't long enough. Rotting in hell for eternity was what he deserved.

'You have a valid point. I could look into it for you but then again he may simply have jumped parole. I need his full name.'

'Enrico Joseph Giovannazzo! Former policeman, bastard extraordinaire and underworld snitch.' Even to herself, she sounded cynical then she realised she'd let more slip out than she should. Her eyes slid heavenwards as she regretted giving Rico's name. She couldn't let James become involved.

'Underworld?' Looking as though she'd more than surprised him James leant forwards.

'Yes, Rico was a crooked cop.' Sipping the last of her juice for something to do and to keep her tongue from gabbing, she then began tracing slow falling beads of moisture down the side of the large tumbler. Memories she thought she'd long buried began surfacing, twirling then stabbing. Nausea rose, along with feelings of terror and hatred.

'And you know this for sure?' A large hand descended then withdrew the glass from her grasp.

Only then did Amy realise how badly her hand was shaking. She shoved both hands into her lap and clenched her fists tight to garner some control. 'How else does a man on a lowly police wage pay for expensive toys like half million dollar cabin cruiser, Porsche sports car, waterside mansion plus every electronic gizmo known to man? I know for certain.'

She dared to peek at his face. James looked sceptical. She wasn't sure if she felt surprised at his scepticism or downright mad that he didn't believe her. 'Look, I know this whole thing sounds crazy but I have proof. Certain papers. Not that I could ever really use them.'

'Why not?' Now he looked intrigued.

Amy bolted upright. 'Are you mad? It was bad enough having Rico after me. You think I want his gang cronies chasing after me as well. That would be signing my own certain death warrant.' Agitated, she sprang from her seat. 'And don't you go poking your nose into his records because they'll be after you as well.' Her breath caught in the back of her throat. Gasping for air she turned her back on James. 'I couldn't live with myself if somebody else died because of me.'

There was a lengthy silence during which Amy couldn't face James. She heard him rise from his seat then his soft footfalls as he approached her.

'Amy, it's obvious you need help and I have the means to provide it. But I need time and so do you. Stay here tonight. Since nobody knows you are here, you will be safe.

Let me finish my role in this court case then we can discuss the best way to handle this mess.'

It took a lot of persuasion by James but after agreeing to stay, since she didn't have a clue as to what else she could do, Amy spent the evening working on the end of the dining room table. It was almost midnight before she closed down her computer, happy with the results of a concentrated effort. Whilst completing her interior designs, a couple of thoughts continually forced their way to the forefront of her mind. This would have to be her final contract. She had no choice but to resign now that Rico had found her. If Rico knew where she was then so did his father and that was way scarier. The other decision she came to had her worried as it meant that somehow she was going to have to return home to collect vital papers and belongings. Deep in thought, she visited the bathroom before retiring to the bed she had been shown earlier. She almost jumped out of her skin when the door to the bathroom opened just as she was about to grasp a hold of the handle. She screamed.

***

Rico draw in a deep ragged breath as he glanced down and recognised the highlighted number indicating who was calling. What the hell was his father doing up at this hour? He tried to calculate the time in Sydney but with a mind blurred by alcohol, he couldn't remember whether there was a two or three hour time difference. Being summer he remembered Sydney had daylight saving but couldn't for the life of him recall whether Perth followed suit. Swearing at his father for waking him, Rico struggled upright on the sofa, knocking the empty whisky bottle over with his foot. Not wanting his father to hear the rattle, he made a grab for the bottle but the momentum and his drunken state caused him to end up on the floor.

He flopped in relief when the ringing ceased, then used his arms to lever his unsteady body upright and eased his backside onto the sofa again. He had only just settled back down and closed his eyes when the phone began again at what sounded like a thousand drums beating right against his ear-drum.

'Shit,' Rico cursed as he flipped the phone open and plastered it to his ear, missed his target then slid the instrument down the side of his head until he heard his father's voice.

'Rico!' The yelled word reverberated through over-sensitive nerves.

'No need to shout,' said Rico then wondered if his words were actually as slurred as they sounded to him.

'Have you got it yet?'

Concentrating hard, Rico forced his voice to sound as though he hadn't imbibed in an almost full bottle of whisky. 'No, Amanda hasn't come home yet.'

'Where the hell are you?'

'In her house.'

'Have you searched it?'

'Of course I frigg'n searched the place. It isn't here. I tipped the place.' His head pounded and his eyes slid closed taking on a mind of their own. He forced them open and figured he should stand and start moving around to get his blood pumping. But the thought was a lot easier than the action. The moment he was upright, the room began to sway up and down, up and down, feeling as though he were on his cruiser in rough seas. Unsteady legs buckled and he plopped back onto the sofa. Even though his body was now steady, the contents of his stomach continued the up and down momentum.

'And I suppose, you useless git, that you've parked your car right outside her front door so she knows you are there.'

'Fuck you. I parked it in a different street.' Rico hung up, switched off the phone then feeling the acid rising, raced to the bathroom where he ejected some of the alcohol before reeling back to the sofa and crashing into the cushions.

Chapter Four

Amy was still screaming when the door swung open. 'Hell I'm sorry,' said James as he slid his arms around Amy and steadied her. 'I thought you had gone to bed. I went for a walk to get my closing together in my head. When I didn't see you still working and with the place so silent, I thought you were asleep.'

For a few seconds, while her hammering heart eased to a more normal rate, Amy welcomed the security and warmth of long arms holding her against a very manly chest. Her nose was squashed up against where she felt the steady rhythm of his heart under a cotton collared T-shirt. It had been a long time since she had been this close to a male body and briefly she wondered why, for once, she didn't feel her old terror rising. Her few relationships over the past five years had ended when things got anywhere near her being held this close, this intimately. When sanity returned, Amy pulled away, feeling suddenly self-conscious.

'I'm fine. You just scared me witless. I had no idea you were back.' Feeling a desperate need to escape, she edged around him into the passage. 'Was that police car still outside my place?'

'No. The only car unfamiliar to me is parked in this street, two doors down. The car is locked and empty. I looked inside.'

Amy couldn't suppress the shudder skipping down her backbone. 'What sort of car?'

'Flashy. Hard top sports model.'

'Far out! Rico! It has to be. He'll either be camped inside my place or watching from somewhere nearby waiting for me to return.' In an action she realised was almost becoming a habit she wrapped her own arms around her upper body, feeling the need for security.

'You can't know that.' James grasped her shoulders gently as though to steady her.

'He only drives flashy cars – ever. If the police are gone, he'll be waiting. He won't expect me to notice a car parked in a different street away from my road. It'll be him.' She dragged free from his grasp turned and headed for the bedroom she'd been allotted. 'I'm going to bed. He can wait.' Good manners sent a stab of remorse through her conscience. James didn't deserve her shortness. Before stepping inside the room, she turned and gentled her voice. 'Goodnight. I really am grateful for your assistance tonight. If you don't mind I'll need a lift into the city tomorrow morning so could you please wake me early?'

Not waiting for a response she shut the door behind her, hearing a muffled goodnight as she crossed the carpeted floor. Without bothering to undress, she lay on top of the still made bed while the makings of a plan formulated in her brain. She needed vital items from her house before she could flee the state. She quickly set the alarm on her mobile phone and flicked the light off. She needed as much sleep as possible but worried her troubled over-active mind wouldn't relax enough for her to find a reprieve from her worries.

Much to her surprise, a familiar tune woke her from a deep sleep. Desperate not to waken James, Amy grabbed her phone and silenced the alarm with one automatic flick of her thumb. A quick glance at the lit up face told her she had managed two hours' sleep. She must have been a lot tireder than she'd thought for she couldn't recall a single minute after switching off the light.

Creeping through the dark, Amy eased the door open then peered both ways down the darkened passage. After sneaking silently past James's partially open door, she headed for the sliding door through which she had originally entered the house. She had deliberately questioned James earlier if the house was electronically alarmed to give him the impression she was afraid for her safety. His assurance that deadlocks kept intruders at bay had relieved her but it was something she hadn't disclosed given that she needed to get out then back in without him knowing what she was up to. As she slowly swept back the heavy drapes to minimise the scraping sound, she felt sure he wouldn't have agreed to her little escapade. It was a stupid idea to be facing the lion in his den but as far as she could figure out, she didn't have a lot of choice.

The click as she turned the key to the sliding glass door sounded mighty loud. She paused - counting up to thirty to ensure James hadn't stirred before she eased the door open then stepped out in her bare feet. The air felt cooler but it was still a very warm night: too warm to be racing around the streets and putting your life on the line. The bricks underfoot felt rough on her skin but she couldn't take the risk of wearing shoes, her only pair of sandals having leather soles and low heels that clicked and slapped making too much noise.

Reaching the front gate, Amy rued the single blazing streetlight as she peered through the semi-darkness for any signs of human presence. Although not overbright it lit up the surrounding area too much for her liking. Complete darkness would have been far preferable. The moment she saw the sports car further down the road, she knew she was right about it belonging to Rico. Even in the gloom, the yellow paint gleamed. Keeping close to the fences and even intruding into the properties to seek the best shadows, she crept towards the car, maintaining a low profile in case Rico had returned and was waiting inside the vehicle. But knowing him as well as she did, she bet he would have broken into her house and would still be there.

Just in case, she approached the car from behind with bent knees then sidled up to the rear passenger's window. Daring to peek inside, she searched the interior. The relief was intense when she saw the car was empty. One up to me, she thought as she knelt by the rear wheel and grasped her thumb and forefinger around the cap on the tyre valve. Once the cap was free, she pressed the tip of her fingernail into the tiny silver stem of the valve, smiling at the steady hiss as the air flowed out. Not satisfied with one completely airless tyre, Amy repeated the exercise three more times before heading towards home via dark shadows of the leafy trees and shrubs along the property boundaries.

A shiver passed through her body as Amy approached her home. She didn't know if it was a shiver from the dampness hovering just above the ground or from the knowledge Rico was so close. Regardless, it felt sinister. She'd had five years to plan for this night but she hadn't expected to have to break into her own home with Rico on the inside. All her scenarios had been based on having to escape with him being outside. But she didn't have a whole lot of choice. She needed to get in to fetch what was lying hidden in a cedar wood chest in her bedroom: a backpack, already bulging with emergency supplies, private documents and incriminating evidence linking Rico to the family underworld gang. It had taken many hundreds of hours over the past five years searching websites on various computers not linked to her, to find all the information she had about court hearings and results. Shock at some of the findings had been a regular occurrence. Rico's father was one nasty piece of work.

Pausing before reaching her front yard, Amy drew in a deep breath then poked her head around the pillar of her neighbour's fence. She'd chosen the house to live in with care. No front fence to impede an escape and easy access all around the building for the same reason. The lack of shrubs for an intruder to hide amongst was now, she decided with a wry grimace, a definite negative for it meant she had little cover to keep herself hidden. Not knowing if Rico was awake and peering through the window gave her the heebie-jeebies. For five years she'd been convincing herself that she was strong both inside and in the physical sense. But now that the crunch had come, she wasn't so sure. Right then she felt vulnerable and beyond terrified. Get over it, she told herself. You can do this. He's just a man: a man who doesn't have a clue what you've been up to since THAT night.

She shuddered then gave herself a mental shake-down before sucking in three deep breaths. She needed to think like Rico. Having ensured Amy had seen him so that she knew he was after her, he wouldn't expect her to approach from the front. She paused and ruminated on the best way to tackle the situation. There was a side gate between the two properties, one she'd used to check on her elderly neighbour before he had become an inmate of a nursing home and the house had been sold. Praying the young family now occupying the house were all sound asleep, she crept down the driveway, cringing every time a sharp gravel stone pressed into her flesh.

When the gate creaked ominously loud as she eased it centimetre by slow centimetre open, Amy held her breath and stood statue still. Hearing no sign of human movement over the normal sounds of the night, she continued to manoeuvre the metal until she could squeeze through the opening. Instead of putting herself through the trauma of closing the darn thing again, she bent and felt around in the dirt from the garden bed for a rock, wedging it under the bottom gap then testing the gate to ensure it wouldn't budge. Before stepping onto the pathway bordering her house, Amy took her time peering up at the two small windows on this side of the house. Both were high: one tiny pane for the toilet and a larger one of opaque glass belonging to the bathroom. Until now she hadn't realised how convenient, apart from keeping the fierce afternoon sun at bay, the lack of windows on the western side of her house actually was. She sent a silent prayer of thanks heavenwards.

Her heart fluttered with fear as she leapt across the garden bed onto the pathway then slunk her body against the brick wall of her house, her nerves on edge, ready to flee at the slightest sign of Rico. Facing the wall she sidled on the balls of her feet towards the front veranda then eased around the corner as though she were a glob of mercury. The curtains to her lounge window had been moved, confirming her thoughts that Rico was inside, or at least, had been inside. He had left a small gap at either end as well as one in the middle of the large bay window. Sucking in a breath of courage, she eased one eye against the nearest gap. Half expecting to come eyeball to eyeball with Rico her heart felt as though it was jammed in her mouth, sweat dripped down between her breasts and she dared not breathe as she peered into the darkened room. All the time her body was in flight mode, ready to turn and run full pelt.

Once her eyes adjusted to the darkened inside, she grinned. She could make out the shape of the dangerous and intimidating Rico sprawled on the lounge appearing to be fast asleep. His short-sleeved cotton shirt had come adrift from the waistband of what looked like blue jeans, exposing several inches of flesh and an arrow of dark hair. Amy shuddered. What a fool she had been all those years ago to think that his body was sexy. Boy, had he taught her different.

Peering further and with her eyes adjusting, Amy noticed an empty bottle tipped on its side on the floor next to a hanging arm. She couldn't make out the label but guessed that if the bottle were from her meagre supplies of alcoholic beverages, it would be whisky. Not that she imbibed in the foul tasting stuff. She had purchased it to flavour a batch of orange marmalade she had made to use up some of the fruit on the only fruit tree in her back yard. Recalling what else she had in the cupboard, and knowing Rico so well, she figured it was the only alcohol he would have touched and if he'd drunk the entire contents he would be well sozzled.

The knowledge eased Amy's fears, but only slightly, as she returned the way she had come and made her silent way around to the other side of the house until she was standing beside one of the other reasons she had rented this particular house - a separate entry directly into her bedroom. She had no doubts Rico would have checked every room and removed the keys from the inside locks but Amy was well prepared. She knelt on the ground, reached under the single wooden step and removed a set of four spare keys, one for each outside door and a special one for the teak chest.

She noticed her usually drawn curtains were pulled right back giving her full view into her room. Rays from a streetlight flowed down this side and she wondered if this was the reason Rico had left the curtain open, so he could see any presence outside with ease. But that didn't make logical sense since there was enough light for her to see equally clear into the room. Drawn curtains would have made more sense. A thought came to her that this might be some kind of trap so she took a great deal of care in examining every single detail in the room seeking out some unusual shape, bulge or shadow indicating a human form.

The room had been searched; the contents strewn all over the place, but even with her clothes spread across the floor and bed the room didn't look a total write-off. She scoffed silently. She didn't maintain a vast wardrobe, always thinking about the time she would have to flee. That time had come and her frugal lifestyle now bore fruit.

To ensure Rico hadn't awakened and was waiting for her, Amy scooted back to the lounge-room window and peered inside. He hadn't moved and this time she could detect the sounds of a regular rhythm of snoring. The thought that maybe he had someone else with him, entered her mind then just as quickly she dismissed the idea. Rico was a bragger, boasting about how he preferred to work alone. At the time she hadn't realised exactly what he meant, thinking it was how he carried out his police duties, but now she knew better - much better.

To make sure there were no other men lying in wait, Amy made her slow way all around the house, peering through every window in search of some unfamiliar lurking shadow. It was too difficult to see in the rooms in the lee of the streetlights but in the end she felt convinced only Rico was inside. Deciding she had wasted enough time, she slid the key into the lock of her bedroom, slowly twisted it with her ear up against the frame listening for the snick of the releasing barrel and with her every sense honed for any other hint of an unwelcome presence.

Once the door was unlocked, Amy took her painstaking time to slide the door along runners she kept free of grit and dust for this very reason. The silent rumble as the door slid open, Amy knew, sounded louder than it actually was. Her heightened nerves and edginess made everything seem louder, longer and more acute than it should. Once inside, she moved quickly. She tiptoed across the room to the teak chest next to a tall bureau of drawers on top of which was a small television set. As she suspected, the wooden box hadn't been searched because the key to the intricate lock wouldn't have been found.

Before opening the box, Amy slowly pushed the door into the passage shut then jammed a rubber doorstop under the crack of the door, making it difficult for Rico to open if he happened to awaken. She knew it wouldn't hold him at bay for more than a few seconds but those precious moments could be the difference between her escaping or not. The chest opened easily on well-oiled hinges and within seconds she was drawing out the only item contained within – her already crammed large waterproof backpack. It was the only thing she really cared about and the only thing she needed. But feeling confident at the muffled sounds of continued snoring, she decided to take a few more minutes to change her clothes.

Having made the decision to quit her job, she wouldn't need her classier office outfit so stripped it off, along with her underwear. Picking up odd items from the floor, she donned fresh bras and knickers under a pair of white cotton knee-length shorts and a deep blue smart T-shirt. The clothes were comfortable and suitable for what she needed to do. They were of adequate class and quality that she didn't look like a hobo and the items were perfect for the continuing summer heatwave as well as giving her the freedom for rapid movement if needed.

Satisfied with her clothes, Amy gathered together several other sets of underwear and a few tops and slacks while ignoring dresses and skirts which were more awkward to flee in. Pulling on a pair of comfortable light sneakers over bare feet, she shoved the clothes in a separate small cloth tote bag, picked up her backpack and slung it onto her back. Then she removed the wedge from under the door before leaving the way she had come, taking the spare keys with her. Maybe, just maybe there would be the opportunity to retrieve the rest of her belongings.

Rico would know she had been. She'd left the door shut and the lid up on the chest on purpose. It was time he was outsmarted, time she repaid a few dues. Her actions would increase his anger but she didn't much care. If he managed to catch her, she was dead in any case. But she'd had five years to prepare for this and she hadn't wasted those years.

***

It was the feel of an urgent pressing on his bladder that roused Rico from a deep sleep. Still drunk, it took quite a few moments of clearing hazy eyes and mind, for him to remember where he was and why. He shot upright then groaned as waves of pain from a thundering head beset him. The long vertical lines of bright light in the gaps of the curtain had him groaning again, but this time for stupidity. He hadn't touched alcohol since being incarcerated and had enjoyed the lack of alcohol after-effects so much he'd sworn to not ever touch the stuff again. And now his one step off the bandwagon had been a doozy. Sunshine careening through the gaps meant morning and he had slept through the night. Cursing under his breath, he staggered to the bathroom, relieved his bladder then searched the house again even though he figured if Amanda had returned, she would have disappeared the moment she had spied him.

'Bitch,' he hissed as he entered her room and noticed the open chest. Recognising the dress piled in an untidy heap on the floor he bent and lifted it up, holding it against his nose then sniffing deeply. 'I still love you, Amanda. God, sweetheart, you have no idea how sorry I am about the entire freakin' ordeal.' He sank to the bed and pressed the dress against his face, drawing in a deep breath to absorb and drown in Amanda's scent. Outwardly he blamed himself for what happened and had readily suffered his punishment in gaol but deep in his gut he blamed his father. The entire fiasco stemmed from his father's obsession to have a son who at least looked the part of someone to be reckoned with. He scoffed. He'd never wanted the life, nor acted the expected way and it had done nothing to endear Rico to his father. And still, even after all that had happened, his damn father was trying to dictate the rules of a life Rico hated but from which he couldn't seem to escape.

Chapter Five

'Good grief!' James spluttered as Amy stepped into the kitchen early the next morning.

She couldn't help but grin at the stunned look on his face with both of his eyes widening and his mouth gaping open. She felt inordinately pleased at his reaction. But seeing him dressed in pressed suit trousers and a sleeveless undervest had given her an equal shock. Seeing his top half so scantily clad, she realised that his hulking size was not because of extra flab but through a solid bone structure. His very frame was enormous but covered in very little excess flesh. His arm and chest muscles were finely honed giving the impression that given his profession and the hours he would remain seated at a desk indoors, he must work out to keep in such impeccable condition.

'Is that the same woman who was here last night?' James took one step forward to study her altered appearance, a spatula waving around in the air and dripping water onto the floor. 'What on earth have you done to your hair?'

'It's a wig.' Amy patted down the short auburn spikes and grinned. 'Do I look different enough?'

'I didn't recognise you. And the clothes, I'm sure they don't belong to Angie.' His eyes squinted as though he was trying to work things out.

'They don't, they're mine.' Trying to act nonchalant, Amy raced for the table and pulled out a chair. She figured that given James was a QC then he was highly intelligent and would soon put two and two together and she would have some explaining to do even though it was none of his business. She kept her eyes averted, toying with the cutlery already set out. She felt, rather than heard him nearing.

'Since you arrived on my doorstep with only the clothes you were wearing, do you want to explain exactly where the outfit came from? And when?' His supercilious voice sounded right next to her ear, his presence felt overpowering.

Amy winced but didn't move. 'My place, two-thirty a.m.' She made an exaggeration about sniffing the air. 'Is something burning?'

A muttered profanity followed by receding footsteps and a clatter as a heavy frying pan hit the metal sink caused Amy to sigh in relief then grin.

His next words came from the other side of the room amidst the scraping of food being shifted from pan to plate. 'What about this Rico you said would be waiting for you?'

'Oh, he was waiting but fortunately for me he wasn't able to resist the temptation of an almost full whisky bottle he found in my scant wine-rack. He was stretched out on my sofa – asleep and snoring and, I suspect, drunk. He didn't see or hear me.'

A plate landed in front of her. 'Care to tell me why you didn't disclose what you were planning to do? I have no doubt you made plans before retiring to bed.'

She couldn't look at him as he settled opposite. 'Would you have let me go?' she said to the plate.

'Probably not: at least not alone.'

'It was safer for me to go alone. I've told you more than once, I can't involve anyone else.' Feeling very hesitant, she picked up her cutlery and sliced off a small piece of bacon. The crisp rasher was perfectly cooked and smelt wonderful. She popped it into her mouth and began chewing with a vain hope that James would let the matter rest.

'I think I'm already involved and I'm big enough and smart enough to look after myself. I don't need some slip of a woman to look out for me.'

Almost choking as the morsel of meat shot down her throat, Amy glanced down at her folded five foot eight length. She certainly wasn't skinny but didn't have too much meat covering her bones. She'd always thought she was well proportioned for her height. 'I'm hardly a slip of a woman,' she protested as she lifted her cutlery and began hoeing into a soft centred egg residing right in the middle of a slice of buttered toast. Even though she rarely ate a cooked breakfast, giving her undivided attention to the meal in front of her was far preferable to facing the man she knew wasn't pleased.

'Compared to me, you are. So what have you got planned for today?' James replied to the top of her head.

She chewed then swallowed. 'It's none of your business.'

'I'm making it my business,' came back so fast she wondered if he was eating but she certainly wasn't game to peek to find out.

She could tell by the tone of his voice that James was trying hard to keep the conversation civil and, she suspected, his temper under control. She wasn't sure how to handle things and was in two minds as to how much she could rely on him. Innate instinct told her she could trust him but fear for his wellbeing if she relied on him for help, held her back.

'I've emailed my designs to my boss, along with my resignation but I have a meeting with my clients scheduled for this afternoon. It's a meeting I can't get out of but lucky for me it is scheduled to be held at the client's premises in West Perth so I don't have to go into my office. Therefore Rico can hang out there as long as he wants. I won't be turning up. Then, since this darn wig is too hot to wear for any length of time in this stifling heatwave, I'm going to spend the morning having my hair done. Then I have to try to contact the sergeant who gave me my new identity. I need to find out how my whereabouts and identity were leaked and how to change it all again.'

'If you wait until tomorrow I can help. My case should be over by lunchtime today.' There was a lengthy pause during which Amy continued eating but she could feel the increasing tension. 'Amy, look at me.'

Hesitating a moment, Amy lifted her face and noticed James's eyes flaring. 'You're wearing coloured contacts.' His eyes screwed. 'That is unless you were wearing a different colour yesterday. What colour are your eyes?'

'Blue - or rather, grey. What you saw yesterday was the real thing. I have two different coloured sets of contacts, these that make my eyes look hazel plus a dark brown set.'

He studied her face for a few moments then said, 'You've planned well for this haven't you?'

'I've been planning every day for the past five years. I have a lot of things ready but I wasn't expecting to be homeless so soon. I need to find somewhere to stay until I can organise another change of identity.'

'Come back and stay here tonight. I can pick you up from your meeting so you won't have to take the chance of being exposed on the streets. I'll be free from one o'clock onwards.'

The idea sounded perfect but Amy had strong reservations. She didn't know this man well enough to trust him or how safe he would be if she involved him. He might be a QC but her last lawyer's credentials hadn't kept her safe and Rico had been a darn cop! 'I can't take the risk.'

'Risk of being seen here or risk of my well-being? Neither is really a risk. You'll be safer here than anywhere by yourself. Nobody knows you are here or that I even know you. At least here you have the law on your side.'

Was he a mind reader? She thought for a moment then added aloud, 'I need to think about this.' She pushed her chair back and rose, lifting her half eaten breakfast from the table as she went. So many things rushed through her mind while she scraped the remnants of her meal into the bin then washed and dried her plate and cutlery.

'Coffee?' James asked as he joined her at the sink.

'Please, white with no sugar.' Amy reached out to take his plate, tugging when he resisted. 'If I'm to stay another twenty-four hours then I insist I share the load.'

'You'll stay?' He finally relented and the plate almost flew into the air as he suddenly released his grip. He grinned as Amy grabbed the plate and slid it onto the sink, groaning at the resultant clatter.

Sighing, Amy paused with her fingers resting on the edge of the metal sink - not knowing why she had agreed but the words had slipped out. Maybe it was meant to be. Another twenty-four hours of relative security would be a good thing. Having somewhere safe to stay would give her an extra day to sort things. She began washing the plate, using a small blob of detergent to dissolve the grease. 'Only because what you said made more sense than anything I can come up with as an alternative right now. My guess is that Rico will have people checking out the hotels for my presence.'

'Who is this man? Would he go so far?' Once again a large hand descended on Amy's shoulder forcing her around to face James. How many times in the past day had she jolted at a man's touch? But it wasn't the touching she shied from; it was the suddenness of the action coming from behind.

She sucked in a couple of slow breaths to calm her racing heart. 'Oh, yes, he had people searching all the hotels in Sydney when I first managed to elude him. I was still in hospital, about to be released when I was almost caught. It was only because a female nurse had seen the state I was in when I first arrived at the hospital and became suspicious when a man asked really specific questions about me. She warned me and I was able to get away by using a back exit. She took me to her home for a few days where she tended to my injuries until I was well enough to leave. I owe her a great deal.

'What state were you in? What exactly did he do to you?' James hung the tea towel he'd been using, on a rail inside a cupboard door then steered her towards the sofa in the lounge and used gentle force to get her to sit. He handed her a mug with whispers of steam curling upwards. The coffee that had come from one of those new-fangled home coffee machines smelt enticing and miles better than the instant variety she was used to.

'I already told you what he did. It was obvious I'd been physically manhandled. I couldn't hide the evidence. And I don't want to talk about it. It's past history.' Amy placed the mug that was beginning to slosh, onto the side table then gripped her fingers together to control a tremor in her hand. She was amazed at how vivid and real the remembered pain was. It was as though it was more than a memory. It felt as though she was going through the horror all over again.

Something in her manner must have been relayed to James for he reached out with both arms and drew her against his still half naked chest. 'You're shaking as though you're in the middle of a force seven earthquake,' he murmured into her ear as he ran one hand up and down her back. 'He did a real number on you didn't he?'

'Please, I can't talk about it, but yes.' Fighting for control, Amy pulled back. Dear, God, she thought she was over all this remembered pain but all it had taken was for Rico to re-appear and five years of determination to be strong seemed to have taken an extended holiday. 'That's all I'm saying apart from I have to move as far away from here as possible and as soon as possible.' Having an urgent desire to be alone, she shot from the seat and headed for the bathroom. 'What time are you leaving?' she called in a voice she new quivered, as she reached the bathroom door.

'Half an hour,' James called back.

To the minute, Amy was standing at the front door half an hour later with her demeanour under control and her computer bag over her shoulder. It contained not only the items she needed for work but also a file with her private identification papers she had retrieved from her backpack. As James neared, wearing a crisp ironed shirt with smart silk tie and a suit jacket over his arm, she held out a large tan, sealed envelope.

'I'm going to have to trust you. You're a QC and I'm hoping one with integrity and on the right side of the law. This contains a letter of instructions and a safety deposit box key. If anything happens to me, open it and follow the instructions. The details of the deposit box are inside. The box contains copies of damning evidence of Rico and his father's activities. I don't think he knows I've got it. They are photocopies but you can only open it if anything nasty happens to me. I insist on that.'

James looked completely stunned as he held the envelope in one hand. He dropped his bulging briefcase onto the floor and turned the envelope over several times, studying all the surfaces. 'First, let me assure you that my ethics are above board, but why me and why now? I have a terrible gut feeling you have just handed me a real hot potato. If there is such incriminating evidence, why don't you use it to put this man away for good? He doesn't have the right to make your life such a complete misery.'

'I've stewed over this during the past few hours. With Rico loose, I feel very vulnerable. It's not only him I have to hide from but also his cohorts and family who are far reaching and have fingers in pies you wouldn't even dream about.'

James slid the envelope into his already overflowing brief case. 'I'm well aware of what type of pies criminals have a hand in making. I'll put this in my office safe but how am I going to know if you are all right?' He opened the door leading into his garage, which was built under the main roof on the side of the house.

Amy edged past him when he indicated with his head for her to precede him. 'I've thought about that as well. I'll ring you on a particular day every week – say a week from now.' She walked down the passenger side of the car while James headed the other way. 'If you don't hear from me within twenty-four hours of the set time – how about noon, then you have my permission to open the envelope.'

James paused before getting into the car, his head just above the roofline. 'How did you get mixed up with him in the first place?'

'I didn't know who or what he was when we met,' Amy continued as James disappeared into the car. She bent to follow suit. 'He showed a different side to his character right up until the night…' She couldn't complete the sentence, waiting until she was sitting in the passenger seat of James's car before going on. 'I've kept those papers hidden all this time but right now something tells me that someone else needs to have access to them. Some innate feeling tells me I can trust you.' She dragged the seatbelt across her chest and latched it into place. As James pressed the remote control for the garage door, Amy felt the nerves and muscles in her body tighten in tension. She peered over her shoulder at the increasing gap of the opening, feeling petrified Rico was going to barge in brandishing a gun, or even worse, his knife. She shuddered at the thought of the knife.

'Are you okay?' asked James as he caught her eye with his fingers on the key that he held still.

'To be honest, I'm terrified but if you didn't recognise me this morning then I guess no-one else will. Let's go.' Amy straightened her back and looked straight ahead hoping to give the impression she was a lot braver than she felt.

James turned the key and the engine of the upmarket sedan purred into life. It was an expensive car but not ostentatious and Amy figured it showed the reflection of the man driving it. He had money but preferred not to advertise his wealth. He let the motor warm for a few seconds before reversing out onto the drive. As he swung backwards into the road, Amy sucked in an audible breath when she spied Rico standing at the side of his car. He was in the process of kicking a very flat front tyre. Amy quickly retrieved a large pair of sunglasses from her bag and slid them over her eyes.

'I take it, that that is Rico,' murmured James as he drove past way too slow for Amy's liking.

'That's Rico.' Amy kept her eyes turned away from the man under discussion and silently willed James to hurry.

'He doesn't look very happy.' The humour in James's voice was obvious. 'I presume you had something to do with the flat tyre,' he added as he turned the steering wheel and the car swung around the corner.

'Four flat tyres.' Amy choked as she tried to suppress a giggle.

'Four!' James burst out laughing. 'And what was written on the note he so viciously tore from the windscreen and tossed onto the road?' he asked when he'd regained his sobriety.

'Umm, something about him being caught unawares while on watch. It wasn't signed but he'll recognise my writing and the derogatory terms I used.' She couldn't help the grin that crept out from the corners of her mouth.

'You are an amazing lady. I think I like you quite a lot.' James glanced at her as he waited to turn onto the main road. Even at this early hour the traffic flow was already quite steady with few gaps into which to pull.

'It was a miniscule payback. He deserves to be caught with his pants down. I was a foolish idiot once but he won't catch me out again. When we do meet up again it will be on my terms and he is in for a very rude shock.'

There was silence as James waited until he had executed a quick turn into the traffic and was driving steadily along Stirling Highway. 'Are you going to explain with a little more detail? Exactly what are you planning? I thought you never wanted to see him again.'

'I don't ever want to set eyes on him again but I figure I don't have a whole lot of choice. I could have taken him out last night. I could have grabbed a kitchen knife and plunged it between his ribs right into his heart. Believe me, I was tempted. He was spreadeagled and dead to the world. But a quick death is nowhere near enough for him, and besides, I'm not about to go down for murder for that mealy-mouthed bastard.'

'Such language,' James laughed. 'Now where do you need to go?'

'Which court are you appearing in?'

'Supreme Court, but I usually park underneath my office block which is within easy walking distance. The short distance gives me a chance to gain a bit of exercise while I gather my thoughts for the upcoming day and also to breathe in fresh air, albeit tainted with exhaust fumes.'

'That suits me fine. I have several city central stops to make before my meeting.'

'Where do I pick you up from, and at what time?'

Amy unzipped the front pocket of her capacious bag and pulled out a sheaf of stapled together papers. After browsing through the small pile she ripped one from its clasp, folded it in half and placed it on the console between them. 'The address is at the top. My meeting is at two and should take at least two hours. Make it four-thirty in case it takes longer. I'll wait outside until I see your car.'

'It might be better if you waited inside.' He caught her eye. 'Just in case and I'll be there at four.'

As she replaced the papers a small rectangular card floated to the floor. Amy bent and picked it up. Glancing at it, she smiled as an idea came to her. She held it in the air and waved it around. 'This might be the answer to my short term problem.'

'Where did you get that?' asked James with a certain curious tone that told Amy he recognised it.

'The man yesterday, who knocked me into the road, then hauled me from in front of the bus. He handed it to me as I stepped onto the bus. He said to give him a call if I needed any help. I'd forgotten all about it. Why?'

Pulling up at a set of lights, James slid the card from her grasp. 'Did you read it?' His face looked as though he was trying desperately not to burst into laughter.

'No, I was going to toss it in the bin but couldn't find one on the bus then forgot all about it.'

James held it out towards her. 'Read the name.'

Grasping the light blue card between thumb and forefinger, Amy studied the darker blue writing. 'Jonathan Ward,' she read out aloud. 'Insurance assessor.'

'The name doesn't ring any bells?' asked James as he drove off again.

'No, should it?'

'What's my name?'

'James Ward.' She paused as things tumbled into place. 'Oh, golly gosh, gee whiz! Ward. Your brother! I remember now, he said his brother was a lawyer!' A shiver ran from the top of her head all the way down to her toes. 'That's real spooky. How weird meeting two complete strangers within two hours of each other and they are brothers. How scary is that?'

***

While waiting for a tow truck to arrive, Rico couldn't help but admire Amanda's actions and her guts. She had outsmarted him but in a sense he felt proud of her.

His smile turned to a frown when the thought changed to his father. How the hell was he going to tell his father that he had let Amanda slip though his fingers? Not once, but twice. Then a vague memory itched through his grey matter – had he really said that to his father then hung up on him? Oh, yeah, there was going to be hell to pay.

He slid his mobile phone from his pocket and switched it on. Six missed calls – and he bet he knew who had made each one of those six. He tapped the down button six times, feeling slightly sick at the sight of six exact same numbers. Should he call back now or wait? He glanced around, hoping to see a tow truck heading his way. No such luck. The only vehicle was a slightly battered red Volkswagen, sputtering a ring of black smoke each time the driver pressed down on the accelerator. New rings were needed, or maybe better to replace the entire engine since the car was near the half century in age. With nothing else to grab his attention, Rico glanced back at his phone. Better to get it over with. He dialled then waited, hoping his father was in court.

A click told him his luck had eluded him again. Then an angry voice bellowed, 'don't you ever swear at me again, you son of a bitch! What the hell is going on there? Tell me you've got it and that stupid bitch is dead.'

Rico sucked in a breath. Dead? His father wanted Amanda dead? 'If I'm a son of a bitch then I guess that makes you the bitch. And no I haven't got it. Amanda didn't come home last night. I searched her place again and I'm sure she hasn't even got it.' He'd ignored the loud indrawn breath at his insult but could feel the tension from his father steaming on the other end of the line. Right then he didn't give a damn. The only thing he could focus on was that he was supposed to get rid of Amanda, as in terminate her life. That wasn't the deal when he left Sydney. It hadn't even been mentioned. So what else was his father up to that hadn't been revealed? A sick feeling invaded his innards.

He only half listened as his father ranted details of what Veteramo and Lo Presti had planned on how to catch Amanda. Rico gave the occasional grunt as response adding in a few, *'Yes, sirs,'* to show he was listening then promised he would keep his mobile switched on as the tow truck arrived.

Rico slammed the phone shut and gripped it so tight there was an ominous crack of plastic. Damn the man. There was no way he could allow Amanda to die. She didn't deserve to die. She didn't deserve any of this fiasco. God, even if she did have the damned file, she hadn't used the information in five years. Had his father given the order to kill to the two cops? There'd certainly been no hint given to him. Why? What was going on? All of a sudden Rico knew for certain his father had a hidden agenda. He swore profusely as the tow truck driver headed his way.

Chapter Six

Despite James having mumbled something about fate and the world moving in mysterious ways, Amy still felt completely spooked as she made her cautious way through the Supreme Court Gardens. With eyes flicking in a constant survey of her surroundings she studied every movement and person for the slightest indication of being either watched or followed. It was a difficult task given the nature of the park with a large number of garden beds containing dense foliage of mature tress and bushes interspersed by several winding footpaths. The gardens on the edge of the main business district had been in existence for many years. A wide variety of summer blooms glistened so bright in the sun's rays that they appeared to be almost iridescent. But to Amy the wavering shadows from the more mature growth took on sinister forms.

Reaching the edge of the park, she stood behind the main gatepost to wait for the walk signal at the intersection. It was not only her fear of being found that kept her as hidden as she could but also to seek shade from the already fiercely hot sun indicating no relief from the sweltering heat-wave. Under the wig she was sweating and itchy and had a desperate urge to rip it off and scratch like a flea-ridden dog.

Now she was alone and out in the open her nerves felt so taut she figured if someone dared to lay a hand on her shoulder as had happened so many times over the past day, her nerves would ping apart and scatter her body in a million bits of gore all over the pavement. She found it hard to convince herself that she wouldn't be readily recognised as she waited with her eyes scanning every single soul milling at the edge of the road.

The moment the little green man showed in the traffic lights, accompanied by his audible staccato beeps, Amy surged forward so as to mingle in the crowd of workers heading towards their offices to begin a new day. If this day was anything like the previous one Amy guessed she was going to find it extraordinarily long and tension filled.

Even though the temperature was already soaring, it was still too early for a hairdresser to be open and banks didn't begin business until half an hour after the shops so she figured a cup of coffee would be her best bet to fill in the time. But which coffee shop afforded sufficient cover? When she found herself automatically heading in the direction of her own office building she did an immediate about face and retraced her steps. Stupid, stupid, stupid! It would be the first place someone would be laying in wait for her. At the first corner she came to, she turned left and finding there were very few people in the narrow street, she broke out into a trot. It took too many seconds for her to realise that to be running, especially in this heat, brought people's attention honing on to her and her alone. Stopping suddenly she sucked in several deep breaths, slid her eyes closed and forced her body to relax before continuing at a more leisurely but tension filled pace.

Her mind swung between opting for one of the popular more modern breakfast bars or a more discreet coffee house in one of the arcades. As she walked in the midst of the densest group of people she could find, she glanced into various eateries, searching the inside for a suitable spot to remain hidden for the next three quarters of an hour. It wasn't until she had crossed the city that she found the right place. With the busy café widening once she was inside, Amy found a table for two hidden behind a potted palm. She tried both chairs before deciding on the one where she had full view of the narrow doorway by peering between fronds of greenery.

Being neither hungry nor thirsty after the more substantial breakfast than normal she'd already eaten, Amy ordered only a pot of black tea when a waitress approached with a glass and bottle of chilled water. While waiting, Amy filled her glass and took a couple of sips while continually scanning the entrance, screwing her face when she spied the dense layer of dust on what she now realised were plastic palm leaves. She was suddenly glad she hadn't ordered any food as she wondered if the level of cleanliness was any indication of the standard of service or quality of meals. Ugh! She shuddered at the thought.

Her fervent prayer that her order would take ages to be delivered went unanswered when the same waitress slid a tray onto her table only minutes later. 'Do you have the daily papers?' Amy asked.

'On that rack.' The young girl pointed with her chin towards a ladder-like construction on the back wall then returned to the kitchen.

'Wonderful service,' Amy muttered under her breath as she wove her way through the small spaces between the tables and picked up a local newspaper folded over one of the wooden rungs. 'Yesterday's,' she said more audibly as she shoved it back and returned to her seat. So far the place had absolutely nothing going for it except for the dirt-laden artificial palm behind which she could remain unseen. Pouring her tea, she wondered if it was an omen of things to come during the day or if things could only improve. She prayed for the latter as she lifted the cup to her mouth, feeling guilty about inspecting the side for traces of old lipstick or stale coffee remnants before daring to take a sip. Even though she detected no smudge, she still rubbed hard around the rim with her index finger.

When you wanted time to pass quickly it seemed to take forever, she thought when she glanced at her watch for the umpteenth time and at last the big hand approached the hour. Time to leave. Thank goodness! Most people had already left and few people had entered the premises during the forty-five minutes she had been drumming her fingers on the table in frustrated impatience. But that made sense since it was opening time for the majority of shops and businesses. All self-respecting workers would be at their stations ready to start a new day.

Amy entered the first hair salon she came to, seeking a vacant appointment spot. She wondered if the salon was as bad as the café when she was welcomed with such open arms and gushing pleasure from the young girl with spiked hair and more scrap metal piercings than she'd ever seen on one face before. For the life of her, Amy couldn't understand how people could eat with a lump of steel threaded through the tongue. The thought of a build-up of food remnants and bacteria around the shaft and under the stud was enough to create a shudder of distaste in Amy as the owner of the abominations lisped her way through questions about Amy's hair. The day was definitely getting worse but Amy didn't have time to seek another salon and didn't really care how bad her hair looked when she left. In fact, the worse she looked would probably be better, she thought as she was shown to a seat at a basin.

She whipped off the itchy, sweaty wig and let her blonde locks fall around her shoulders then took one last look in a mirror halfway across the room, at the person she'd become used to over the past five years. 'I want it in a bob tapered in at the back and coloured a natural looking red,' she said with more determination than she felt. When would she ever be able to see her hair in its natural pale gold? She sighed as towels and capes were draped around her shoulders and the process of her third identity began.

Ninety minutes later, Amy inspected her new look in a mirror, the back being reflected in a second smaller mirror held by an apprentice. The young hairdresser had done a brilliant job and was far more capable than Amy had envisioned. But it was going to take some getting used to. Taking a second look, Amy was startled to realise how much she looked like her mother now that the colour was closer to the fiery red of her mother's hair. She smiled as she wondered if James would recognise her this time. After paying the bill with cash, she headed straight for her bank, feeling far more confident she wouldn't be recognised.

The heat hit her like a full steam locomotive as she stepped from the air-conditioned salon and slid her large sunglasses over her eyes. Sweat broke out within minutes, fogging up the lenses. Turning towards the wall at the front of a building, Amy removed the glasses and wiped the moisture off with the corner of her blouse. Smaller lenses would be more appropriate but she purposefully chose the biggest glasses she could find in order to hide as much of her face as possible. She set the glasses back into place, pulling them away from her face a fraction and dropping them lower on her nose to allow more air to circulate. Even though she felt sure neither Rico nor any cohorts he had searching for her wouldn't be able to identify this new person, Amy remained vigilant as she set off again and strode down an arcade, crossed the main street at the end then entered the main branch of her bank.

Inside the door, she stood still and glanced around, wondering which section would be best to go to. What she needed was more than a brief visit to the teller. She needed privacy and, she imagined, more time than regular customers so she headed for the business section and joined the short queue.

When her turn came and she disclosed what she needed, she was met with a frown and shaking head. The simple action told her a great deal. Her day wasn't getting any better.

'You should have rung and notified us that you needed that much cash,' said the stern middle-aged man, his beady amber eyes peering at her over the edges of half lenses. He reminded her of a prowling feral cat.

'I didn't know until after closing time last night that I would have to close my account,' responded Amy in just as stern a voice as she drew herself up to her full height.

'How about a bank cheque?' The man punctuated each word with a stab of his black ballpoint pen on her withdrawal slip, adding several smudgy dots to her signature.

'Can't. Since I'm closing the only account I have, I won't be able to cash a cheque so I need the cash but first I have to pay off my credit card and close that account as well.' Past experience had taught her that bank transactions in her name could be a trail to her whereabouts. She'd been through this before. She was also well aware that to clean out her savings account in cash would create problems. These days, banks didn't like to carry large amounts of money in cash drawers in case of armed robbery and thirty odd thousand dollars was a lot to be carrying around but like most things in her life right then, her options were limited.

The man's heaved shoulders and defiant face sent Amy a definite message that he was going to be difficult. How to placate him? 'I'm sorry,' she began, 'but it is of vital importance. I need my money right now. I know it is very inconvenient but this is the head branch so you must have sufficient cash somewhere in the building.'

There was a long pause after an overloud harrumph before the man spoke again. 'I'll speak to my supervisor.' The cold, pointed tone did not bode well but the fact that he had relented even though it was just a fraction, gave her hope.

'I'd appreciate that.' Amy smiled as she plastered the meekest look on her face that she could muster. The man disappeared behind a walled partition then returned a few minutes later.

'You have identification?' he asked.

'More than you will need,' Amy replied as she delved into her bag and withdrew a zippered vinyl document case. Opening it out, she leafed through the contents until she

came to all her identity papers including her Amy Masters'
birth certificate and passport. It wasn't until the man
opened the passport out, ran his ink-stained thumb along
the binding and began comparing the picture inside with
the real person standing in front of him that she realised she
looked nothing like the photograph.

'I've just had my hair cut and coloured and if you wait
just one second…' Amy couldn't help but grin at the man's
astonished gasp when she deftly removed her coloured
contact lenses in front of him. She slid each into the palm
of her left hand, wondering what on earth she was going
to do with them until she could find a bathroom of some
description. And they would be covered in grit, dust and
germs. Far out! 'You'll see that my eyes are grey.' She smiled
then a thought suddenly occurred to her and she slid her
right hand back into the bag. She withdrew the receipt
from the hairdresser. 'Look, cut and colour.' She pointed
to the printed piece of paper, thankful she hadn't tossed the
innocuous scrap into a bin.

'I'll need to observe you sign this withdrawal slip to
compare signatures.' The man slid the paper through the
narrow horizontal slot then followed it with his pen.

Amy grinned. Things were beginning to look up.
'Certainly, not a problem, I'll sign as many pieces of paper
as you want.' She grasped the pen he held out to her
and holding the paper down with her still clenched fist,
signed, hoping her scrawl looked similar to the one on her
passport, which had been signed when she first received
her new identity. At the time she had been hesitant at the
unfamiliar name.

Her grin turned to a hesitant frown when the man
studied both signatures, then the one on the back of her

credit card. He then stared at her in silence for what seemed like an eternity.

'I'll be back,' he eventually said before vanishing into the same hidden nook.

The man was gone so long Amy was beginning to feel really concerned. What if she couldn't get her money today? It was Friday. She'd have to wait another whole two days. It was too long. She had hoped to be long gone by Monday. Her worry levels increased when the man returned accompanied by another who looked even more forbidding. This second man, much taller, reminded her of James and the way he could look so stern.

'Can I ask why you are closing your accounts?' asked the newcomer.

Amy pondered for a moment. 'It's really nobody's business but my own. It's my money and I need it urgently. I have to catch a plane tomorrow.' A ping of guilt for lying was ignored.

'You're not running from the law are you?" asked the first teller.

Amy laughed: an ironical snort. 'Quite the opposite actually, I'm running to the law.' She paused, wondering how much she could disclose. The truth may appeal to these men's consciences and she wouldn't be around long enough for it to matter. 'The man who raped me has been released from jail and found where I live and if I don't get on that plane tomorrow you'll probably be reading about my dead body in the paper.' Liar, liar, her conscience shouted. 'Hence the change in my appearance and the need to close my account in a hurry.' A thought came to her. She didn't want to involve James but she would if she had to and right now she needed every advantage possible. Besides, he'd offered his services. 'Look, I have a local QC acting for me. Give him a call to verify my claims.' She delved into her bag for the third time and searched around with her fingers until she felt the couple of business cards in the pocket. She withdrew both then handed over the one James had given her as she walked with him to the Supreme Courthouse.

Amy held her breath as both men studied the small card. Her breath eased out when the more senior man nodded to his underling and said 'Okay, release her funds. I've heard of this man.'

Raising her head skywards she acknowledged a God she'd lost faith in when trying to get Rico charged, as the manager returned to his hidey-hole and the teller began the lengthy process of closing down both of her accounts. While she waited, Amy wrapped the two tiny round lenses in a tissue and placed them in the end of a case holding her drawing pencils. It was the only place she could think of where the lenses would be relatively safe from being crushed.

It took another twenty minutes before she hurried from the bank with more cash than she cared to acknowledge, hidden in the depths of her laptop bag. She'd had to squish in the bundles of one hundred dollar bills around all the other contents giving the bag a definite bulgy look. She was only too glad her bag was of the larger variety. She began the trek up to the elite office section of the city, West Perth, for her appointment. She could have caught the free Cat bus service but with hours to spare, walking would help fill in the time.

***

With his car mobile again, Rico spent several hours penning plans, screwing them up then shoving the crunched balls into his pocket. Whilst sitting in three different cafés during the morning he'd fielded an equal number of phone calls from his father. With each call, Rico's concern deepened. There must be some reason why his Dad was sounding more and more desperate, the threats more demanding and verbal abuse stronger. This made Rico even more determined that his father wouldn't succeed in whatever sneaky plans he was withholding from Rico. He needed to find Amanda and tip her off. He needed to keep her safe.

Decision made, Rico concentrated harder on his father's words, lapping up any clue as to Amanda's whereabouts. He had no doubts that Lo Presti and Verteramo were as crooked lawmen as was his father. Why else would they be carrying out the dirty work? He also doubted they would have any difficulty in tracking Amanda therefore it was important that he kept tabs on these two henchmen even though he didn't have a clue what they looked like.

Chapter Seven

Beads of sweat were dripping from her brow and down both the front and back of her torso when Amy shouldered open the glass door of her destination. She'd stopped off in a café for an iced coffee to break what had felt like a marathon walk with the heat draining her physical stamina. Her less than normal hours of sleep didn't help matters.

The blast of cold air as she stepped inside was so welcome she stood right under the ceiling vent for several minutes to cool off before crossing the cream marble tiles to the receptionist who was eyeing her with a curious look. Having been here twice before, Amy recognised the young lady but couldn't recall her name, but it was obvious and very pleasing that said lady was having difficulty in recognising the stranger acting like such an idiot, cavorting this way and that underneath a single vent. Using the corner of her blue cotton blouse, Amy bent to wipe the moisture from her face before glancing at her watch. She still had thirty minutes before she was expected, enough time to make a few phone calls. She crossed the floor and approached the desk.

'Amy Masters, I have a meeting at two.' At the stunned stare from the woman opposite her Amy lifted her sunglasses from her brow.

'I didn't recognise you.' The lady pointed to Amy's head. 'Your hair, it's so different!'

Amy felt pleased but tried to act as though her changed looks was an everyday occurrence. 'I like a change every now and again. Saves me from getting in a rut. Look,' she peered at the woman's nametag, 'Michelle, I know I'm early but I have a couple of phone calls to make. Is there somewhere I could sit with a little privacy? And some cold water would be most appreciated.'

'Certainly. I believe the conference room is waiting. I was told you would need to set up for a Power-point presentation. It's all ready. There's hot and cold refreshments waiting. Follow me.'

Amy hadn't realised she felt so tense until a held breath gushed from her lips and her shoulders slumped in relaxation as she followed Michelle down a short passage then into a large room set up with a long oval polished jarrah conference table. Six chairs were grouped around one end with an already set screen at the other. Cable ends were just waiting to be plugged into her laptop. Along one wall was a credenza with glasses, cups and the makings of tea and coffee all ready. A tray covered with a draped clean tea towel held promise of food, reminding Amy that she hadn't bothered to eat during her brief stop. Seeing the tray caused an involuntary tightening in her stomach and she realised she was hungry. Daring to peek under the cloth, she lifted a corner. Suppressed aromas of fresh pastries wafted upwards and the sight of glazed apricots and apples nestled in creamy yellow custard caused an embarrassing gurgle as her stomach relaxed.

'This is perfect, thank you.' Tucking the edge of the tea towel back under the tray Amy then filled a glass with water from one of three jugs, ensuring at least two ice-blocks plopped into her glass. She took a sip, groaned in pleasure as the coldness zinged against the back of her dry throat then she quickly consumed half the glass before filling it again. Satisfied, she turned to Michelle. 'Umm, apart from letting Keith know that I've arrived, if any one else asks after me, can you not let them know I'm here?'

'What do you mean?'

Far out, what could she say? Amy thought long and deep. How could she explain this when she didn't understand herself the deep pressure of dread that had settled across her shoulders and into her stomach? So far the day had gone reasonably well, if you didn't count dirt-laden palms and stubborn pernickety bank tellers. Much better than she had anticipated but an insidious niggle kept eating away at her innards. She lifted a hand to her head. 'The hair, there's a real nasty man looking for me. I can't give you the details but if he finds me then I'm as good as dead.'

Amy's words were met with an indrawn hiss then a mouth that opened and refused to close. Wide brown unblinking eyes stared at her in the stunned silence.

'Five years ago, this man raped me and left me for dead,' Amy added in an undertone.

Michelle might have been excellent at her job, but the words that slid from her shocked mouth were better off not heard by any of her workmates or customers of the company. An embarrassed blush rose up her cheeks as her hands automatically flew to her mouth. 'I'm sorry I didn't mean to say that.'

Amy smiled - what else could she do? 'That's okay, I shocked you but what I said is the truth. I had better warn you though - it might not be Rico who comes looking for me. He has…' how could she explain this? 'He has people working for him. Think criminal gangs of the worst kind and you might get the gist.'

Another series of four letter words shot from Michelle's mouth causing her to blush even more. 'I'm really sorry. I promise I won't let on, about you… you know…. I won't say anything. Wow! Gangs? Really truly?'

'Of the worst kind.' Inside Amy was grinning at the naïve awe of Michelle who couldn't be more than eighteen. 'Now, if you don't mind I need to make a couple of phone calls.'

'Oh, oh… of course.' Michelle spun away then headed for the door. 'I'll let Keith know you are here. And please, if you need anything else call me on the extension over there.' Michelle indicated an internal office phone sitting on a separate small desk in the far corner. 'Just press three.'

The moment Michelle left her in peace Amy settled into the nearest chair, removed her folder of personal papers and searched through until she found the phone number she was looking for. She dialled Sergeant Michael Simpson's number then waited, listening to the ringing until the phone rang out. Every five minutes she repeated the call but there was no answer. This sent the niggles of unease she'd been having all day into overdrive. The number was Michael's personal mobile and he'd never not responded before.

As a last resort she put in a call to Michael's office, the headquarters of the Federal Police in Sydney. Her unease strengthened to major stabs by the time she was passed from one person to the next only to be told that Michael was on temporary leave and couldn't be contacted. In all her previous dealings with him that was unheard of. What was more concerning was that even if he were on leave, surely he would answer his personal mobile phone. She was chewing on the corner of her lip with her hands unconsciously wrapped around her upper body when the door opened. Completely spooked, Amy shot up then around on one foot then slumped back into the chair.

'Keith, it's only you.' The words rushed from her mouth.

'Only me, who else were you expecting?' Keith neared her then paused, his face taking on a concerned look. 'Are you okay?'

'I'm fine,' she lied as she snapped her mobile phone shut, slid it into her bag then began setting up her laptop computer. By the time she had the programme up and running and had tested the remote control, the other four company executives had just settled into the seats. She was ten minutes into her presentation when her boss, Brendan, rushed in, excused himself then slunk into the only vacant chair.

Guilt stabbed at Amy for even though she had emailed these improved designs to him this was the first time she hadn't gone through the details with her boss before a presentation. But he hadn't rung so she figured he was happy with what she'd done. For the next two hours all thoughts of Rico were cast from her mind as she concentrated on displaying and explaining her designs for the interior of a new office building the company she worked for was designing.

After jotting down the few required minor changes in her ever-present notebook, Amy began packing up her gear. 'I'll email the changes sometime in the next few days,' she said as she zippered her bag.

'Take your time we don't expect you to spend your weekend working.' Keith offered her the plate of pastries.

Amy wavered before declining the food. She felt ravenous but her desire to leave as soon as possible outweighed her hunger. 'I need to tell you that I've tendered my resignation. I've promised to see this job completed so I will work on these changes immediately.'

'Resigned? Why? I thought you enjoyed your work.' Keith indicated the coffee pot with one hand, inclining his head in question.

'No thank you, I need to leave.' She waved away the percolator as Brendan joined them. She hadn't given him the true reason for her hasty departure. 'I do love my work but something, umm, urgent has come up and I have to fly east.'

'A job offer?'

When Brendan bristled at Keith's question Amy shook her head in negation. 'I wish. No, and it's going to be hard to find such a perfect position again.' She smiled at Brendan. 'Something personal has come up but I can't talk about it.' She shoved the remaining few items in the bag that contained so much it was difficult to zip shut then headed for the door. 'I have to go. Brendan, I'll email you with a fuller explanation as soon as I can.'

As she stepped into the passage, Amy glanced at her watch. It was earlier than she had anticipated with at least thirty minutes before James was due to pick her up. With her head down while thinking where she could hide out for the next half hour, she strode down the passage and pushed open the door leading into the reception area. 'See you later, Michelle,' she called as she passed the desk.

Then she came to a grinding halt when a man rose from the square of seats in the waiting area. A shiver of fear quivered from head to toe at the vague recognition. He was quite tall with broad shoulders and wearing a suit that hadn't seen the dry-cleaners for too long. It was the shape of the man rather than the unfamiliar facial features that brought back a recent memory. She felt as though she had become paralysed and unable to move for she felt certain he was the one who searched behind the bins at James's house. How in heaven's name did he track her here?

'Ma'am, have you seen this woman in here?' As he approached the man held out a photograph. Coming to her senses, Amy realised he hadn't recognised her. She swept her eyes towards the proffered photo then felt her heart miss a couple of beats before kick starting again. The photo was of her. She should have expected it but actually seeing herself was an enormous shock. She slid a quick glance towards Michelle who shook her head but whose face was contorted in fear. Amy didn't dare raise her eyes to look directly at the man since she hadn't had time to replace her contact lenses. Staring at her own reflection she knew her eyes would tell the truth. She didn't find her eyes particularly attractive but she knew the shape and colour were distinctive, especially this close. To keep her face out of direct line of vision she reached out with one hand and gripped the edge of the photo, fighting to swallow her gasp when she realised how recent it was. The background was of her office building and the clothes were the ones she'd had on only yesterday. This was taken as she went into work yesterday morning.

She scrabbled in her mind on what to do. Instinct told her that this man was one of Rico's cronies. Why else would he be looking for her and why else would he have such a recent photograph of her? He might be a law enforcement officer but if he was, and he hadn't shown a badge, then he was as crooked as Rico.

'Err; I think she's at a meeting back there. They've just called for refreshments so I think they'll only be about another fifteen minutes.' Releasing her hold on the photo, Amy began walking towards the front door, calling over her shoulder without actually turning her face. 'Look, I have to hurry.' She patted her bag. 'Banking. I have to get to the bank in time to do the banking.'

Amy was out the door and striding down the path so quick the man had no option but to accept her word. She hadn't missed his grin of triumph from the corner of her eye as she'd fled. She also hadn't missed the gasp of shock from Michelle at her overt lie. God, she hoped Michelle didn't spill the beans. The minute she was out of sight of the building, she hastened her steps then slowed again when she remembered there had been two police officers the previous day and officers tended to work in pairs. To make it not blatantly obvious she was searching for the car and the other man, she moved to the kerb, slid her sunglasses over her eyes then glanced both ways down the street as though to cross.

Her breath stalled when a second man emerged from the driver's seat of a dark blue sedan directly across the road. He had a mobile phone plastered against one ear and was looking straight at her. Adrenaline screamed through Amy's veins. Running would be obvious, as would not crossing the road when she had made every indication that it was what she had intended. Keeping her head twisted and as low as she could, she waited for the stream of traffic to pass then ran through a gap but turned on an angle so the man would only see her back. Reaching the other side, she strode down the pavement, keeping her eyes glancing into the windows of buildings for any sign of being followed. She strained her ears for the slightest sound of following footsteps or the man calling out for her to stop.

Reaching the first crossroad, Amy turned right, walked steadily until she was certain she was out of the man's vision around the corner then broke out into a frantic run. As she jogged, she scrabbled in the front pocket of her bag for her mobile phone and James's business card. It was difficult reading the number and dialling as she ran, the large bag slapping wildly against her hip and her sweaty hands making everything slippery. She didn't ease her pace as she placed the phone against her ear and held the bag still with her other hand. It felt like hours before James responded.

'James, change of plan,' she panted. She sped around the next corner, swerving to avoid a business-suited man coming the other way and ignoring his call to watch out. 'Those same police officers that turned up at your place were at the office where I had the meeting.' Her breath came in gasps as she panted out her words. 'They had a photo of me – taken only yesterday morning. They were waiting.' She heard James mumble something but her heavy breathing, the slap, slap, slap of her feet on the concrete pavement, the rustling of the bag against her slacks and the up and down jolting made it difficult to make out his words. She had to stop but didn't dare. Glancing around as she kept on running with the phone against her ear, she searched for somewhere, anywhere, to hide. In the backstreet, the buildings, mostly old houses turned into boutique offices, were small and close together.

She shot down a driveway and found herself in a small car park behind what was once an old brick cottage but had been restored into offices. There was room for just three cars, an industrial rubbish bin of dubious age and a narrow row of unkempt bushes along the back fence-line. If she got caught here, there would be no escape. In an effort to keep intruders at bay, the surrounding fences were too high to clamber over unless she used the cars to give her leverage. 'James, I need to meet you somewhere else. How did they find me?'

'Did you make any calls on your mobile phone?' James asked.

'Yes, several. Why?'

'Is your phone a fairly recent model?'

Amy stared at said phone before answering. What difference did it make how modern her phone was? 'Yes, I purchased it about six months ago? Why?'

'With the right equipment they can trace your position by triangulating from mobile phone towers. Listen hard. You're on King's Park side of West Perth aren't you?'

'Yes, about two blocks away.' Two blocks with two nasty men after her: the odds weren't good.

'Do you know Jacob's Ladder?'

'Yes, I think so. I've seen it but never been up it though.'

'Good. I've just left home so will be driving along Mount's Bay Road. Once you cross King's Park Road you can use the bush as cover. Go down Jacob's ladder and I'll meet you at the bottom in fifteen minutes. I'll be waiting for you. Do you understand?'

'Yes.' Amy was bent over double, dragging air into her lungs with her bag hanging from her neck and almost reaching the ground. Great droplets of sweat dripped onto the grey bitumen but sizzled and evaporated the moment they hit the hot surface. Her clothes already felt hot and damp and were clinging like a second skin. She swiped at her face with her bare arm but it felt as though the amount she swept away was replaced within seconds.

'Amy, get rid of the phone. Dump it. Now.' A click told Amy that James had hung up.

In a state of disbelief and shock, Amy stared again at her own phone for several seconds. 'My phone? They can trace where I am by my phone?' She shuddered then dropped the still open phone as though it were scorching her fingers. Feeling a surge of sheer fury, she lifted one foot then stomped on the abomination again and again until it was so mangled only the cracked glass face gave it any indication it was once a phone. After staring at the remnants while forcing her body to calm, she scraped up the pieces and hurled them into the waste bin.

Then a thought came to her. She hadn't switched the phone off. Could they still be tracing the phone? She had no idea how such technology worked but she figured she had to get out of there and fast. She wavered between retrieving the phone and attempting to remove the sim card but one peek in the huge bin and she knew it would take too long for the mangled plastic was at the very bottom amidst torn plastic bags of something that looked as though it had been fermenting for several years. It both looked and smelt gross.

Hitching her bag across her chest then over her other shoulder Amy retraced her steps, pausing at the entrance to the drive to work out exactly where she was and which was the best way to go. With two blocks to go before reaching the busy King's Park Road she would be vulnerable out in the open but what else could she do? Standing there like a stunned kangaroo caught in headlights of an oncoming car was just plain stupid.

She set off at a brisk walk. Power walking was good for you but she figured doing it in blistering heat wasn't what the health experts intended. Buildings were close together with tiny gardens affording little cover. The only positive she could see were the many mature street trees casting shadows all the way along the concrete slabbed footpath. Searching both ways up and down the street for any sign of two men or a blue car searching for her, Amy checked she was headed in the right direction then strode briskly but not with the frantic speed she'd used before. Her entire body was exuding perspiration by the litre but knowing it wasn't going to stop any time soon in the relentless heat, she ignored it, concentrating only on the cars as she moved, using the shadows of the trees as she strode, thankful for even the briefest of moments out of the sun's direct rays.

It was amazing how many cars were blue when you didn't want to ever see another blue car in your life, she thought as she neared King's Park Road. She hesitated before exposing herself on the footpath of such a busy road. There were two lanes of continuous traffic going each way with a wide, well-maintained island consisting of mowed lawn and a long garden bed filled with blooming pink roses, in between: a good thirty metres without a skerrick of cover. She waited for a break in the traffic, sucked in a deep breath then shot forwards, jogging across the first two lanes. She slowed as she crossed the island, her eyes studying each car as it whizzed past. Not daring to stay exposed a moment longer she took a chance at the first break, knowing there wasn't really enough space between cars for a really safe crossing.

A blare of a horn as a driver had to brake to avoid hitting her barely registered as Amy kept on running once she'd reached the other side of the road. She headed straight for the area of bush behind a wide swathe of beautifully mown lawn. Keeping to the fringes of the bush, she kept jogging until she felt she was in line with the top of Jacob's ladder: a back breaking number of steps leading from the top of the hill to the river below. She'd heard of it, seen it but had never used the steps. Coming to a halt, Amy paused as she stared across the road. She had at least a hundred metres of being out in the open to reach the bush on the other side. This was all too hard.

Before taking the first step, Amy studied the area both ways. Traffic here at the beginning of this major tourist attraction was lighter with only a single lane each way but there was still a steady stream. Were they searching for her yet? She glanced at her watch. The fifteen minutes she told the detective was long gone. Had they put two and two together yet? Both men had seen her. Had Keith been asked? Or Brendan and Michelle? Not wanting to get too many people involved she'd refrained from asking either Keith or Brendan to keep her presence quiet. Stupid, stupid, stupid!

She licked her lips, wincing at the salty taste. She had to assume they were searching for her red hair, long frame, white slacks and deep blue blouse. Far out, she couldn't be any more obvious if she'd tried and this morning she thought she had dressed as conservatively as possible.

The breath she sucked in before taking off was purely for courage. She was either going to make it or get caught. Praying that the two men were still searching the streets where they'd last seen her, Amy took the first tentative step then increased her speed, pausing only long enough to ensure she didn't get splattered by a car as she raced full pelt across the road. She was almost at the kerb when a flash of dark blue registered. Adrenaline surged and she doubled her speed, not daring to waste time to check out the car.

Not knowing exactly where they were, it took Amy a while to find the top of the steps. She knew James would already be at the bottom waiting for her to appear. How long would he wait before he gave up and came searching for her? She ran, one hand skating along the handrail as she jolted down the steep stairway while the other held her flapping bag against her side. Beneath the bag, she knew her clothes were soaked, the rush of wind causing a cool dampness. Sweat poured from her body and trickled down her face carrying the taste of salt to her lips that felt as though they were chafed. Her lungs screamed for more oxygen as she panted in short gasps. She passed others going down, barely registering the aura of tourists by the hanging camera, backpacks and gaudy dress. A couple of hardy souls dressed in exercise gear were labouring upwards, causing Amy to wonder exactly how many steps there were. She could see the bottom when she slipped and hurtled down several steps on her knees before she could manage to grasp the metal posts to stop her fall. A yell from above had her scramble to her feet and get them moving again. It had to be the two men. She heard herself whining as she pounded on downwards. It felt like there were thousands of metal steps by the time she spied the huge man pacing around at the bottom with his eyes turned in her direction.

James. Never had a man looked so good to her. She ran straight into his arms and collapsed against his body, her chest heaving as she dragged in great gulping gasps of air. The moment his long arms wrapped around her she promptly broke down and began sobbing. 'They are just behind me, coming down the steps.'

***

'She's in Mayfair St, between Colin and Outram Streets in West Perth. Now get over there and find her!'

At the yelled words from his father, Rico reached over to the back seat and grabbed a hold of the road directory with one hand, the other keeping the phone against his ear.

'And she's a redhead now!'

'What? Red? Are you sure it's her?' Flabbergasted, Rico jolted around, the directory slipping from his fingers. Finding it impossible to reach the book, he juggled the phone from one hand to the other, unclasped his seatbelt then levered his body upright using his feet to push up until he could twist far enough around to grasp the pages and haul the book into his lap.

'Of course it's her. We have a trace on her phone. She's making a call now. Get her!' A sharp snap followed by dead silence told Rico that his father had hung up. Sliding the phone back into his pocket he began rifling through the pages with his other hand. 'Mayfair,' he mumbled as he ran a finger down the street names, flicked a page then scanned three columns. 'Mayfair – Cool… Meadow… Willetton, shit, what was the suburb? Ah, yes, West Perth. Map 1 B3.' Instead of wasting time tracing a route through pages of maps, Rico leant forwards and set directions on the Navman set on the dashboard of the rented car then followed the directions, praying he managed to reach Amanda before Lo Presti and Verteramo.

Turning the corner into Mayfair, he slowed to a crawl and scanned the interiors of parked cars as he passed them. There was no sign of any human wandering around, nor in any of the vehicles and who would be sitting in their car in this heat? Reaching the end of the street, he pulled into a vacant parking space and eased out of the car. Rico zigzagged from one side of the road to the other, peering down driveways and into windows but not really knowing what to look for, except a redhead with a body to die for and the longest of legs. God, how he had admired those legs that seemed to go on forever!

'Hey, Rico!' He spun around at the sound of his name being called then searched for someone he recognised. Two suited men were huddled over something at the top of a driveway. One looked up and stared at him. 'You are Rico, aren't you? Your father said you would be coming.'

God, they've found her, was all Rico could think about as he walked slowly towards the two men. 'I take it you are Lo Presti and Verteramo.' He knew of the two men but had never met either. They were cops but earned the bulk of their money doing his father's less than honest deeds: dirty untaxed and untraceable money, for dirty and dishonest work. Fearing the worst, Rico ignored the proffered hand of the taller of the two. As he neared them, he noticed that both were red-faced with rivers of sweat pouring from their brows. They'd been hoofing it for some time. 'Did you find her?'

'The bitch gave us the slip. Found this.'

Rico glanced down at the man's hand, frowned at the mangled mess of plastic and metal then smiled inwardly when he realised what it was. But how on earth did Amanda know to get rid of her phone – if it was hers. 'Are you certain it's Amanda's?' He had to know for sure.

'It's the phone we were getting the signal from and it was the number we were given so as sure as we can be.'

'So you're not a hundred percent certain that the woman you were following was Amanda?' He certainly hoped not.

'We're sure. She's wearing a red wig, white slacks and bright blue top. Should be easy to find.'

Hope soared, as did the need to get back at his father. 'So easy that two detectives being paid a huge sum of underhand money, lost her trail.' Laughter gurgled up his gullet then spilled out. 'Ring me when you find her again.' He gasped out before fighting for control. 'I'm going back to wait for her to return home.' With his lips twitching, he turned away and ambled along the footpath, calling over his shoulder, 'Don't let the heat get to you, fellas!'

He ignored the, 'Bastard!' thrown back at him.

Chapter Eight

After spending several minutes gazing at the stairway, James assured Amy that no one was following or if they were, they were staying out of sight. Amy was more than thankful when James gave her time to calm then gather together her shattered emotions. His hands ran in gentle circles along her back and arms while he supported her shaking body against his torso. Her tears soaked his shirt but he said nothing other than, 'Calm yourself. You're safe. Take your time.'

Amy heard and felt him but couldn't control her tears or the way her body trembled. She was still shaking when she felt James shift his position and tucked her under one arm. She stumbled on legs that were shaky from the exertion as he began leading her across the dry grass towards the edge of the road but he steadied her. Swaying on her feet, she saw through her soaking eyes a bleary image of a man-made lake across the other side of the road then his car came into view. It was parked on the pathway of the small cul de sac.

'It's damned hot out here and we need to get you home,' said James as he pulled his arm from her shoulder then withdrew car keys from a pocket. He grabbed her again as she swayed then fell against the side of the car. 'Steady up, Amy, I'm guessing you are a tad dehydrated.'

She heard the *bleep, bleep,* of the remote unlocking the door then felt her body being shuffled away from the car before James opened the door and assisted her inside. He leant over her and strapped her in then reached into the back seat. As he withdrew, he handed her a bottle. 'Get this into you. It was cold when I bought it.' Twisting the top open he removed the plastic cap and wrapped her fingers around the cool plastic. It wasn't exactly cold any longer but the water felt like manna from heaven.

It took a moment for Amy to control the shaking of her hands as she stared at the bottle. Then she lifted it to her mouth and poured, gulping the entire contents without pausing. She ignored the dribbles that ran from the corners of her mouth and down her chin until the bottle was empty then she swiped the excess moisture away with her forearm. 'Boy, I really needed that.'

James eased his massive frame into the driver's seat then twisted and reached into the back seat. When he straightened he held a second bottle of water in his hand and offered it to Amy. 'There's more if you need it.'

Feeling guilty and knowing James had been waiting in the stifling heat for at least half an hour Amy shook her head and pushed the bottle towards him. 'No, I'm fine now.

We'll be home soon. If I drink any more I'll probably make myself sick.'

'You look as though you've just completed a marathon.' James took a long swig from the bottle then recapped it. He then opened the console between them, pulled out a small travel pack of tissues and held them out.

'I feel as though I've just run three of them.' Amy swiped at another wave of moisture from her forehead with her arm before taking the proffered package. 'I'm sorry about breaking down. I don't do the tear thing any more but it was such a relief to see you. I was petrified.'

James swung the rear vision mirror around in her direction. 'You were scared. You have every right to relieve your fear with a few tears. Take a look.'

Knowing how ghastly she felt, Amy didn't really want to see what she looked like but she dared a peek. 'Far out!' Her face was bright red, her hair as wet as if she'd just come from under a shower and was hanging in limp strands. Moisture was still steadily beading on her overheated skin.'

'I like the hair style.' There was definite humour in his voice.

'It looked all right when I left the hairdresser.' Then she gasped as a sudden thought came to her. 'We'll have to stop at a chemist or supermarket on the way home. Those two police officers saw me with red hair. I'm going to have to change the colour again as soon as we get home.'

'Pity,' murmured James as he turned the key and the engine purred into life. 'The colour suits you.' As he edged to the kerb, he added, 'What is the real colour of your hair?'

'Honey gold, but I haven't seen my natural colour for five very long years.'

James eased onto the road running back into the city then made all the road changes until they were headed west, the lowering sun blinding them until he dropped down both sun visors. 'Tell me what happened.'

As he drove, Amy related her story, only ceasing when James pulled into a pharmacy. 'Stay here,' he said as he unfolded his body. 'What do you need?'

Amy leant over to glance in the mirror. Her face was not a lot paler but the entire packet of tissues had removed most of the moisture. The air-conditioner turned up at full blast had gone some way towards stopping the steady flow of perspiration and lightening the redness. 'I guess the only way to go now is black. And I'll need a pair of hairdressing scissors.' She ran the fingers of one hand through the still wet strands. 'I have to alter the style again.'

As James walked away, she opened the door and half stepped out. 'I need some contact lens solution as well,' she called. James waved in acknowledgement. While waiting she retrieved her lenses from their hiding place and unwrapped them. She was still picking off minute pieces of tissue remnants when James slid back into the driver's seat. He sat staring at the tiny coloured pieces of plastic held on the end of two fingers then placed one hand under her chin and twisted her head to gain eye contact.

'What happened?' He dropped the package into her lap.

'The man in the bank compared my passport photo to the person standing in front of him.'

'Before or after the hairdo?'

Amy grinned. 'After. I had to convince him my eyes were grey.'

'Can I make an inference that the man waiting for you saw a redhead with grey eyes?'

Amy sighed. 'Yes."

'Maybe that was a good thing. It would have convinced him that it was actually you he saw, so now they will be searching for a woman of that description.' James pulled onto the road and headed the short distance home, which was completed in contemplative silence while Amy rid her lenses of as much shredded paper as she could.

The moment they turned off the highway Amy began searching the street for any sign of Rico or a blue sedan. She doubled up moments before they passed her street, and remained with her head on her knees until after James had pulled into his garage and the remote controlled doors had dropped completely down.

James sat for a moment, the engine still idling. 'I saw no cars. You said he raped you but there's more than that, isn't there?'

Amy shot her head up, alarmed at his perception. She stared at him for a moment. 'How did…?' she stuttered. 'Yes, but I can't talk about it. It's too…' She glanced away then made to exit the car, the old memories rising up and swirling around. She felt James drop a hand on her forearm and the gentle squeeze. She knew it was a sign of understanding but couldn't face continuing the conversation. 'I'm going to have a shower and do something with this hair,' she called as she dragged her bag from the back seat then fled inside.

She heard James follow, his leather sandals padding loudly on the tiles. 'Amy,' he called as he reached her.

Amy paused but didn't turn around.

'I'm sorry if I brought up bad memories but it would help if I knew a few more facts so I can gain a better understanding of what you are up against. I have to tell you that I did a bit of research on the web this afternoon.'

With panic rising in a sudden burst Amy spun around. 'I asked you not to poke your nose in.'

'I used the firm's web name, not mine. We employ a lot of people. I searched under the surname but the only

Giovannazzo I could come up is a District Court judge in New South Wales.' He paused at the long hiss escaping Amy's mouth.

'That's Rico's father. So you understand why it was so hard for me to get the authorities to act. He's also a member of a family underworld gang. In fact I think he's the big boss.' Amy spun back around and headed for the bathroom.

James shot after her and grasped her hand before she could get inside the door. 'You can't drop a bombshell like that and not explain any more. How do you know he's a member?'

'I have spent the past five years doing a great deal of research using computers in libraries and internet shops under different Google names, so nothing can be traced back to me. I have paperwork. If you study very closely the trials he has presided over you will find a certain pattern of criminals who were obviously guilty being let off on technicalities or being given very minor terms. Plus there were certain papers and notes in Rico's desk that linked his father to what Rico was up to. I traced quite a few leads I gleaned from those papers. And since there is a very strong family link to a major gang in Sicily, which is where they came from, I suspect papa is the head of this particular family gang. Now I'm going to have a shower.' She pulled away and slammed the door in his face.

'I'm going for a walk to check out your place,' she heard James call after he had banged on the door. She yanked the door open.

'Don't you dare!'

He was standing right there, grinning. 'I walk these streets every day, sometimes twice a day to keep fit. It's a common occurrence for me to be roaming around. I'm just going to be walking past your place, not knocking on your door. I want to see if anyone is hanging around. How long do you need for that stuff,' he pointed to the package she had grasped against her chest, 'to work.'

'Probably about three quarters of an hour.'

'I'll be back before then. Don't answer the door, I'll take a key.' He tapped her on the end of her nose and departed, leaving her standing there with her mouth agape.

After ripping the paper bag and spilling the contents onto the vanity top, Amy poured a small amount of contact lens solution into a small drinking glass used for rinsing the mouth after teeth brushing and dropped her lenses in to soak while she showered. Toothpaste dregs she could handle germs she couldn't. Then she picked up the pair of scissors and ripped the price tag off, noting the cost so she could repay James. Undressing so that loose strands of hair didn't stick to her clothes she then began hacking away at her hair, clump by wet bedraggled clump, dropping the pieces into a small refuse bin that stood at the end of the vanity unit. She kept cutting until her remaining hair fell around her head pixie style, the uneven ends not mattering so much. She wiped down the bench and tiled floor with a damp flannel to remove most of the loose hairs then read the label on the bottle of hair dye.

Under an almost cold shower to cool her overheated body, Amy applied the dye before soaping the layer of perspiration and dust from her limbs and torso. While waiting the required twenty minutes for the colour to set, she wrapped a towel around her body and carried her laptop bag into the bedroom then set out a clean set of clothes. Used to bright contrasting colours, she stared at the outfit laid out on her bed for a few moments before swapping the T-shirt from dark vivid green to a plain white to match the white denim shorts. She had to remember to dress more conservatively so she didn't stand out.

Back in the bathroom, she took her time rinsing out the dye and ensuring her skin was thoroughly cleaned and showed no signs of dark dye. She jolted back in shock when she finally stood in front of the mirror above the vanity, the dripping black strands of hair feathering around her face. The change was so dramatic she didn't recognise her own image. After staring for a few moments she twisted her head this way and that to see more of her head and to make sure there were no obviously long bits or definite hacks to indicate an amateurish job. Then to get an idea of the overall picture she placed her contact lenses over her irises. Staring at her image, she wasn't satisfied that hazel eyes went so well with ebony black hair. She needed the darker colour. She wrapped a towel around her body and stepped out into the passage.

The sound of male voices brought her to a standstill in the open doorway.

'What were you doing snooping around number thirty seven?' Amy ceased breathing when she recognised the voice as the police officer that had confronted her earlier.

'I wasn't snooping around any house. I was walking the streets as I do every day.' James replied.

'You were studying the property closely.'

'I was probably studying several of the properties closely if that is how you perceive things. I have to look at something as I walk. I can't walk around with my eyes shut.' James sounded sarcastic.

'No need to get smarmy with me!'

'And there's no need to be so officious with me. You have a problem with the locals walking around their own streets?' Amy grinned. James sounded as though he was becoming like the forbidding person she'd glimpsed a couple of times.

'Do you know the lady who lives in number thirty seven?' This question had Amy bristle then stand at attention, holding her breath to hear clearly how James would answer.

'I've met her a couple of times since I moved here. Just like I've met quite a few of the locals on our regular rambles. We've chatted on occasion.'

Very clever, thought Amy. He's telling the truth but at the same time evading the truth. She began to see the lawyer in him.

'Why, has something happened to her?'

'No, her husband is looking for her. She seems to have disappeared.' Amy sucked in a breath and must have made a sound for before she could unfreeze, James's head appeared around the corner of the entry hall.

Then a second head emerged, recognition turning Amy into a solid statue. 'Who is that?' The man barged past James and strode quickly towards Amy.

'Mrs Giovannazzo?' Before she had a chance to say a word the man reached her, lifted a hand and yanked hard at her hair.

Amy squealed in pain then without thinking slapped the man across one cheek. How dare he? Gathering her thoughts together in a hurry she stared at the man and voiced her thoughts. 'How dare you?' she yelled in the broadest of Scottish accents. Having grown up with Scottish parents she had no difficulty with the brogue.

Both men stared at her in shock. 'The name is Cathy and it's Miss.' Amy said as she gripped at the slipping towel and hoisted it higher. 'And if you'll excuse me, I need to get dressed.' She glared at the man then stalked down the passage and into her bedroom, slamming the door before slumping against it.

'Come back here,' she heard James call moments before a loud knock sounded on her door. Startled she stood stock still, unable to figure out why James wanted her to face the officer.

'I need to talk to that woman.' The officer yelled so loud Amy checked that the door hadn't opened then suddenly realised James had been talking to the detective and not her.

'That woman as you call her, happens to me my girlfriend,' she heard James add. Amy bolted upright at the blatant lie.

'And what does your wife think of you entertaining your floozy in her house?'

The silence was so profound it was deafening. Amy felt her heart race as she waited for James to say something.

'What makes you think I have a wife?' James's voice was so quiet Amy could tell he was furious.

'The wedding ring.' There was a definite sneer to the tone.

'My wife is dead. The ring is pure self-defence. It didn't take me long after Glenda passed away to realise that a single man with a more than adequate income was fair game for unscrupulous gold-diggers. Replacing my ring was the only way I was able to stop the onslaught.'

Amy wondered how much of what James said was true. She believed from the way he had spoken the night before that James was still in love with his wife and hadn't got over his grief yet.

'Cathy is my first serious relationship.' Amy's head shot up. Now he was really lying and she hadn't thought he would go that far. A strange sensation of warmth tingled through her veins at the knowledge James would lie for her.

'She looks very much like the woman we are after.' Something very hard lodged in Amy's throat.

'Looks alike? How? If I recall, Amy is a blue-eyed blonde."

'She's about the right height and build.'

'She's about the right height? And that gives you the right to barge into my home, uninvited and then physically assault my woman? I trust you have a search warrant.' There was quite a lengthy pause. 'You questioned Cathy without announcing you were police officers, you were not invited into my home and you didn't request permission to enter.' James began sounding very officious.

'What are you, some kind of lawyer?'

Amy moved closer to the door at the sound of a distinctly different voice, guessing it to be the detective's partner.

'QC,' was all James said.

'Shit!' Amy couldn't tell from which man the muffled imprecation came.

'A very appropriate choice of word, my friend, since the two of you are in it up to your necks. I will be pursuing your illegal actions today. Expect to have charges laid against you.' Another pause ensued. 'James Ward.' Amy envisioned him holding out his hand just as he had done with her.

The same swear word she'd heard moments ago, was uttered by both policemen before Amy heard James laugh. 'I see you recognise the name.'

'You are the one…'

'The one who had one of your colleagues put in jail today? Our investigations haven't concluded. Maybe I should be adding your names to our list.'

The voice faded, along with three sets of footsteps and two other muffled voices. At the sound of a closing door

Amy began dragging her clothes on, her mind in turmoil. What did James mean? What case had he been on? What was he investigating?

Amy was so wrapped up in replaying all she had heard that she forgot one particular sentence until she opened the door and stepped out into the passage. James was standing leant up against the opposite wall, one leg crossed over the other and his arms folded over his chest. With his head cocked to one side he gave the impression of being completely at ease. He peered up out of the corner of his eye.

'Mrs Giovannazzo, I presume.'

***

Rico paced, waiting for Lo Presti and Verteramo to return. Personally, he thought the two men were fantasising about the woman in the bloke's place around the corner being Amanda. And the fact that the man had walked past the house while they were searching the inside, yet again, was pure coincidence. As Rico pointed out to his two unwelcome guests, prior to being incarcerated he had jogged around his local environs every day. It happened all over the country so why should here be any different.

But Amanda had stolen in during the early hours of the morning, so she must have been close by since he was certain she didn't own a vehicle. But then again, she could easily have borrowed a friend's car and she'd had more than a couple of hours in which to make the raid. What a damn mistake that had been: drinking on the job. God, his father would have skinned him alive if he'd been here.

A sudden vibration at his chest broke his thoughts. Glancing at the number lit up in the lighted window, Rico grimaced. It was as though the damned man was reading his mind. He paused before flipping the instrument open. Better get it over and done with.

'Tell me, you've got it!' his father barked.

'Why don't you ask those two idiots who let her get away? They know the lay of the land better than me and they were on her tail. It's my guess she put two and two together because they let her see them. How else would she have known to dump her phone? She's probably half way to woop-woop by now, thanks to your henchmen.' Even as he spouted the words, Rico knew his father would explode and lay the blame at his feet. It was always Rico's fault.

'Don't you dare speak to me like that. If you hadn't gone crazy in the first place, none of this would have happened.'

'And who was it that got me hooked on the damn steroids. No son of yours was going to look like some weak-kneed poofter,' he parroted in a cynical tone. 'I think those were your exact words.'

'Didn't do you any bloody good did they? You're still a weak-kneed poofter. Christ, don't tell me I'm going to have to fly over there and sort this out myself. Where are those two idiots?'

'Chasing imaginary ghosts. We've searched this place again. There's nothing here.'

'She could have hidden it elsewhere by now.'

'She didn't know we were on to her and she hadn't been back here before I searched the place. Personally I don't believe she's even got it. If she did, why in hell's name didn't she hand it over to the Feds? There hasn't even been a sniff of her having it, no questions, no enquiries – nothing in five years.'

'Like I said before, she would have held off until your release.'

'But it implicates you more than me and my guess is she hates you more than me.' Rico paused as another thought came to him. 'Amanda didn't know I was being released.'

'Just find her and get it back. I'll give you another twenty-four hours.'

Rico sighed when the click was followed by silence. His father was wrong – he had to be wrong for nothing else made any sense. Anybody could have been in his house - even his father's most trusted men could have stolen it for their own security. Hell nobody was safe from treachery in this stupid game.

Chapter Nine

Amy bristled but felt her cheeks flame. 'You assume wrong.' This was really none of his business but he deserved some sort of explanation. She couldn't help but feel she had involved James far too much but she had a deep gut feeling she could trust him. He'd had so many opportunities to give her up and yet he had gone so far as to lie for her, even claim to be in a relationship with her.

James straightened but Amy could see his mind cogitating. 'But you were married to him.'

'For about twelve hours.' With her arms folded, she watched her right foot swing backwards and forwards just scraping the floor in an arc, but not feeling comfortable about revealing facts of her life, she didn't dare look James in the face.

'Twelve? No one in this country can be married for only twelve hours. They won't even consider a divorce under twelve months.'

'Tell me about it.' Amy straightened then stalked past James with her head held high. 'Physically married for twelve hours but legally for way too long. In the end the marriage was legally annulled.' Not knowing what to do and hating having to relate a past she was so incredibly ashamed of, Amy kept ambling through the house feeling agitated and uneasy. All she really wanted to do was hide away in some dark corner and force bad memories from her mind. She felt, rather than heard, James follow close behind.

'When did he rape you? After you walked out? You know that it's hard to prove rape when you are actually married. Especially so soon after the ceremony.'

James's words fired Amy up. She didn't know if he was deliberately trying to provoke her but she felt anger surge as she spun around to face him. 'How dare you pass judgement when you know nothing about it!' She stormed back the way she had come, snatched her backpack from the floor and flung it onto her bed. While James began trying to pacify her, she hurled the contents onto the floor until she came to a small but thick folder. Still ignoring James's platitudes and apologies, she shuffled through the contents until she found what she was after. She yanked one photograph from the others then flung it onto the floor. As she shoved the rest back into the folder she screeched at James. 'You tell me that that is an acceptable way to leave your bride on her wedding night!' Then she flung herself onto the bed, knocking the backpack onto the floor with a thud and buried her head under clenched fists. She wanted to cry but found she couldn't as waves of shame engulfed her.

'Holy…' James bit back the second word but Amy figured what it would have been. 'He did that to you? On your wedding night?'

The sensation of terror and pain washed through her as the memories surged back. Amy knew she was trembling but had no control over her body. She felt the mattress give on one side as James sat on the edge. He pulled her up gently, twisted her around and settled her onto his lap before wrapping her in his arms. In the past five years, no one had ever held her like that or shown such incredible warmth and tenderness. She'd always put on a brave stoicism that she'd never really felt, to give the impression she wasn't cowered by what had happened. She'd never told anyone close to her the exact details of that night. Only those at Rico's trial had seen any of the photographs. She'd not shown all of them to anyone other than her lawyer. It was not something she was proud of. She'd been taken in by a suave psychopath and duped in the worst possible way.

It was then that five years of held in emotion began tumbling out. Amy wept and kept on weeping. She just couldn't seem to stop. Every time she thought she had control, took a couple of deep breaths between unladylike sniffs, the tears started rolling from her eyes again. James simply held her, one hand gently cradling her head against his shoulder while murmuring the occasional calming phrases including, 'Let it all out, Amy.'

Amy had no idea how long they had been there when she finally ran out of tears. Even when the moisture ran dry, James continued to hold her until she began wriggling to be released. He lifted her from his lap and laid her lengthways on the bed. 'Stay there a minute.'

He was only gone for the claimed minute, returning with a damp flannel and a towel. Settling his hip on the edge of the mattress, he gently wiped the moisture from her face then patted it dry. 'Are you okay?' he asked.

Amy nodded. 'I'm sorry. I never cry and yet in less than two hours I've leaked like a broken dam wall twice.'

'Do you feel up to dining out? Maybe somewhere casual. A pleasant atmosphere with other people around might give you a chance to gain some normality. You've had a tough twenty-four hours.'

'I can't believe it's only been a day, it feels like a lifetime.' A hiccough slipped out and for a minute she thought the tears were going to start again. To overcome them she forced a smile. 'A casual meal sounds nice, besides I don't have any glamorous clothes with me. I've only packed for practicality.' She waved a hand around towards the floor.

James grinned at her wildly strewn belongings. 'I can see that but maybe the floor isn't the best place to hang them. Feel free to use the wardrobe, it's relatively empty.' He stood to check the contents of the robe, opening doors and drawers and shifting the meagre contents into just the bottom drawer and shoving the few hanging items to one end. 'It's all yours.'

When he turned around Amy was sitting up glaring at him. 'I can't stay. You are way too involved already, which could put you in danger.'

'And exactly where do you propose to run to?'

'When I can get in contact with the sergeant in the Federal Police, I'll be able to organise something. I'd been trying to ring him from the office, where… hell I'd been hanging on for five minutes at a time.' She glanced at James. 'Is that how they found me? Can they really track my mobile calls?'

'With the right tracking gear, yes, and the police have the equipment although I'm guessing that it was used illegally in your case. In our country they need special permission to trace private citizen's phone lines especially with no legitimate reason and there would be no reason if you haven't broken the law.' His raised eyes asked the question.

'Certainly not!' Amy sent him back a contemptuous glare.

'I take it you couldn't get through to this sergeant.'

'No. After being passed from one person to another I was told that he was on temporary leave and not able to be contacted. I found that hard to swallow because it was his personal phone number I was ringing at first. He's never not got back to me straight away before.'

'Give me his name and all his contact numbers. My position might gain better information. Given that they were responsible for your identity change they shouldn't be passing you off like that. I presume you were given the standard procedure to only contact in emergency apart from your regulated updates.'

At first Amy was astounded at his knowledge and stared at him in amazement. 'You seem to know a lot about this.'

'I've dealt with identity changes before. It doesn't often happen in our country but I know the ropes.' He rose from the bed. 'Now, how about we change into something suitable and find us a pleasant place to dine? You deserve a few hours of relaxation.' He chucked her under the chin as he departed.

Within twenty minutes during which Amy had spent most of the time with soaked tissues over her eyes to reduce the red puffiness, they were driving along the highway and passed a couple of eating spots. James slowed at each, gave the premises a perusal but kept going. Catching Amy's mystified look he grinned. 'I'm looking for somewhere with a crowd and not too upmarket. We're not dressed for those two establishments.'

Amy gave their attire a closer scrutiny. She hadn't cared what she had dragged on after slipping off her shorts. She'd just picked up the first thing that came to hand from the floor, a pair of navy slacks and a serviceable cotton blouse in a lighter blue. At least her garments matched and she was reasonably neat and apart from being a bit creased her clothes were clean and of acceptable quality for most occasions. She didn't have a vast wardrobe but always bought quality garments that could be easily mixed and matched. James was wearing jeans and a smart short-sleeved button-down shirt. With her sandals and his casual loafers she knew he was right.

'There's a nice place in the main street of the Claremont shopping precinct. I ate there a couple of weeks ago. The food was quite good. You can sit either inside or on the open veranda,' said Amy.

'I know the place.' James sped up and headed west but kept glancing in the rear vision mirror. He said nothing so Amy assumed he was just being a cautious driver since the traffic flow was rather heavy.

Quite a few cars carried passengers that looked as though they were headed to the beach to find relief from the still hot evening. Bright towels wrapped around the necks of youngsters told the story, as did the sight of packed Eskies and fold up chairs in the boots of wagons. It was an ideal night for a picnic on the white sands of the vast coastline, thought Amy as James turned right and searched for a parking spot in the street. It wasn't until they were almost at the end of the road before James pulled into the curb.

When James grimaced as he alighted from the car, Amy wondered why he wasn't happy. By the time she had opened the door, James was by her side to hand her out. Not used to that kind of treatment she smiled at him. 'Thank you.'

'You may not thank me in a minute but please don't take this the wrong way.'

Before she could ask what he meant, James swept her in his arms and kissed her. When she struggled he lifted the corner of his mouth and mumbled, 'We are being watched,' then settled his mouth over hers again.

Amy shuddered at the onslaught then relaxed, the warmth of his kiss dissolving her tension. She was just beginning to enjoy the experience when James lifted his head and gave her a devastating smile.

'Not bad at all: in fact very pleasant. I think we might have convinced them.'

Wriggling from his embrace and feeling mortified, Amy looked around, searching for anyone watching. 'Convinced who?'

James slid his arm around her shoulders and headed her back down the street. 'Keep looking ahead and smile as though you are enjoying our romantic stroll. Our detective friends are parked across the road.'

Amy stiffened before relaxing into the embrace and dropping her head against James's shoulder. The mere thought of those two sent a shiver down her spine. But she could play the game if it meant getting them out of her life. Keeping her head still she swung her eyes until she caught sight of the car. 'Why are they following us?' she muttered under her breath as she turned her head slightly towards James.

'I don't think we convinced them that you aren't who you really are. Keep your head down in case they try to take a photo of your features.'

A stab of sheer terror shot through Amy. Close scrutiny of a photo would reveal her features despite her altered hairstyle. She turned her back to the car and acted as though she were having an in-depth conversation with James until they entered the bistro-type restaurant.

'Inside or out?' asked James as they stepped onto the wooden veranda then crossed the floor to the main entry.

'Since I'm the star feature, as far inside as we can get.' Amy pulled away and, ignoring the prominent sign saying, *Please wait to be seated*, almost raced to a vacant table near the back. She dragged out the nearest chair and plonked down with her back to the road.

As James eased out the opposite seat with far more grace and aplomb, he grinned. 'It's polite for the gentleman to sit with his back to the other patrons and allow his lady to have full view.'

Amy's scowl caused him to laugh. She knew he was being facetious.

'I hate using a mobile phone in restaurants but I'm going to see what I can do about our friends out there,' said James as he withdrew the instrument from his shirt pocket.

'How?' asked Amy.

'I have a few contacts in high places.' James scrolled through his regular numbers list and pressed the call button while Amy watched, feeling intrigued. What did high places mean? Her eyes popped open when he began speaking.

'Is the Commissioner in? I'm sorry to be disturbing your meal but it is important. James Ward.'

There was a break of several seconds during which James just gave Amy an enigmatic smile. 'Chris, my apologies for disturbing you but I have a bit of a problem. Two of your detectives are following my lady and me. They barged into my home earlier and assaulted Cathy. Yes, physically attacked her by yanking at her hair and making wild accusations. It was only when I spouted all the protocol they'd not followed that they realised I was a lawyer.' There was another lengthy break before James continued. 'Chris, I have a feeling these two are moonlighting and on the darker shade of the law. If I'm right, then they are working for an Eastern States criminal gang member who has recently been released on parole. Enrico Giovannazzo. He is in breach of his bail conditions so I'm guessing he has absconded… Sydney.' Another lengthy pause ensued. 'They've been watching the house of a lady who lives around the corner from me. Amy Masters. She was followed and chased but managed to escape. I suspect they are using police resources to trace her mobile phone… no she is safe for the moment but in hiding. She's too scared to return to her house. This Rico character is also on the scene… Thank you. Umm, I only have the name of one man; the other didn't give me his identity. Paul Verteramo – Detective Sergeant. I have a feeling we might need to investigate these two next on our list.'

Amy stared in amazement as the meaning of the conversation registered in her brain. Who was this man? Then she recalled the earlier conversation she'd overheard from outside her bedroom. She waited until James completed his call but the waiter arrived with menus before she could ask a whole lot of questions that were spinning around in her head. James suggested then ordered a bottle of white wine when Amy nodded her agreement. It seemed to take ages for the waiter to fill water glasses, spout off the specials for the night and remove the unwanted red wine glasses. The moment he left, Amy opened her mouth to speak but James lifted the menus and handed her one.

'Decide what you'd like, we'll talk over dinner.' Then he promptly studied his menu.

Feeling completely frustrated, Amy glanced down at her menu and called out the first thing her eyes focussed on.

She didn't care what she ate. She wanted explanations. For a full five minutes she watched James as he read every damn word on the two pages of the simple bill of fare. When he finally looked up he was grinning and she realised he was deliberately stalling.

'Bastard,' she muttered under her breath.

His shout of laughter had heads turn in their direction. 'Such language!'

'You are deliberately stalling. Were you talking to the Commissioner of Police?'

'Yes.'

The one word answer accompanied by a grin, further inflamed her frustration. This was going to be a very long night. 'What investigation were you talking about?'

'Ah.'

There goes that single word again, Amy thought. Such a simple expression can sound so frustratingly enigmatic. 'Ah is not an answer.'

'No it's not but I shouldn't really be discussing this with you.'

'Shouldn't doesn't mean won't. Besides with all the secrets I've been carrying around for five years, I'm hardly the type to be spouting off private matters. The information I have is probably as volatile as yours.' She grinned back at his raised eyebrows.

'Care to elaborate,' asked James.

'You first.' She shrugged her shoulders to give the impression she was as cryptic as he.

'I can see you are a smart cookie. All right, it's no secret that our new Commissioner is working hard to flush out a small band of corruption in the Police Force. I'm part of his group of investigators. I get to take the culprits to trial and put them in jail after Internal Affairs have collated all the facts.'

'Today's case?' Amy asked. 'I heard you mention something to our two friends out there, earlier.'

'I'm hoping those two won't be there very long. Chris promised to have them called in to headquarters to give an explanation as to what the hell they were up to. His words, not mine.' James lifted his head to search for the pair, his frown telling her that they were still watching.

'You didn't answer my question. Was that what today's case was about?' Amy folded her arms across her chest to show she meant business.

'Yes. There is one less crooked cop on the beat. He'll be serving several years in jail.'

'Is this why you believed my story? After all it sounds pretty fanciful.'

'It sounded so off-beat that it couldn't possibly have been made up but...' he paused as he shifted his eyes from the road to her face. 'I couldn't find any details in my web search this afternoon. I searched for an Amy Masters receiving medical treatment or being involved in a court case. I couldn't find any details of Enrico Giovannazzo having been sent to trial.'

'That's because I wasn't Amy Masters then.'

'I realise that now but there was no Giovannazzo either.'

'That mystifies me about the trial but I used a false name when I took myself to hospital so that he couldn't find me. But you don't need to search for those details. I have a copy of all my medical records,' she paused then sighed, 'and the photographs.'

'The photograph you showed me was horrific.'

'And that was taken a day after they sewed me back together.'

'What?' James sat forward, his eyes flaring.

The waiter arrived with the wine and to take their orders. This time it was James who tried to hurry the process while Amy sat back and wasted time revisiting the menu. She didn't read a word but needed the time to collect her thoughts and calm her racing pulse. Recalling the image on the single photo she'd allowed him to see seemed to shrivel up her insides into a tight ball of tension. She'd chosen a full-length photo of her naked back depicting thirteen horizontal black bruises surrounding vicious red welts from her shoulders all the way down to her ankles. When a violent shudder beset her, she grabbed a hold of the edge of the table to force her body to stop. It wasn't until she felt James hug her tight that she became aware of her surroundings.

'Amy?' From some far away place she heard his voice. One final shake and she became conscious of James kneeling by her side.

She opened her eyes and forced words past the blockage in her throat. 'I'm sorry. Sometimes the memories just take over.'

'Do you want to leave?'

She wanted nothing better but it didn't matter where she was, at work or in the middle of the street, when the pictures overtook her mind she had to fight them away. 'No, I'm fine now.'

As though afraid to release his hold James remained kneeling, keeping one hand rubbing across her shoulders. 'What would you like to order?'

It was only then that Amy spotted the black trouser clad legs of the waiter standing to the left of James. Every detail of the white apron reaching to his knees became imprinted on her mind, right down to the repaired section of stitching down one side that hadn't quite met with the original line of thread. Far out, she thought, how many times can I embarrass myself on the one outing? Without lifting her head higher than the waiter's waist, she mumbled, 'I'll have the fish of the day.'

While James completed the order, he remained by Amy's side. Then he was silent for a moment as though not sure what to do. 'I'm fine, James. Truly.' Amy forced a tentative smile.

'You sure?' James pushed his body upright from his haunches then slid back into his seat but kept one hand wrapped around Amy's. She felt glad of the human contact. It was something she'd missed so much even though it was her that had shrunk away from other people touching her.

'Yes, I'm sure.' She finally found the courage to look at his face. 'Can we not talk about the photo or what happened? Please?'

James seemed to chew on his words then agreed. 'Let's keep to general topics while we eat so we can enjoy the evening.' Then he immediately began telling Amy about his daughter who, she soon learned, was taking a year off to travel the world before beginning her university studies.

***

He'd got lost twice trying to follow the vague directions passed on from the pair of idiots via his father. As far as he could make out, some lawyer had rumbled them. Typical. By the time Rico had figured out, *some outdoor eating establishment*, actually meant enclosed veranda with most of the tables indoors, the two morons were no longer parked directly across the road. There was no sign of a dark blue sedan let alone one with the quoted number plate.

Now regretting hiring such a distinctive car, Rico drove to the end of the road and parked in the darkest recesses of a railway station car park then walked back to the restaurant, turning to visually check how well his car was hidden. Dark shadows from overhanging trees and the side of a building dulled the yellow but damn it, the vehicle still looked what it was: expensive and luxurious.

Amanda was supposed to be sitting in the far rear left hand corner. Standing across the road, it was almost impossible to make out the features of anyone inside the dimly lit building but he was almost certain there was no blonde or redhead apart from the bottle induced platinum hooker sitting on the veranda with a group of young lads. And that scantily dressed, dumpy girl most assuredly was not Amanda. For starters, there was no way Amanda would wear anything remotely that gaudy and nasty. Amanda always had class.

Rico moved past the building before crossing the road then ambled slowly past the clear plastic curtains rolled over the opening to keep the blustery wind at bay. He smiled at those nearest him as his eyes searched the insides. There were mostly couples, two groups of four and a larger group. He paused on each female, searching for some familiarity and dismissed most as too short, too thin, too fat, wrong hair. The only woman snagging at his memory bank had the right shape but had short black hair and she had her back to him. Was she wearing a wig? Impossible. The hair was way too short to be hiding the bulk of Amanda's shoulder length blonde locks. No the hair was natural, of that he was certain. He ducked out of sight when the woman's partner glanced up. Hell, was that the same man who walked past Amanda's house? Even if it was, Rico was better off returning to the house in question to wait.

Chapter Ten

Stepping out of her bedroom, Amy slammed into a hard but moving target then screamed. Having heard James turn off the shower only a second before, she hadn't reckoned on him being in the passage so soon. She paused. It was impossible for him to have reached her door in that second, which meant that the only reason there would be another human being in the house would be Rico or one of his cronies. She screamed again as fingers descended onto her shoulders and shoved her backwards.

'What the hell?' The crackling masculine voice muttered the imprecation at the same time Amy spotted bare feet moving into her line of vision.

Bare feet? She shot her head upwards and kept on going up. He was very tall and skinny. Almost as tall as James but nowhere near as well built. When she realised that the man was only young with features almost identical to James's, there was no mistaking his heritage. A light flicked on in her brain. There was a son as well as a daughter. It looked as though this young man's body had just kept on growing, using up what little flesh he had as growing bones stretched his skin taut while the torso and limbs attempted to outgrow his covering.

'Jason!' The single word erupted from behind her at the same time as she heard the bathroom door swing open. 'I wasn't expecting you until after lunch.'

Expecting him and James had said nothing! Amy swung around then her eyes widened in shock. James was wearing only a dark blue towel grasped around his hips. He hadn't even had time to knot it. Water droplets glistened on his skin and clung to the dark hairs on his chest. By the look of his messy hair, James had dried that part of his body first and her screech had interrupted him. Water was puddling onto the tiles at his feet.

'Caught in the act.' There was definite humour in the young man's voice.

Amy felt her face heat from the inside and knew it was going a bright shade of scarlet.

'You've been keeping secrets from us, Dad. But it's about time.'

Amy twisted back around, appalled at the innuendo.

'Keep your mind above your belt, son. Amy is a guest and there's nothing going on.'

Amy swung back to look at James. She must have looked shocked because he grinned at her. She felt more than shock. Try horrified.

'Isn't that what they all say when they've been caught red-handed? She's pretty, Dad.'

Pretty? With her hacked hair sticking this way and that. She'd already caught a glimpse of it in the dressing table mirror. She looked like a freak show. Amy shot her head back around to stare at what she now presumed was James's son: a son that had never cracked a mention so far and she wondered why. His grin was wolfish. Time to wipe the grin off his face: off both men's faces.

'The name is Amy and despite the fact that I'm standing in the passage in my night-clothes and your father, I presume he is your father, is wearing nothing...' she glanced at the towel that had slid lower revealing the very top of a mass of dark pubic hair, 'but a towel that is dangerously close to revealing more than he wants.' Amy slid James a supercilious grin as he hitched up the towel. 'I can assure you,' she turned back to Jason, 'I slept in the guest bedroom and your father slept in his room. All night,' she emphasized as an afterthought.

When Jason slid his eyebrows up to indicate he didn't believe a word of what she'd just spouted, Amy pulled herself up to her full height and stuck her hands on her hips. 'I don't sleep around. Especially with some stranger I've known for all of thirty-six hours. Your father very kindly allowed me to stay here when...' She groped around for the right words when she couldn't think of a logical explanation.

James interrupted. 'Amy found herself in a bit of bother when some crook broke into her house. She had nowhere else to hide out. She lives around the corner, number thirty-seven. Until we can get things sorted, she's staying here.' James sounded rather irate. 'And, son, if I ever do take up with a woman it's none of your damned business what I do in the privacy of my own home and I don't ever want you to make wild insinuations without finding out the facts first, especially in front of said lady.' The bathroom door slammed.

'Phew,' Jason muttered under his breath then held out his hand towards Amy. 'I'm sorry. I was out of line. I'm Jason.' He waited until Amy had released his hand before he grinned and added, 'but you are still very pretty and Dad needs to find himself a new woman.'

Knowing the hint for what it was Amy felt a desperate need to put a stop to this. 'Jason, from the little I know, I think your Dad is still in love with your Mum. It takes quite a long time for someone to complete the grieving process. When my mother was killed by a drunken hit and run driver ten years ago, my Dad went to pieces. It was three years before he had any desire to seek friendship from other women. He joined a few community organizations, dated several ladies and maybe had physical relationships but if he did I never knew. I hope he did. He was too nice a man to live like a monastic hermit. Give your Dad time. He'll know when he's ready to let go.'

The indrawn breath as Jason stared past her, told Amy that James was standing right behind her. She twisted her body around expecting James to be furious with her interference. He had donned a pair of tan shorts leaving his now dry chest bare.

'Thank you for that, maybe now the kids will understand and stop pestering me.'

Amy was relieved to see the gentle smile hovering around his lips before he turned and walked away, disappearing into his bedroom. She turned back to Jason. 'If you'll excuse me, I was about to take a shower.'

When Amy emerged fifteen minutes later she heard the mumbling of male voices from the vicinity of the kitchen. Not in the habit of eavesdropping and not wanting to intrude on private family conversations she wasn't sure what to do. After the more than substantial meal the night before she wasn't over hungry so breakfast wasn't a priority. To waste time while she thought, she dumped her belongings in the bedroom, straightened the bedclothes, tidied up then paced. Maybe a walk would ease her angst, she thought after her tenth turn around the room. Since walking suited her, assisting her to think, she slid on her comfy old walkers and snuck down the passage, only pausing for a second when she heard her name mentioned. Curiosity bit but she hardened her resolve to not interrupt and eased the key around in the deadlock of the front door then slowly turned the handle so as not to make any noise.

The fact that someone might still be hanging around watching for her didn't even enter her mind until she stepped past the coloured metal side fence and the glint of bright yellow reflected onto the back of her retina. She turned and fled back to the front door, cursing under her breath when she realised she didn't have a key. The sound of a car door slamming caused a surge of adrenaline and she pounded on the wood panel with one fist and frantically pressed the doorbell with the other hand.

'Please hurry,' she whispered several times while she attuned her ears for the sound of approaching footsteps. She felt too afraid to yell out for Rico was sure to recognise her voice. Then she remembered having used a Scottish accent and was about to call for James when the door swung open.

'Thank, God,' Amy gushed as she raced past a stunned looking James. 'Shut the door, its Rico,' she added over her shoulder as she sped down the passage and into her room. Gripped with panic, she swept all her scattered belongings into her backpack and other bag she'd brought from home then shoved everything into the wardrobe. One quick scout around of the room to ensure there was no evidence of her presence she grabbed her laptop and dived into the robe pulling the door closed behind her.

'Amy?'

She stiffened at the sound of her name and didn't dare breathe.

'Amy,' James continued calmly, 'he didn't come near the house. He's heading towards your place.'

The door opened revealing James standing back and in the background Jason was peering over his father's shoulder. Amy tried but no words would move beyond the blockage in her throat. She hadn't realised she was shaking so much until she attempted to step from the wardrobe and took on an embarrassing sway. James grabbed her as she wobbled.

'You're terrified. I won't allow him to come near you.' James guided her across the carpet and gently lowered her to the bed then sat next to her, keeping one arm around her shoulder. 'I wish you wouldn't jerk every time I touch you. You're giving me a complex. I promise I won't hurt you.'

Amy just stared at him. 'I jerk?'

'You do. Every single time, which makes me wonder why. I'm beginning to wonder if you have ever had another relationship since you were so brutally beaten.'

Amy froze and went silent. James was too darn perceptive.

'You haven't, have you?'

'Not that it's any of your business but I've been on dates.'

'Single, once only dates? Have you had a lasting relationship with the one man? You're how old?'

The fact that Jason was hovering and overhearing every word and she was feeling very uncomfortable about the nature of the questions as well as how close to the truth James was, caused Amy to clamp her mouth shut.

'I've outlined the basics to Jason. He needed to know why you were hiding out. I also told him to call you Cathy and that if anyone asks, such as the punk in the yellow sports car, to tell them that you and I have been dating for four months. We need to come up with a few more facts such as profession, where you live and an explanation for the broad Scottish accent.' James stood then reached out with one hand turned upwards as though to ask permission to touch her. 'Let's talk over breakfast which is probably stone cold by now.'

When Amy remained sitting wondering if the man had supernatural powers since he was able to read her thoughts, James slid his hands under her armpits and physically hauled her to her feet. 'I've drawn the blinds closed so nobody can see inside and Jason locked the gate into the backyard. Nobody can get in without making a lot of noise and if Rico did manage to break in he has to get past the both of us.' To make sure Amy followed, James swept one arm around her shoulder and virtually forced her into the kitchen where he sat her at the table while Jason began serving up cooling omelettes that had been sitting in a covered pan on the side of the stove.

James waited until they were all seated before he started asking the questions Amy knew were coming. She'd already left a few hanging by not knowing how to answer. 'How old are you, Amy?'

'Thirty-two.' She kept her eyes glued to her fork as she took infinite care in filling it.

'You don't look older than twenty-five. I take it that you are an interior decorator.'

Amy glanced up.

'From the designs you were doing the other night.' James added.

'I'm actually a trained architect. That's how I met Rico. I was commissioned to design a new beach house for him. But after I changed my identity it was suggested I also change my profession so I went into designing building interiors. That way I was not wasting my training, didn't have to retrain and could still do what I loved but with a few modifications.'

Both men raised their eyes at her revelation. The surprise was something she had grown used to. Architecture was still classed as a man's domain by those who didn't know how many women were in the profession. Although, she had to confess, there was still a glass ceiling in place as far as women winning design awards or being given the opportunity to climb the ladder.

'And the Scottish accent? It was so true I couldn't believe what I was hearing.'

Amy smiled. This bit was easy. 'My parents were Scottish. They emigrated when I was two. I grew up listening to them and until I went to school, spoke with just as broad an accent. I soon learned that to fit in I needed to develop the Australian twang.'

'So you are a British citizen?'

'Australian, my parents took on citizenship but I had dual passports.'

'Had?' James replaced his cutlery and sat back watching her but looking thoughtful.

'When I changed my identity by deed poll, I let my British passport lapse. It would have been impractical to go through the process of identity change in two different countries.'

'Hmm.' James looked introspective then added, 'but if you reverted to your original maiden name, you could theoretically renew your original British passport and return to the U.K. without any problem.'

Amy ceased eating and pushed her half eaten breakfast to one side. She hadn't really been hungry and even though it was quite tasty, the tepid warmth had taken the edge off the eggs being irresistible. 'I'm not sure. How would I stand legally?'

'I don't know for sure but I could make some enquiries. It does give you an option on how to avoid this relentless pursuit. You could simply leave the country.'

'There is nothing simple about getting the mafia off your back. They have a wide network throughout the world. It won't take them long to track me down. Rico knew my maiden name.'

'Mafia?' Jason said as James leant forward.

Ignoring his son, James asked, 'Why did you marry him?'

Amy sucked in her breath then folded her arms across her chest feeling mortified and very uncomfortable. 'Because I was sucked in. During the months that we dated, Rico was the epitome of a gentleman. He went out of his way to charm me, take me on wonderful dates. He never made a wrong move. I had no idea about his other life or seedier dealings. It wasn't until… ' she paused and heaved a breath into lungs that felt as though they were being clamped flat in a huge vice.

'Until your wedding night, I get the picture. And you haven't been able to trust a single member of the male species since.' James stared at her with a mixture of empathy and triumph for guessing right. 'I can't say that I blame you but you are still young enough to meet someone, fall in love and marry. Then have a couple of kids and become a happy family.'

An unbidden mewling sound escaped Amy's lips. She just had to escape so she shoved the chair back and attempted to leave but James was quicker and swept an arm around her waist. He drew her backwards as he rose. Then he clamped her against his body. 'I said something that really upset you didn't I? I'm sorry.' He paused and Amy guessed he was thinking. Then almost as if he was thinking aloud, he muttered each statement that he'd just verbalised. 'You paled then baulked at the kids and family bit.'

Amy felt herself being swung around then held at arms length with James's fingers gripping tight at her shoulders. Knowing it would be useless to try, she didn't attempt to free herself. Instead she dropped her eyes and stared at the small strip of floor between them. She studied every minute detail of the tiles, noting the pattern of smudges in the pale blue ceramic and how the grout in between was a darker blue and how there were a couple of grains of instant coffee granules melted onto the surface. James hadn't washed the floor in the past couple of days. Maybe she could do it for him. All the time she could feel the tension in the silence that indicated Jason had stopped eating as well and somehow she knew he was staring at her with his mind swirling. The atmosphere felt expectant and oppressive.

She'd already figured James was an intelligent man with a logical mind that seemed to be adept at reading her thoughts. He'd have to have been smart to gain his exalted position but his next words threw her.

'What the hell did he do to you? You showed me only the back view, which was horrific enough. The front was a lot more gruesome wasn't it?'

When she remained silent, he shook her gently, she guessed in angry frustration. But for some strange reason she couldn't fathom, she wasn't frightened by his action.

'Amy, look at me!' He released one hand and grasped her chin, forcing her head up. 'Hell, you look like a ghost. You're so pale. He beat you into a pulp didn't he?' Not waiting for a response his arms went around her in a surprisingly gentle grip and drew her into the arch of his body. 'God, Amy, I'm so sorry.'

While she was being held in an unbelievably warm embrace, Amy heard James talking to Jason.

'Jas, can you clean up and put the coffee on? Then go into Amy's room and fetch me her backpack.'

His arms tightened when Amy wriggled to free herself. He was being high-handed and she didn't do the male domination bit any longer.

'I think it's time I learnt all the facts so we can set about finding a solution to Amy's problems. She doesn't deserve to be spending her entire life scared witless and running away from this cretin.' Then he planted his mouth against her ear. 'You and I are going to have a long heart-to-heart. We need to get comfortable.'

***

Rico was at a stalemate. After spending the night alternating between keeping an eye on Amanda's place as well as trying to peer into the lawyer's house, he felt beyond tired and fed up. Ignoring the time difference, his father had woken him from an uncomfortable sleep folded in the front seat of his car at four in the morning. The phone call was, as usual, unpleasant, preventing Rico from getting back to sleep until about six. Then the oppressive heat caused by an already hot sun, had driven him from the car, plus the desperate need for a toilet and decent shower.

Breaking into Amanda's house was a breeze now that he had done it several times. She hadn't been back and he guessed she wouldn't return again. He smiled as the tepid water flowed down his back. He had to give Amanda credit; she was one smart lady, but he already knew that. Her logical clever mind had been just one of the things that had attracted him to her. Her vibrant personality had been another although there had been a shy reserve underlying her determination to appear in control of her world. She tried to keep her lack of self-confidence hidden but he always knew it was lurking beneath a façade; especially about her looks. Amanda had never believed that she was beautiful but damn it she was drop-dead gorgeous.

Using female scented shampoo, he rubbed the foam into his hair, lapping up the sensation of hard fingertips easing the tension in his head. He rinsed off then slathered pink, sweet-smelling soap against his skin until it tingled. He was going to smell like flaming roses but what the heck. It wasn't as though he was going to get up close and cosy with anyone other than Amanda – when he managed to track her down again.

Best bet at the moment was the lawyer's house. Maybe it was Amanda, but he wasn't yet convinced. He needed to see her up close. But first he needed to change his clothes, toss the old ones in the machine and then raid the fridge.

Chapter Eleven

'Lounge or office?' James asked as he eased his hold then immediately grabbed her around the waist when she fought to escape.

'No man is ever going to order me around again.' Amy gritted her teeth then completely relaxed her body like a rag doll and flopped straight down to the floor, sliding from his hands.

James immediately dropped to his haunches and held out one hand, palm up again to show submission but his folded bulk blocked her escape route. 'I didn't mean to come across as overbearing but, Amy, you have to admit this man is still dictating your life. You aren't free to live a normal life. He is effectively controlling you and everything you do: where you live, or at the moment, don't live, your social life, what sort of job you have, even keeps you from visiting your own sister and the nephew and niece you've never seen.'

Amy flinched at the words; now sorry she had revealed so much over dinner the night before. But James was right. Even when Rico was in jail he had been controlling her. She'd never seen it in those terms before. The thought made her mad. She'd worked so hard to become physically strong so she could counterattack if some male threatened her again. She thought she had become emotionally stronger but now she could see that it was only in some aspects she had mastery over her emotions. Since James had mentioned it, she had become aware of how she flinched whenever either he or Jason brushed against her and it shouldn't be like that. Anger surged. The bastard still controlled her life. She stood, pushed past James then stalked through the house.

'The office,' she called to James. 'Let's plan how to take the bastard down in the office. I want my life back,' she yelled even louder then plonked down in the office chair and planted her feet on the ground with her arms crossed over her chest feeling full of determination.

James followed, his grin of triumph obvious as he swung the other chair around from facing the desk and sank in a more genteel manner.

'And you can wipe that smug grin off your face,' said Amy moments before she saw the ridiculous side of his actions and grinned back.

'You're kind of cute when you're mad. I'd like to be around when you give Rico his comeuppance.'

'Oh, he'll get it. I'm just biding my time.'

'I could have him arrested right now if you want. He's stalking the neighbourhood. A few concerned neighbours could make discreet phone calls to the police. Plus, I'm fairly certain he has jumped bail but until I receive confirmation I can't go down that line. You said he tried to grab you and force you to go with him. That's abduction. But since he didn't succeed, you can't prove it. Then there's the breaking and entry into your place; there's probably fingerprints. If I stretched the grey matter I could come up with a couple of other charges.'

'And I could have killed him the other night. It would have been so easy. He deserved it but since it was my home, I would have been the prime suspect. He's not worth a jail term.'

'So, how do you want to approach this?' James leant back in his chair with his elbows resting on the armrests and his fingers splayed tip-to-tip.

'What are my options?' Amy followed suit, leaning backwards but her fingers wrestled with each other in her lap.

'Why don't you ring your Federal officer and see what he has to say? You could alter your identity again.'

'Can't, I don't have a phone. Some hotshot lawyer told me, no, ordered me to dump it.' Her grin was supercilious but she wiped it from her face when Jason appeared at the door with two mugs held in one hand. Hot tendrils of steam twirled upwards as he handed one to her then the other to his father.

'Jason,' said James, 'you are the techno whiz. If you wanted to buy your girlfriend a mobile phone as a surprise gift, is it possible? You know, without signing contracts and such like.' James settled his mug on the desk.

'Sure, you pay for the phone outright and put the account into credit. But it means you can only use up the credit. You purchase so much credit at a time. Why?'

'Would you be able to do that this morning?' asked James.

'Yes, but I don't have a girlfriend at the moment and I have my own phone.'

'I'd like you to buy one for Amy. She had a slight accident with hers yesterday.'

Amy couldn't help but grin at the vision of the so-called accident as James spun around and opened a drawer of the desk. He pulled out a pile of business sized cards, shuffled through them then held up what looked to Amy, to be a credit card.

'Use this.'

'No!' Amy yelled then cursed under her breath when the coffee she'd forgotten she was holding sloshed onto her hand and stung. She stood and placed the mug on the desk. 'Sorry, I didn't mean to yell but I have money of my own. I'll pay cash.' She shoved the scalded spot in her mouth and licked it to ease the stinging heat as she retreated, backing out the door then headed for her bedroom. With her hand still in her mouth she lifted her backpack onto the bed then unzipped the front pocket. She withdrew a bundle of cash she'd received from the bank.

'How much cash are you carrying around with you?'

Startled by a voice so near, Amy swung around to see both James and Jason standing in the doorway. 'I closed my accounts yesterday. I know Rico can track my movements through bank withdrawals. Besides, it's none of your business.'

'But it's not safe to be carrying that kind of cash around. I have a safe in the office. I keep sensitive documents locked away when I'm not using them. Bring the whole backpack. I need to read through the paperwork you say is incriminating. And the Federal officer's number. I'll use my position to see if I can't get some joy.' James reached over and hefted the backpack from the bed then returned to the office, leaving Amy staring after him.

Jason grinned at her. 'You can't stop him once he sets his mind on something. Give him the merest sniff of wrongdoing and he's off righting the world. I always thought he used his size as a silent intimidation to get what he wanted.' Still grinning Jason held his arm out as indication for her to go first.

'You're not much smaller and once your body fills out you're going to be just as intimidating. How tall is he?'

'Six-five.' Jason followed her down the passage.

'And your sister? Did she inherit his genes as well?'

'She takes after Mum.'

'I bet she's pleased,' Amy murmured as she sat back down.

A snort of laughter came from James. 'Glenda was five-ten.'

'Oh,' said Amy, 'then I feel sorry for Angie. I'm only five-eight and I feel like I'm too tall. I've found that men aren't so keen on dating taller women.'

'This man is,' said James. 'I'd look downright ridiculous squiring some five foot sylph on my arm.' A wolfish grin crept out from the corners of his mouth as he held out his hand. 'Money.'

'How much for the phone?' asked Amy as she counted off five hundred dollar bundles, each still with the elastic bands around it. She handed Jason one pile. 'Buy me at least a hundred dollars of credit. How does that work?' She kept the other two bundles and gave the rest to James who moved to a wall safe hidden behind a false wall behind a row of shelving inside the cupboard.

'I need a full name and address for the phone,' said Jason. 'You put the credit on a phone card and top it up every time it gets low.'

Amy glanced at James. This name business was going to be a problem. 'I need a new name.'

'How about Cathy?' piped in Jason. 'It's already stuck in my mind.'

'And your mother's maiden name,' said James. 'Does Rico know that?'

'It was Douglas. No, Rico wouldn't have known. He never met my mother and I only ever called her Mum. I think it is written on our marriage certificate but I was handed that and still have it. I doubt he ever saw it. I can live with Cathy Douglas. Maybe use Heather as my middle name.'

'Why Heather?' asked James.

'It was Mum's name.'

'As long as Rico didn't know.' James turned his attention to Jason. 'Use our address, son. It'll do for now. At least until we can get things sorted. Changing addresses is not difficult later on. Another phone attached to this address won't send up a red flag. And besides, I've already indicated that someone called Cathy is my latest love interest to those two idiots yesterday. We didn't give them a surname.'

'Love interest?' Jason sounded very curious and looked hopeful.

James frowned. 'Don't go there, son. It was a furphy to get rid of some nosy detectives. Which reminds me, I must find out what happened to them. How about shooting off to find that mobile phone, Jas? Take my car.'

After Jason left, James remained standing leant up against the wall next to the closed but uncovered wall safe with his hands in his pockets and one leg crossed over the other. An uneasy sensation settled into Amy's innards as she watched changing emotions flicker over his face. He was staring into space and looked as though he was stewing over some major problem. Now knowing how forthright he could be, his lengthy hesitation began to eat at her. What was so difficult for him to broach? She waited until the tension became too much to bear.

'What is the problem?'

James straightened then glanced at her. 'I'm tossing up whether or not to ask a favour.'

'Must be a huge favour if it takes this long to stew over.'

He smiled. 'Huge for me, could be even bigger for you.'

'Now I'm intrigued, ask away. If it is in my power to help you, I will. You're doing a lot for me and I have no other way of repaying you.'

'I'm not looking for repayment. I have the position and means to give you a proper life and with my court case over, I have some spare time. What I want to ask may sound ridiculous but something Jason said earlier has had me thinking.'

When James straightened then began pacing backwards and forwards across the room, Amy's tension heightened. Jason was right. In an enclosed space, even as large as this office was, James's bulk was overpowering. 'Can't you sit down? You're height and the pacing feels intimidating.'

James paused, stared at her for a moment then smiled. 'Sorry, I've been told that many times but there's not a lot I can do about my build.'

She felt relieved when he sat but when he said nothing for way too long, she began to worry. 'Just spill it out,' she finally blurted to break the tension

'Okay. It's just that I noticed how pleased Jason looked when he thought that... you and I... were...'

'Having a relationship?' Amy offered since James was stammering and stuttering all over the place. It amused her that he was so uptight about the incident.

'Yes. They've both been hounding me for months to start getting out again. Angie even set up my profile on one of those Internet singles sites before she went away.' He grinned. 'She didn't ask my permission or even tell me. I started receiving all these strange emails in response to my profile from women wanting to meet up. It took me a while to figure out what the kids had been up to. Jason blamed Angie between his guffaws of laughter and vice versa. But they were both in on it. Maybe it is time, but it is so hard to make the leap.'

'Hard? Why hard?' Amy leant forwards and placed a hand on his arm.

'Because I feel so damned guilty! Even kissing you to show those two detectives we were an item caused me a sleepless night because I felt guilty.'

'Why? I don't understand. Why feel guilty about kissing me?'

'I felt as though I was being unfaithful to Glenda. God, I know I shouldn't. She's dead. But I was haunted by feelings of guilt all night.'

Amy leaned forwards again. 'Tell me about her. When did you meet?'

A gentle smile erased his stern features. 'First year in high school. She was in my English class. I think I must have fallen in love with her that first day. We just connected. We were sweethearts all through high school. I knew at age seventeen that I was going to marry her. We both went to university and were going to wait until I completed my law degree before we made our union official but Jason decided he was going to come onto the scene.' It amazed Amy that James actually reddened.

'I was fortunate I had a bit of family money behind me. Things were tight but we managed. We married at twenty-one. Too young but we both knew it was right.'

'That's such a beautiful story. Glenda was a very lucky lady.' Amy squeezed his hand.

James looked up. 'I was the lucky one. Glenda was the love of my life, a wonderful wife and mother and my best friend. It devastated me when she became so ill. I wanted her to fight the cancer that last time for purely selfish reasons. I didn't want to live without her.'

Amy felt tears well. 'But in the end you gave her permission to let go. Because you loved her so much you didn't want her to suffer any longer. I can only imagine how hard that was for you.'

When she noticed James was fighting to keep his emotions in check, Amy knelt on the floor in front of him. 'I know my Dad was at peace with the world when he died. He told me the last time I saw him just weeks before he passed away. He had accepted his mortality and I'm guessing Glenda had too. You gave her your total love and support for, I'm guessing, around twenty-something years? No, probably longer if you count the years at high school. She died knowing only that kind of happiness and I'm certain she loved you just as much. If I put myself in her shoes, I'd want you to find happiness again. I wouldn't want you to never love again, to spend the rest of your life grieving and lonely.' Amy reached up and grasped his hands. 'If the positions had been changed, would you have expected her to spend the rest of her life mourning you?'

'No, of course not, I'd want her to marry again.'

'Then what is the difference?' Amy sank back on her heels. 'I'm taking a stab in the dark here. I bet she spoke of this before she died. I bet she told you to find love again.'

The sheepish grin gave Amy the answer before James even spoke. 'You're too smart for your own good, Amy Masters.'

'You'd better get used to calling me Cathy Douglas. Now that we've got the reason for your favour behind us, what exactly was the favour?'

'Ah!'

'You have a habit of saying that word.' Amy rose and settled back into the chair.

'I was wondering if you'd be my date tonight. My brother turns thirty-five today and there's a small celebratory party tonight. It's the reason Jason came home this weekend. There will be a few family and friends.'

Amy sat back feeling dumbfounded. 'Your date?'

James eyed her with a look of consternation. 'You look as though you are horrified at the thought.'

'No, just stunned. This is the same brother who sent me flying in front of a bus before dragging me away from the same bus?'

'Jon is my only brother. But if you agree I need to warn you about him. He's a bit… spoilt would be a good word. My Mum had difficulty in conceiving after I was born. When Jon arrived seven years after me, my parents were over the moon. The fact that he was a sickly child and didn't thrive until a hole in his heart was fixed at age twelve meant that he was rather spoilt. I'm not saying I was neglected. I wasn't. Mum and Dad made sure of that, but Jon was treated as special and consequently grew up believing the world owed him everything. He's never maintained a long-lasting relationship with any woman mainly because he hasn't yet learned that females were not put on this earth to be slaves to his wants. He will make a play for you. He makes a play for every woman he comes upon thinking he is irresistible. But he would never harm a woman, physically. He does have that much respect. Apart from that he's a nice bloke.'

'So if I agree to be your date, I keep away from him.'

James laughed. 'He's not that bad. He'll just try to get you to go out with him.'

'Even when I'm with his own brother! He'd try to steal his brother's date?'

James hesitated. 'I'm not really sure since I've never been in this situation before. I was married before he was old enough to date but if you are single, you'll be fair game. There is another reason I'm asking you. I'm hoping that by escorting you, I can lessen this feeling of guilt I have every time I even think of another woman and maybe it will help you to learn to trust again. I have no intention of mauling you but to show every one you are my date, I'll probably touch you every once in a while. Such as put my arm around your waist or my hand in the small of your back and maybe by the end of the night you won't jump out of your skin every time a man so much as brushes up against you.' James's enigmatic smile gave Amy the inkling that it was probably her own reactions that had brought this whole thing on and he was only using his reserve as an excuse.

'Just a date?' Amy asked, feeling more than a little apprehensive. What if he meant to take things further?

'Just a date. I'm not about to jump your bones. I don't think my conscience will allow me to go any further for quite a long time. I've never slept with any other woman apart from Glenda.' He swept his brow with one hand then his fingers brushed restlessly through his hair before scratching the nape of his neck. 'God, just the thought brings me out in a nervous sweat.'

When Amy giggled, James shot his head in her direction looking astonished. She swallowed an outright laugh. 'I can't believe such a suave and sophisticated man who has been married for so long is more nervous of having sex than I am. The very thought terrifies me. It's not the actual sex bit that petrifies me. It's getting up close. I freeze. I've been to counselling and even tried the hypnosis bit but I wasn't a good subject. I think maybe the fact that the hypnotist was male might have been the reason. I couldn't relax with just him and me in the room. I know not every man is like Rico. I keep telling myself that but the few times a man has got anywhere near even suggesting it, I've turned tail.' Amy felt her face redden at what she had just disclosed. 'I can't believe I'm talking to you about this,' she mumbled with her chin seeking to hide somewhere inside her chest.

Not daring to look up, she heard James say, 'I've never opened up to any one else either. It just occurred to me that we both have hang-ups about similar things but for entirely different reasons. Maybe we can help each other take the tiny first steps. So will you be my date tonight?'

When she spied his hand reaching out to her, Amy forced her body not to jerk and accepted his touch with as much grace as a stiff body could. But at least she didn't jump. 'How dressy is tonight?' she asked as she peeked upwards. 'All my going out clothes are back in my house.'

'It's a barbecue. Jeans or slacks will probably be the norm. You haven't said yes, yet.'

Amy smiled. 'Yes, it will be my very great pleasure to be your date tonight.'

***

Rico scratched his head as he looked around Amanda's backyard. Where else could she hide things? He'd spent too long searching the grounds for possible hiding places, even though he felt sure Amanda didn't have anything of his. It wasn't logical for her to have kept it this long and not used the information especially since it incriminated his father and other people much more than it incriminated him. Hell, his name wasn't even in the damn file. The only way it related to him was that it was in his possession. God, he wasn't stupid enough to put his own name on such incriminating records. Even his father didn't realise that little gem.

His eyes scoured the fences, shrubs and garden beds. He'd already examined them closely and found nothing. He stared at the house, traversing the back wall up and down then across before lingering on the roof.

'Damn, the roof space!' he muttered as his eyes continued on their path then paused at the base. There was a step up into the house, which meant a space between the ground and the floor. Bending low he walked slowly around the house, searching the brick build-up for any gaps or loose bricks. The front portico was concrete, poured against the walls but the side was brickwork. At the step leading into Amy's bedroom, he got down on all fours and felt around with his fingers, shivering at the feel of cobwebs then brushing frantic fingers against the paving bricks on the path to remove the sticky strands before inspecting his body for venomous creepy crawlies. God, he hated spiders.

Satisfied there were no cracks big enough to contain stolen items he went back inside, searched for the manhole in the ceiling then placed a chair underneath the hole that looked way too small for a man to fit through. It was quite a struggle to hoist his body high enough then wriggle into the roof-space. If it weren't for the sunlight streaming through the gaps in the tiles, he wouldn't have been able to see a thing. In the centre of the house he could stand upright as he searched between rafters, taking care to avoid the mass of electric cables.

Nearer the edges he had to squat or kneel. His fingers were groping under insulation batts near the steam vent over the bathroom when his phone rang. 'God, not now, Dad,' he cursed as he brushed dust from his fingers then flipped open the phone.

'Dad, what is it this time?'

'Where are you?'

'Searching the roof space in Amanda's house.'

'What the hell for?'

Give me strength, he thought. 'You wanted me to be sure I searched everywhere – well I'm searching and I'm still convinced she doesn't have it nor ever had it.'

'I'm sending you another man. Those two idiots got hauled over the coals and a rapid transfer to different ends of the state. We're going to have to dispose of them.'

Rico bolted upright, cracking his head on the beam above him. 'Christ!' He squatted down again as he rubbed the already swelling ping-pong ball sized area.

'You've found it?' The excitement in his father's voice was unmistakable.

'Hell no,' he said then added in his mind, and I'm not giving you the satisfaction of knowing you are the cause of an injury! 'Just an electric cable in the way. There's nothing here.'

'What about under the house?'

'Looked. Zilch. Who's the new man?'

'Salvatore Zappacosta. He's a hit man. Reliable. I've used him before.'

Rico slid his eyes closed as he swore inwardly. A hit man in his father's outfit meant torture before certain death. 'Dad, if you'd let me do this my way instead of continually interfering we would have Amanda by now. Those two blockheads were like a runaway bulldozer in tactics. God only knows how they managed to become detectives.'

'Well you haven't done any better!'

'Only because those dunderheads had the subtlety of a brick dunny! I've got a plan and I sure as hell don't need any interference from anyone else. Now please quit ringing every thirty minutes and let me get on with it? If I'm in close range I won't be able to talk to you and if I don't answer my phone you get on your high horse. Give me a break!'

On the verge of losing his temper, Rico snapped the phone shut, crawled until he could stand without losing more skin then dropped to the chair and replaced the manhole cover.

Still convinced Amanda was never returning home, Rico decided to concentrate on finding her. He gave himself twelve hours to check out the woman living with the lawyer. To this end, he made the decision to turn in his Porsche and hire a plainer car. Amanda would recognise the Porsche but she would never believe he would drive a plain, common old sedan. Hell, he had enough trouble believing he had even thought of it.

Chapter Twelve

The warm needles of water pinging on her back eased the tension of tight muscles as Amy leant her head on her arms, which were resting against the glass shower partition. Her head ached from the unbroken hours spent at her computer. She'd stuck to the task until the design job was complete and the final drawings emailed to her boss with a copy to the customer. Even though she attempted to force all thoughts from her mind in order to ease the pain in her temples, she couldn't. While she'd been working locked in her room, James had been reading the thick wad of papers she had copied after stealing them from Rico's filing cabinet and desk. Her self-imposed exile had been deliberate on her part, telling James she wanted to concentrate on completing her contract. She hadn't even gone out to the kitchen for coffee during the afternoon and she figured her aching temples were as much from dehydration and lack of caffeine as from overwork.

She knew she was being cowardly but the shame she felt about becoming involved with Rico had prevented her from facing James. During the afternoon she'd heard mumbling and laughter emanating from various rooms of the house and this was another reason she'd remained in her room. She hadn't wanted to interrupt what she felt was important catch up time between father and son. From the conversation she'd had with Jason while he explained and showed her all the features of the phone he'd purchased, she'd learnt that Jason was studying at the School of Mines in Kalgoorlie, was twenty years old and only came home during the term on special occasions like tonight's family get-together. He had vacation work with one of the mines, earning him enough to live on for the rest of the year.

Amy smiled at the thought of the evening ahead. Going as James's date was rather nice but at the same time daunting. Jason had been relentless in his teasing once he'd found out. Knowing the two men were waiting to have their showers, Amy straightened, quickly soaped her body, shampooed her hair and rinsed off. After roughly drying her skin, she wrapped the towel around her body and knotted it under her arm then collected all her bits and pieces and checked that the bathroom was tidy before opening the door.

'It's all yours,' she called as she strode down the passage towards her room. She was still attempting to style her hair into some resemblance of class using a hair dryer James had found in his daughter's room when there was a loud knock at the door. Switching the appliance off, she sighed at her image in the small mirror. Instead of a flat, hacked look all she'd succeeded in doing was creating a fluffy hacked look with a bit more body.

'Come in,' she called.

The first thing she noticed were the sharp creases in the jeans James was wearing. She couldn't suppress a grin. 'I can't believe you actually press your jeans.'

James grinned back. 'I don't, the drycleaner does.'

'You get your jeans dry-cleaned!'

'Not always. Only when I'm snowed under with a case. It's quicker to drop off all my trousers and suits in one bundle than sort through. Jason is right, you look pretty.' His eyes ran all the way up her body and then they settled on her hair.

Amy felt her cheeks warm. 'The hair needs a professional touch. It's all uneven and jagged. Did you want something?'

'I just had a call back from the Federal Police in Sydney. When I spoke to them earlier I insisted on more details about the whereabouts of Sergeant Simpson. They had been rather cagey so I outlined what has been happening over here. It appears he is missing in action. They haven't heard from him in over a week. They searched his house. His personal mobile is switched on and attached to the charger. That's why it has been ringing out. His car is there. Everything looks normal except they can't find him.'

Amy felt ice flow through her veins then her knees buckled as though they couldn't hold her up. She swayed then plonked onto the bed to prevent falling. 'Far out! Rico. Michael is dead. I just know it. That's how Rico found me. Using his position, his father would have made enquiries and found out who was on my case. Oh, God. When will this ever end?' She knew she was shaking, could feel her body tremble as she wrapped her arms around her torso. The bed sagged and an arm went around her shoulders.

'You don't know that, but it does sound mighty suspicious. The timing is right. I've discussed a lot of details with the inspector in Sydney. But I don't think it was Rico for the man disappeared before Rico was released. I checked. So Rico isn't responsible but he has jumped bail and they were looking for him. New South Wales Police are sending over two senior officers to extradite him back over the border. That is if he is ever caught. I'm sorry but I thought you needed to know. They gave me some local contacts to organise a new identity for you. We'll get started first thing Monday morning.'

'Did you tell them Rico was hanging out here?'

'Yes, but the yellow car hasn't been around since early this morning. I'm guessing Rico realises it won't be long before the authorities start putting two and two together. He probably thought he would be able to snatch you very quickly.' He lifted her chin and smiled at her. 'But being the smart intrepid woman you are you've thwarted his plans. He'll have to go underground.'

'He won't be far away and he won't give up. I can't stay here any longer.' Amy pulled free and stood then started pacing around, her actions mimicking the turmoil in her mind.

'You are safer here than roaming around out there.' James waved his hand around indicating the door and window. He rose from the bed then neared Amy. 'Let's forget about it for the next couple of hours. I'm taking you out on a date and we are going to enjoy the evening.' Both of his hands settled on her shoulders then he lowered his frame by bending at the knees and peering up so he could catch her lowered eyes. 'I promise I won't let him get near you. And to make sure, I've rung the Commissioner to give him a few more details. He's having this area put under regular patrol surveillance until Rico is caught. Are you ready to go?'

'I'm ready but I don't like this.'

'Don't like going on a date?'

Knowing he was teasing to break the tension, Amy smiled. 'That's not what I meant and you know it. Do I have to go?'

'I'm not leaving you here by yourself, so either we all stay or all go. You'll be safer with Jason and me amongst a group of family and friends. Come on.'

Amy figured she had no choice but to follow for two reasons. She didn't want to be the cause of him missing his brother's birthday celebration and because James slid one arm around her shoulders and virtually forced her to go with him. She grabbed a small bag containing her female essentials of comb, tissues and lip-gloss as she was swept past the dressing table.

Fear engulfed her as they left the safety of the garage. Amy's eyes skittered in all directions seeking any sign of Rico or a bright yellow car. Even with the forever present sunglasses covering her eyes, the lowering sun temporarily blinded her as they headed west. It took a few moments for her pupils to adjust to the glare and re-focus after turning into the next street but by the time they had turned onto the main highway, her vision was clear once again. For the entire journey to North Perth, she kept glancing around; ever afraid she would spot a yellow sports car, her nerves tensing whenever she spied any vehicle of a similar colour.

'Relax, Amy.'

She heard the words at the same time James settled his fingers around her screwed up fist. Realising she needed to do exactly as James intimated she released a long breath and forced her muscles to relax.

'Easier said than done,' Amy mumbled in response, 'and you'd both better start calling me Cathy.'

'Cathy, Cathy, Cathy,' parroted Jason from the rear seat.

'I guess I'd better introduce you as Cathy Douglas tonight,' said James as he removed his hand and settled it back onto the steering wheel.

With Jason repeating Cathy every couple of minutes for the rest of the journey, the three were laughing by the time they pulled into the driveway of what Amy assumed was Jonathan's house. She didn't know whether it was pre-arranged but she felt intense relief when James moved to one side of her and Jason the other as they walked along the short pathway towards the rear of the brick home. The rumble of voices and a burst of laughter indicated the guests were in the backyard.

The moment they stepped through the open gateway all talking ceased. The silence was profound causing the three of them to stop in their tracks. Amy didn't dare look up but could feel the pressure of all eyes boring into her. 'Is something wrong?' she hissed through the side of her mouth.

Jason giggled. 'I think they're shocked that Dad has a woman with him,' he whispered.

'Might be that they are wondering if Jason is your toy-boy or if I'm having some sort of mid-life crisis and found me a young floozy.'

The chuckle at the end of James's whispered words told Amy that he was finding the moment hilarious. 'Floozy?' she hissed back.

'Sorry,' came from James at the same time as Jason spoke.

'You could kiss her, Dad.'

'Better still, we could shock them even more and both kiss her,' responded James in a tone that inferred he was finding it hard to not burst out laughing. Amy couldn't see what was so amusing.

'Don't you dare,' hissed Amy as she turned slightly towards Jason.

'I dare.' James had no sooner spoken than he swooped down and planted a brief kiss fair square on Amy's open mouth.

She heard Jason laugh as he wheeled away and joined the guests. 'Way to go, Dad,' he called over his shoulder.

Mortified was not an apt description, Amy thought as she gaped at James. Words failed her. James was grinning as he lifted one finger under her chin and forced her mouth closed. 'Come and meet my folks.'

'Your parents! You kissed me in front of your parents?'

And to completely humiliate her he leant forwards and pecked her on her forehead. 'I did and I must say that despite feeling guilty as hell, it felt so good.' He dared to laugh as he grasped her elbow and led her towards the large group of people from whence loud gasps had emanated at the second kiss. Without counting, Amy estimated thirty people had been privy to her moment of mortification.

As she was led forwards, she took in her surroundings. Mature shrubs lined the fence-line giving the yard privacy. Instead of lawn, a large area had been paved with reconstituted limestone blocks. A patio shaded most of the paved area; the ripple of corrugated iron in a pre-painted cream mirrored what looked to be a new roof on the house. At one side a modern barbecue held pride of place with fairly new benches and cupboards each side. Well-placed large pots containing a variety of shrubs and trees around the edges made the area look classy yet comfy. Someone had a good eye for decorating.

Amy was tugged to a halt in front of an elderly but spry looking couple.

'Am… um, Cathy, these are my parents, Maureen and Graham Ward. Mum, Dad, please meet Cathy Douglas. And before you give Cathy the third degree, she's a recently acquainted friend who lives around the corner from me.'

Amy was more than thankful for the qualification as she forced a smile she knew must look very brittle, onto her face. It certainly felt as though her skin was about to crack then shatter.

'But you kissed her!' exclaimed a joyous looking Maureen.

'And I'm waiting for the slap on my cheek for being so presumptuous. It was a dare from Jason. Don't read anything into it. This is actually our first date.'

For a minute Amy felt pleased at the explanation but shuddered at the last sentence. First date meant that there would be many more, or at least several. She dared toss a glare in James's direction before she was engulfed in the other woman's arms.

'Cathy, you have no idea how glad we are to meet you. First date or not, our son has finally asked a woman out. I didn't think I'd live to see the day.'

Then Graham Ward, who was as big a man as his eldest son, grasped her. Despite her size, Amy felt smothered when her face came up against a smart casual short-sleeved shirt and long arms held her clamped to his chest. 'Welcome to the family.'

Sheesh, Amy thought, this is taking things a bit too far. She wriggled free of the bear hug only to be thumped on her shoulder. She knew she jerked at the sudden attack from behind but couldn't help the reaction.

'She's beautiful, big brother. How come a crusty old man like you hooked a gorgeous young thing like this?'

No sooner had she heard those words than she was kissed again, this time by a man she assumed to be Jonathan. His words, the tone of his voice and the kiss that lingered just that little bit too long, didn't inspire her. He sounded jealous. Then she dismissed the thought, putting it down to what James had told her about his brother. Maybe she was a bit biased and on the defensive. When his hand lingered on her shoulder then slid down her spine with sensuous pressure into the small of her back, she figured her first thoughts were the more accurate. Not liking his attitude she stepped away and lifted her head to study the man with what she hoped was contempt. She was half afraid he would recognise her, especially when he peered closely.

'Do I know you?' he asked as he studied her face.

James stepped into the breach. 'I don't think you've ever met my neighbour. Cathy Douglas, this is my brother, Jonathan Ward. We call him Jon.' He turned to Jonathan. 'You can look but don't touch. Cathy is with me.'

The words were definitely a threat, for which Amy felt thankful. She was even more pleased when after the usual round of *Happy Birthday's* and gift giving James ushered her away and remained with her as he made a slow round of the guests, introducing her as a friend and pausing to chat. His solicitous care during the evening, especially when the food was served, was gratifying. Amy relaxed more and more until she found she was enjoying the evening a great deal. It had been a long time since she'd enjoyed such an outing.

After visiting the bathroom, Amy was wending her way back outside and had just reached an arched opening in the passage when an arm shot out from behind the brick wall and snuck around her waist. She couldn't suppress the scream of sheer terror that was cut short by an open mouth clamping over hers. Instinct told her it wasn't James. He knew of her fear and wouldn't pounce on her with such suddenness. Immediately going on the defensive, she lifted one foot and jammed her heel as hard as she could onto the man's foot.

He grunted before lifting his mouth from hers. 'Wildcat,' he mumbled.

Since the man didn't release her, Amy swung one arm back then elbowed him in his abdominal region. She didn't care where she jabbed him but it must have been just under his ribs because the air whooshed from his lungs. The moment he relaxed his hold, Amy dragged her body away.

'How dare you!' she screeched as she looked up. It didn't really surprise her when she recognised Jonathan but still she felt shocked at the liberties he was taking.

'Oh, come on, you let James kiss you. Can't figure what you see in a stuffy old lawyer.' The smirk on Jonathan's face was sickening but the slightly slurred words indicated the man had enjoyed a little too much of the birthday cheer that had been freely flowing all evening.

'I happen to like this particular stuffy old lawyer. He has more etiquette and appeal in his little finger than you do in your entire body. You, I find to be obscene and immature. I can't believe you would make a play for your own brother's partner. You disgust me.' She turned and made to escape but a lurking figure at the end of the passage brought her to a standstill. James looked furious.

'I thought I told you not to touch.' James sounded as though he was holding onto his temper by the thinnest of threads. His voice softened as he held out one arm in invitation. 'Are you all right, Cathy? I heard you scream.'

As though drawn by a magnet, Amy ran the final few steps and almost plastered her body against James. When his arm swept around her she realised she was shaking from head to toe. She hated that she still reacted so badly to sudden movements, especially from out of her line of sight. It had been five years and she thought she was mastering her fear but Jonathan had scared her witless, visions of that ghastly and unforgettable night flooding through her brain the very moment she had been grabbed. Logic said her reaction wasn't normal but no matter how hard she tried, she couldn't control the way she reacted towards men. She was still muffled against James's chest when she felt it move and heard the rumble of his voice.

'I'm really disappointed in you, Jon. I never believed you would go after my woman. Cathy is right, you are an immature oaf where women are concerned and it's about time you grew up and realised that women weren't put on this earth to be your playthings. If you want them to respect you, then you have to learn to respect them. Treat them as equals and something special. Sometimes I find it hard to believe we were brought up in the same household. You have never learnt any of the values instilled in us. Thank you for the evening but I can't stomach being in your company any longer.'

He turned Amy around and began shuffling her ahead of him. Then he paused and Amy felt him half turn. 'If you ever again make a pass at any woman I am dating, I swear I'll flatten you.' Then he slung one arm around Amy and headed her towards the backyard. 'I apologise for my brother. Are you okay? You looked as though you were about to pass out with fear.'

'He scared me with how sudden he grabbed me. I now understand your warning. Has he ever been married?'

'No, thank God. No woman has put up with his nonsense long enough to get hooked. Let's just say our goodbyes and go home.' He paused in the open back doorway. 'I'm sorry; I'm assuming you are ready to leave.'

'I've enjoyed myself but after that little episode have had enough. But if you and Jason want to stay, I don't mind. I'll just act like a leech and stick to your side.'

James let out a deep chesty laugh. 'I'm good to go and Jason has to catch a flight back to Kalgoorlie tomorrow. Are you feeling better?'

'Much better, thank you, although I must say that it wasn't just because it was your brother. Any sudden touching like that sends my adrenaline into overdrive: especially from men. It's something I've been working on to overcome but with Rico turning up I'm afraid things have gotten a bit more tense than usual. I shouldn't have reacted so badly.'

James ceased walking and turned to face her. 'Yes you should. Jon was way out of line and it's been less than three days since Rico turned up. How many scares have you had in those few hours?' He looked at her quizzically, a sympathetic smile hovering around his mouth. He was right but it didn't ease the awkwardness she felt.

After a round of the garden saying goodnight and collecting Jason on the way, they began the homeward journey. They were only a couple of kilometres from home when Jason leant over from the rear seat and tapped his father, who was driving, on the shoulder.

'I'm not one hundred percent certain about this but I've been watching the passenger side mirror and I have a feeling we are being followed.

***

Rico's mind wasn't on his driving with his adrenaline still surging full pelt at almost being caught out when Amanda stepped through the gate seconds ahead of the lawyer and the man who, Rico assumed, was the son. After following the car earlier, he'd been roaming the area, peering over the fence and through cracks, his eyes tracing Amanda's movements. Despite the ghastly hair, he knew it was Amanda, his wife, the only woman he had ever loved. He hadn't been able to drag his eyes away from her once he knew for sure it was she. Her melodious laugh replayed in his mind. He remembered it well, had dreamed the sound so often in gaol.

Even now, thinking about how the lawyer had settled his hand in the small of her back, slid an arm around her shoulder, smiled at her and tended to her every need, made stabs of what he knew to be pure jealousy, feel very painful. Amanda was his – he should have been the one with her. 'God, I was a fool. Those damned steroids!' He fisted the steering wheel.

'Oh, Christ!' The pain brought his mind back to the present and at the sudden slowing of the car he had been tailing he realised he was almost sitting on the bumper bar. He jammed a foot on the brake then knew he had slowed too quickly, making his presence obvious.

Gripping the steering wheel, he eased back then allowed two cars to sneak between him and Amanda. Realising he didn't really need to follow the car any longer for he knew where it was headed, he decelerated even more but then the lawyer's car made a sudden turn into a car park. He slowed, drifted past then drove on.

'I'll talk to you later my lovely one.'

Chapter Thirteen

An immediate tensioning of abdominal muscles caused constriction in Amy's throat. Automatic breathing ceased while the hard knot in her throat made swallowing or speaking impossible. Sounding as though they were far away, she heard James and Jason speaking to each other.

'Are you sure?' from James.

'The same car has been behind us for ages.'

A red mist descended over Amy's eyes. She blinked it away then forced words from her throat. 'Is it yellow?' When her voice came out as nothing more than a squeak she coughed to clear the passageway to her lungs. A rustle from next to her preceded James's hand grasping her clenched fist. It was only when he touched her that she realised how tense her body had become.

'Relax, Amy. There are hundreds of thousands cars on our roads. Two of them could easily be going in the same direction. Look how fluky it was that you met both Jon and me on the same day.'

'That wasn't a fluke, it was downright spooky.' Her voice was at least sounding normal. 'Is there any way we can check out that car behind us? It could be one or both of those two who came barging into your home.' She twisted in her seat in order to gain a clear view of James's features.

He kept his eyes on the road but she noticed him keep glancing into the rear vision mirror. 'I can guarantee it's not them. One was sent to Esperance and the other to Broome on some cooked up urgent need for more men in those regions. I spoke to the Commissioner. They are officially under investigation by Internal Affairs. They were using police resources for their little private job. Their names have been included on my brief.'

'Verteramo is an Italian name isn't it? Do you think he could be mafia?' asked Amy. It was something that had rattled around her brain since hearing the name.

'Possible, but they could just be on the take doing private jobs on the side. I keep hearing the term, Mafia, but really that organisation has been virtually wiped out in this country. But we do have plenty of organised crime and some of it is family related. The speed in which they were on your case so soon after Rico arrived in the state makes them appear to be all the more suspicious though. I have an idea. Jason, keep an eye on the car you thought was following us as I walk Amy, err, Cathy inside then amble in behind us. I want to know what it does.'

The indicator went on moments before James steered into an all night fast food restaurant. 'Since we missed coffee, let's buy a drink,' he said as he pulled into a parking bay then immediately stepped from the car. Within moments he was by Amy's door, pulling it open.

Amy wondered how much adrenaline a body could actually produce as she eased from the car and glanced around. Hers must be running out after all the surges she'd had over the past few days. James immediately shielded her body with his, cutting off her vision. Even though she was anxious to spot the car, relief surged through her at the gesture. Then she figured it was not the wisest idea to be obviously searching around. The driver would disappear straight away if he thought he had been spotted.

The brightness of the internal lights hit her as Amy entered ahead of James. He guided her to a table in a rear corner and pulled out a plastic chair for her. 'What would you like?' he asked.

'If they make hot chocolate, I'd prefer that to coffee. Otherwise I'll have black tea. Caffeine this late will keep me awake for hours.'

'I imagine you're going to have trouble sleeping regardless, so chocolate it is.' As he turned away and headed for the counter, Jason joined him. The two men chatted briefly then glanced her way before Jason headed for the men's room causing frustration to mount in Amy. What were they keeping from her? She was about to move over to the counter when James pocketed his change and turned. He grinned, further increasing her unease.

'You look as though you are about to throw something,' James said as he approached.

'I just want to know what's happened to that car.' She plonked back down from her half risen stance.

James took his time to sit. Amy felt sure it was deliberate. He was still grinning when he finally settled back in his chair and looked up at her. 'Patience is a virtue,' he said.

'Enough with the smart adages - just tell me!'

The darn man had the nerve to just grin at her before he said, 'The car slowed, drifted past then kept going. Jason didn't see it return.'

'Wonderful!' Amy's sarcasm was obvious by the way James hooted with laughter.

'They already know where you live, are probably sure I am Amy Masters or Amanda McPherson as they knew me, and will be waiting parked under the same street light Rico was.' She paused as an idea came to her. 'What's the betting Rico has changed cars?'

'Possible since he knows you recognise the Porsche but I thought you said he always went for flashy vehicles. According to Jason this was a normal silvery grey sedan. He thought a Ford or Mazda.'

When a yell from the waitress interrupted them, James immediately went to retrieve their drinks from the counter. Jason joined them moments before James returned and handed out the three cardboard drink containers.

'What do we do now?' asked Jason.

'Finish our drinks and go home,' said James. 'The police are already making regular patrols of the area. I'll let them know of our suspicions. They can add the car's description to the list. Trouble is it probably fits the description of a third of the cars on the road.'

'I got a partial number plate.' Jason grinned at his father's stunned look.

'Well done, that will help narrow things down.' James shoved his drink to the centre of the table. 'This stuff is disgusting. Let's go home and enjoy real chocolate in hot milk.' He glanced at Amy. 'The milk will help you sleep.'

It only took five minutes before they were home. Despite a quick drive around the local streets there was no sign of any hidden blue or yellow vehicles but the absence only increased Amy's tension. There was no way she would believe Rico wasn't around – somewhere. Her house had been in darkness but that didn't mean Rico wasn't inside. Her unease didn't decrease one iota as they chatted over the promised milky nightcap, nor when she dressed for bed and slid between cool cotton sheets. She discarded the quilt, knowing any extra warmth would not be needed during the summer's night even though the intense heat of the previous two day's heatwave had decreased by ten degrees. Now it was just plain hot instead of stifling. Hot was bearable.

It took quite a while before Amy felt her muscles begin to relax. She listened to the men chatting quietly in the kitchen then to the hushed noises as they prepared for bed: a toilet flushing, the splash of water into a basin, the silence then padding of footsteps that paused at her half-open door. Then there was the quiet voice of James. 'Jason is sleeping in Angie's bed tonight so there'll be one of us either side of you. We're keeping the doors ajar. Call out if you need us, even if you are even slightly afraid.'

Overwhelmed at the consideration, Amy felt tears well as she called, 'Thank you.' It was all she could manage to get out before choking up with emotion. Instead of fighting back the tears as she had done for the past five years, she allowed them to trickle down her cheeks. They were warm happy tears of gratitude instead of angry or terrified tears. She could do the happy thing since she couldn't be seen or heard. Releasing her emotions felt so good and she realised she should have allowed herself to release her fear and anger years ago. Then she focussed her thoughts on how fortunate she was to have blundered her way into James's backyard. Was it fate that had his gate open as though begging her to enter and welcoming her? Were the Gods looking down on her and saying she'd had enough and it was now time for things to turn around for her? The more she thought, the more she realised that after all this time she was beginning to trust again. Despite those first few minutes of disquiet after meeting James, instinct told her she could trust this man and his son. A warm, fuzzy sensation swamped her innards as she relaxed and her eyes drifted shut.

Amy was awake in an instant, a fresh supply of adrenaline surging through her veins. She attempted to rise but couldn't; a heavy weight held her clamped to the mattress. Her scream of fear was stifled by a large hand pressing over her mouth blocking off the escape of sound. Her eyes swept around the darkness, landing on the dark shadow hovering over her. She bucked on the bed trying to dislodge what she knew to be a man. One long leg slid over her lower body to prevent her kicking legs from becoming free. Panic stricken, she wrenched her arms free from the constraint of the sheet tightened by the man's weight and began punching wildly. The pain as knuckles hit hard flesh was ignored.

Grunts of pain gushed into one ear, followed by the whispered words, 'Amy, it's me. You must keep quiet.'

It took a moment for her senses to assimilate and the message to reach her terrified brain. Then all of a sudden she recognised the pleasant aroma of aftershave at the same time the familiarity of the voice encoded. 'James?' The word was nothing more than a mumble under the still tight fingers but she ceased fighting and James must have read her submission as recognition for she felt his head close in on her ear.

'You must keep quiet. Jason heard someone outside Angie's room rattling the window. This was the only way I could wake you without you screaming. I'm sorry I scared you.' A hot breath swept into her ear along with the barely whispered words but with his mouth so close she made out every word.

The pressure eased on her mouth but only a little. 'You promise you won't make a sound?'

When Amy nodded in the dark James must have felt it for his body eased away and his hand lifted. Now that her eyes had adjusted to the gloom, she could make out his frame kneeling on the floor by the bedside. Her heart still palpitating wildly, she sat up, her arms automatically winding around her torso to keep her terrified body from splintering apart. She knew it was ridiculous but her immediate thought was to get her heart checked out. How many scares could it take?

The sound of her window rattling gave her an instant answer. Her body tensed in an all out effort to imitate stone. She didn't dare breathe. James eased his body up and took a single step towards the window. Amy felt suddenly bereft then mentally chastised herself. He was only one step away but it felt like a million and that she was alone.

A thud from outside was followed by a muffled oath. James stepped back to the bed and held out his hand. The moment she grasped it and his long fingers encased her hand, her tension dissipated. With his touch she felt safe. Instinct told her Rico was outside but the sure knowledge that James and Jason wouldn't let him harm her gave her such an overwhelming sensation of security. It was something she hadn't felt since the day she married.

An arc of lights swept through the narrow gaps in the closed Venetian blinds, briefly lighting up the room. James leant down and replaced his mouth against her ear. 'That will be the police. I rang before I came in here but I'm surprised they came so soon.'

He drew her upwards. She slid her legs from the tangled sheets and stepped onto the floor then was enveloped in his arms. They stood together watching the car lights sweep back. The car whispered to a standstill somewhere outside then two doors snicked shut. It was obvious the officers were attempting to be as quiet as possible but not quiet enough for footsteps ran past the window then they heard a scrabbling. By the sound, Amy figured Rico was climbing the back fence for it sounded like knees and feet hitting corrugated metal.

Two separate beams of light swung in wild arcs. Torches, thought Amy. A nearby shout was followed by the thudding of more running feet. Neighbourhood dogs with sharp ears chorused their warnings. More limbs thumping into metal told Amy that the men were on Rico's trail.

'I hope they catch him,' Amy said aloud, knowing that there was no need to keep silent any longer.

'So do I,' said Jason from the door.

Amy spun around and stepped away from James, feeling guilty about being caught in what she knew was merely a security embrace but would be perceived as more intimate. Even though she had nothing to feel guilty about, she felt her cheeks flame. Then to cover her embarrassment she turned back to James and punched him in the chest. 'That's for scaring the living daylights out of me. I thought you were Rico.'

He caught her hand to prevent further onslaught. 'That's a fine way to show your gratitude. You may as well turn the light on, son.'

When the light flashed, Amy saw that James was grinning. She fisted her other hand but it was caught mid-air.

'Are you fighting me out of pure relief or because you are imaging what you'd like to do to Rico?'

'It's what's left of my adrenaline looking for retribution. What I want to do to Rico is exactly what he did to me.'

James eased his stance and released her hands. 'You still haven't given me those details but I imagine it was fairly horrendous given the little you've disclosed. Are you ready to go back to sleep?'

'Sleep! You think there's any hope I'll be able to sleep now?' She headed for the door barging past Jason then stalked down the passage towards the kitchen. 'I need a drink - preferably of the alcoholic variety. My nerves are shot to pieces and my body is full of enough adrenaline to kick start at least fifty dead bodies.' Reaching the kitchen she searched the fridge for any signs of wine. By the time James and Jason reached her, she was peering in the walk-in pantry having found the fridge devoid of alcohol except for a couple of beers and she hated beer.

'How about a shot of Cognac? I believe brandy is good for calming nerves.' James opened an overhead cupboard and pulled out what Amy knew to be a very expensive unopened bottle of vintage Cognac. She enjoyed the occasional really good brand but wasn't about to deprive James of such a luxury.

'You don't have to open that. It's one of the best. Wine will do.' She pushed the bottle away.

'It was a gift for my fortieth. I've just never had the need to open it. I have a feeling now is the right time.' Without waiting, he wrenched the seal from the cork and lifted two glasses from the same cupboard. 'Jason?' he asked with a lifted eyebrow.

'Not for me, I'll stick to beer.'

With the intention of savouring every drop to enjoy the smooth sting of the fiery liquid, Amy took a small sip from the proffered bulbous crystal glass, a real brandy balloon; such exquisite luxury. A loud thump on the front door and the Cognac went straight down her throat as her body jerked. She coughed to catch her breath after the brandy burnt a fiery path all the way down her gullet to her stomach.

Laughing, James set his glass down then tightened the belt on his light cotton robe to cover the expanse of naked chest peeking provocatively through gaping lapels. The padding of bare footfalls echoed down the tiled passage in the silence. Amy heard the door swing open then three distinct voices, the only one she recognised being that of James. Louder footsteps from booted feet came her way. Hoping she was halfway decent, Amy glanced down at her clothes. A short T-shirt type nightie covered the important bits from sight but the outline of her breasts and slight mound below her waist under a fabric that wanted to cling like a second skin did nothing to ease her chagrin. She grabbed a chair and sat, leaning towards the table like some crazed hunchback to hide as much of her female attributes as she could. Knowing she had been in full view to both James and Jason caused her damned cheeks to heat again.

Jason seemed unconcerned about wearing nothing more than short cotton pyjama pants. It wasn't something Amy had been aware of before but now that she'd had time to realise how little each was wearing, embarrassment hit like a typhoon. When the three men entered the kitchen her eyes were firmly planted on the glass she had wrapped her hands around, hoping everyone would think she was warming the Cognac to body temperature. She wondered how long it would take for the liquid to begin bubbling since her body felt as though it was at boiling point.

'Amy, this is Sergeant Mick Rogers and Constable Brian Donnelly.'

Amy dared to glance up without sitting back. James looked at her with a quizzical frown then grinned. Damning the man for being able to read her so well, her heat level rose. He really was an infuriating devil the way he could suss her every movement and thought.

'Ma'am,' said the Sergeant, 'whoever was here managed to elude us. He had a car parked three streets down. We got the plate number and are waiting for the details but I'm betting the car was stolen. They often are. But it's not the same plate as the one earlier and this car was smoky green.'

Amy felt her shoulders rise then slump as she glanced at James. 'So Rico could be back tonight,' she said to her glass. Then what the officer said, registered. 'Not the same number? Green?'

'Maybe the first car wasn't following us,' said James. 'It's possible.'

'Regardless, we'll be keeping watch for the rest of tonight,' said the sergeant. 'Mr Ward here has given us a brief outline. He told us that this man broke into your house and you've been too scared to return. We'd like to send our forensics team in as soon as possible. See what we can find. You need to lay charges.'

Thinking about how she had snuck into her own home in the middle of the night, Amy looked up. 'You think that will stop him?'

James butted in. 'Amy has no faith in the police. Rico was a former officer in New South Wales. Her story is quite long and convoluted and involves crooked members of legal fraternities and organised crime gangs. I'm ploughing through some quite revealing paperwork that is going to rock the authorities in more than one state.'

Taking on a mind of its own, Amy's head shot up and her eyes widened. 'Those papers, they're really important?'

'Explosive is the word I would use.' James dropped a hand on her shoulder and gave a gentle shove. 'I feel certain you wouldn't be aware of exactly how damning they are.'

Amy gasped when she realised the shape of her breasts were so outlined she might as well have not been wearing any covering. 'Far out!' she murmured under her breath as she dragged the top of her arms forward and leant towards the table again. She wasn't game to lift her head when a mobile phone rang. All she was game to do was to listen intently to the one sided conversation of the Sergeant while she was bent over like a hunchback.

'The car was hired by one Matteo Giovannazzo.'

Completely forgetting about her exposed body parts, Amy bolted upright. 'That's Rico's father. I can't believe he would be here. He wouldn't be so stupid!'

There was a stunned silence, broken when James offered an explanation. 'Matteo is a District Court judge in Sydney.'

'You're kidding!' The new voice told Amy that the constable had spoken.

The sergeant wasn't quite so couth. He swore then mumbled an apology. 'Sorry Ma'am. This puts a whole new light on matters. I need to discuss this with my superiors.' The man paused. 'Look guys, how about everyone getting a bit of shut-eye. We'll have a patrol car keep an eye on the area for the rest of the night. I know who you are, Mr Ward and I'm mighty pleased you are cleaning out the riff-raff that are giving the majority of us officers a bad name. The Commissioner asked us specifically to be on your case. I believe you rang him earlier. I need to speak with him then I'm sure we are all going to have to get together to sort out this mess. Ma'am, we are on your side. I can guarantee Brian and I are the good guys. Some time in the morning, I'd like to escort you back to your place with a forensics team. We'll need you to tell us if anything has been touched or is missing. We'll also try to lift some prints from the fence and house here. But now, get some sleep.'

***

From his position perched behind a slatted wood fence, Rico observed the goings on three doors down and across the road. He didn't have to be told who the hood dressed in black from top to toe and who slithered over the front fence of the lawyer's house, was. Salvatore Zappacosta. He was tall, lean, lithe and, Rico suspected, deadly. The moment he spied the man, Rico called the emergency number to report an intruder skulking through the neighbourhood backyards, specifically citing the house number he was observing.

He waited, watching the man until he heard the sounds of approaching cars. Then he made a rapid retreat, through the same backyards he'd used to arrive, until he reached his new hire car several blocks away. Amanda would be safe for the night, giving him a chance for a decent few hours sleep.

Chapter Fourteen

Not bothering to cover her mouth as she yawned, Amy dragged on the same clothes she'd worn the night before. Even though she was aware of waking several times after only short periods of unconsciousness she hadn't slept much after the police had left. Now she felt bone weary tired.

With the slats of Venetian blinds firmly closed it was difficult to make out objects in the gloom so Amy went by touch. With her arms waving before her she crept to the window and parted two wooden strands. The sky contained only streaks of salmon and pale grey along the eastern horizon over the hills but her mind was too alert to attempt going back to sleep. During one of her fitful interludes of tireless brain activity between snatches of rest, she had come to the conclusion that to stay with James would only endanger his life. Last night proved it.

With the decision made to move out today, she unfurled the blind to give more light then began to very quietly pack her belongings. James wouldn't be pleased but it was her life and her decision.

When she remembered there was a damp load of her washing still sitting in the machine and that she couldn't retrieve her money from James's safe without the man himself to open it, she plopped onto the already stripped bed feeling frustrated. She'd hoped to leave before James was awake. Maybe she still could. A phone call to meet him in the city to pick up her cash wouldn't be so difficult to arrange.

Bundling up the used linen she snuck past Jason's slightly ajar door, continuing on down the passage on tip-toe to the laundry where she emptied out her damp clothes into a basket then shoved in the sheets along with a scoop of laundry powder.

'What do you think you are doing?'

Amy yelped as she spun around, spilling the last remnants of powder onto the floor. James stood lolling against the doorframe in a seemingly casual stance but Amy sensed an alertness about him. Dressed in knee-length khaki shorts and matching collared T-shirt, he had a coffee mug in one hand making it obvious he'd been up for quite a while. Now why hadn't she heard him?

'And here I am trying to be quiet so as to not waken you.' She dropped the lid of the machine so he couldn't see what was inside for she knew he'd be less than pleased. 'I'm just collecting my washing. I need to hang it out.'

His smile was more like a gloat. 'You're supposed to put in the powder before you wash, not after.'

His casual swagger across the small room along with his manner told Amy he knew darn well what she was up to. She felt her cheeks redden as he lifted the lid. 'Clean sheets after only a couple of nights?'

'I… umm… '

'Had plans to sneak out without telling me?' James finished for her. 'Don't think I wasn't ahead of you. I suspected you might try this.' He leant back against the machine and swept one arm towards the back door in invitation. 'Go ahead. Step outside with you backpack. See if Rico is waiting for you. Since the only way you can leave at this hour is by walking, let's see how far you get before he bundles you into a car. Maybe your father-in-law is waiting out there instead. You want to go and hang your washing out as a test run?' It took only one step for James to reach the half-filled laundry basket. Then he lifted it onto the bench from the floor and clicked the drier door open. Without saying another word he transferred her clothes from basket to drier, slammed the door shut then set the timer. The machine hummed into life with a rhythmical click, click of clothes tumbling in the metal drum. To further heighten her chagrin, he set the washing machine going.

Feeling both mortified at how he had raised an eyebrow at her lacy lingerie, and put out by his high-handed actions Amy crossed her arms over her chest and straightened. 'I was going to wait until you got up.'

He laughed an all-knowing chuckle. 'Only because you couldn't get your money without me opening the safe. We need to talk. Seriously,' he added after a pause. 'Let's convene to the kitchen. I'll make fresh coffee.'

Without waiting for her, James walked without the extreme caution Amy had taken to not make any noise. She did notice that Jason's door had been pulled shut but wondered how any person could sleep with the racket of two machines running. By the time she joined James in the kitchen he already had fresh grounds in the coffee machine. Even more mechanical rumbles ensued when he pressed the button, creating enough ruckus to waken the dead.

'How can Jason sleep with all this noise?' asked Amy as she slunk into a kitchen chair.

'It's almost impossible to wake him in the mornings before his body is ready.'

'He heard the prowler last night.'

'Jason hadn't been asleep. He had been working on an assignment and had only turned his computer off about ten minutes before.'

Apart from the modern mechanical whooshes and rumbles there was silence until James settled two mugs of coffee on the table. 'Why are you leaving?' he asked while pulling out a second chair. The quietness of his voice didn't deceive her for one second; it held a distinct ominous tone.

'If I'm not here, you won't be pestered.' Knowing the coffee was too hot to sip Amy wrapped her hands around the mug and gave all her concentration to watching the steam rise and the tiny bubbles in the froth pop then settle in tiny darker craters amongst the cream foam.

'I can't prevent you from leaving but have you thought about where to go that would be any safer.'

She wasn't game to look up. 'I'll find a hotel or guesthouse. But it will be for only a couple more days then I'm leaving the state. I still have my passport.'

'In the name of Amy Masters! How far do you think you can get before he follows? His father has the means to track you via airlines, trains or buses. He's a judge. He can write his own warrant.' The scrape of a chair gave Amy the only indication James was moving closer so she was half prepared when his fingers curled under her chin and lifted her face until they were eye to eye.

'I've been up for about thirty minutes, reading those papers you gave me. Where did you get them from?'

'From a filing cabinet and desk drawers in Rico's place.'

'How? You claim you weren't aware of his secret life until after you were beaten and I'm assuming you didn't willingly go back to his place after that night.' James moved to a separate seat directly across from her. His unblinking stare made her feel uncomfortable.

'The moment he was arrested, my lawyer organised two armed bodyguards for me as well as a removal truck. In the week before the wedding, I had transported all my belongings from Dad's place to Rico's house. But I stayed with Dad. Rico and I had never... you know... slept together. I needed my things but wasn't game to return until I could be sure Rico wouldn't turn up. I spent four hours in Rico's house. I discovered that he had opened most of my boxes and rifled through them. My important papers were missing so I searched for them. While the removalists carted my belongings to their truck, one guard kept watch until they drove away. The other man remained stationed outside the door to Rico's office. With the filing cabinet and bottom drawer of the desk locked, I searched for the keys. They were hanging on a hook at the very back under the desktop. I had to search the files to find my papers. What I found in those files made the hairs on the back of my neck stand on end. It stunned me to realise what sort of man I had so stupidly married. It also terrified me, especially after what I had been through. I made two copies of each paper I thought was incriminating, on Rico's copier. One copy you have and the other is in separate bank security boxes.'

'You gave me the keys in that envelope.' James appeared to be at ease, reclining back in his chair but Amy wasn't convinced. Far out, but the man was good at his job. She pitied any one who had the nerve to actually lie to him.

'That envelope contains instructions and only one key. There are four separate boxes in four separate banks. The first box, to which you have the key, contains twenty-five thousand dollars in cash, one file and the other keys. Each of the other boxes has a similar sum of money and another file full of papers.'

'You stole money from Rico?' James shot forward.

'No way! Its money I already had in my previous account plus what I've saved over the past five years since escaping. I was twenty-six when I married him and had been working in a well-paid job for quite a few years. I've lived frugally and saved as much as I could for this very situation where I can't work and need to escape and possibly live for a while without being able to earn an income. I needed to be able to lay my hands on ready cash at a moment's notice.' Amy stared at James until he eased back into his chair.

'Sorry. But something has me puzzled. Where did you get the cardboard files, in which you stowed the papers?'

Amy wasn't sure what the relevance was. What did it matter where eight cheap common files came from? She figured they were so common almost every household in the country had a pile of them. 'There were boxes of them in a cupboard in Rico's office. I felt certain he wouldn't have counted them to see if any were missing.'

'He may just have done exactly that.' She twisted her head to follow him as James stood and took a few steps towards the door.

'Huh? Why on earth would he? There were dozens of them just shoved every which way in a large cardboard carton. I took two of each colour so there wasn't an obvious lesser amount of any one colour.'

'I'll show you.' James vanished, returning less than a minute later. In his hand he carried all four files filled with papers. From the size of the pile, it appeared that all the papers were there. Their absence certainly gave her room to pack more clothes in her backpack and made it a great deal lighter to carry. He sat next to Amy then separated the files, placing them in a neat row on the table.

'I've scanned all the paperwork. Some I have read more thoroughly. Most are photocopies.' He paused as he tapped three of the files. 'But not all.' He removed the paper from the fourth file. 'Did you check that the files were empty?'

Amy thought for a minute, trying to recall her actions on that day. She had worked frantically while ever afraid someone would turn up, especially Rico even though she had been assured he would be held for at least twenty-four hours. But after scanning the papers she was even more afraid of his father turning up. 'No, I just shoved the piles inside and numbered them 1, 1A, 2, 2A and so on.'

'Then I'm guessing that either one of them already contained some papers or you may have inadvertently picked up a separate pile from the desk because these,' he flicked through the papers until he came to a plastic folder, 'are not copies but are originals.' He held them out.

Amy felt her chest tighten. Some innate feeling told her that the thin clear plastic folder held something very important. There was certainly no recollection of having seen any plastic folder before. 'What are they?' She didn't want to touch the plastic, knowing the contents were like lethal poison.

'Probably the most important of the lot.' He waved them in the air then slapped them onto the table in front of her.

'These papers alone are enough to put not only Rico, but his father and several other prominent people in jail for life.'

A sensation of pure dread pressed into Amy's body. She knew how incriminating the rest of the papers were. She was in a quandary. On the one hand she was desperate to know what was written on each and every sheet. But at the same time she didn't want anything to do with them. Caution won her internal war. She tucked her fingers under her armpits to prevent them from reaching out.

'It's also more than likely the reason Rico is still after you. He probably wants them back.'

'But, but...' Amy took a deep breath to control her shattered nerves. 'He couldn't know I have them. I didn't even know.'

As James sat opposite her, he shuffled through the papers. 'He must have known, purely by the absence of your belongings, including the private paperwork he had filed away, that you or someone close to you had been in the house. It would be natural to assume that same person stole these. He may or may not know you have these others.' James swept a hand over the files. 'It depends on how carefully you replaced everything.'

'I was super careful. I copied one file at a time, replaced the papers in the exact same order and touched as little as I could and used latex gloves I found in Rico's wardrobe while I was removing my clothes. That box of gloves alone gave me the heebie-jeebies. The desk had little on top so it was easy to lay the papers out. Therefore I'm certain I didn't scoop that up with the others.' She pointed to the folder that took on insidious grotesque features in her mind. She dropped her head onto the table, banging it three times for stupidity and out of sheer frustration. 'Why, oh, why didn't I check those folders?' She glanced up then straightened. 'Do you really think this is why he's still after me?'

'I can't be sure but if someone stole these from me, I'd be mighty upset and pretty desperate to get them back.'

'Far out!' Amy flopped forward, this time protecting her forehead on her upturned hands. Despite attempting to think about what she could do, her mind felt as though it was in a vacuum, all logical thought eluding her. When she was certain all her brain cells had completely scrambled she straightened. 'What am I supposed to do now?'

'Nothing,' said James as he stacked the paperwork into one neat pile.

'Nothing!' echoed Amy, her voice rising.

'There's nothing you can do. The incriminating paperwork is here. It needs to be handed onto the proper authorities so they can lock these criminals away for good.'

'No!' Amy yelled. The very thought of what would happen to her then, alarmed her to such an extent she lost control of her voice.

'Calm down.' A hand settled on hers. 'I'll make copies of everything then ensure that the right people receive it, not,' he smiled at her gasp of alarm, 'anyone corrupt. Not all people in authority are crooked. I can assure you the right people will deal with this. But these crimes didn't occur in our state.' He tapped the files again.

'I'm as good as dead aren't I?' mumbled Amy.

James laughed. 'No. You will be protected. I've already arranged for you to meet the relevant people to give you a new identity, tomorrow. It will take a couple of days at the very least. That's why I propose you stay here for those few days.'

Amy shot upright. 'No way! You're already implicated by assumed association with me. Even though Rico can't be certain I'm here, I'm not staying.' She stood. 'I'm moving out today.'

James pulled her back down into the chair. 'I can't make you stay but you need to think very seriously about what you are going to do. I understand your hesitation after all that has gone on. Last night tells me Rico is as certain as he can be that you are here. I've tried to imagine myself in your shoes and I agree your concerns are valid. But you are going to be far more vulnerable out there by yourself.' His hand wavered in the direction of the front door. 'I do have a suggestion that will keep you relatively safe while we still work together until you can gain your new identity.'

His grin was not very comforting, telling Amy he was up to something she wasn't going to like. 'I'm going to like this even less than staying here aren't I?'

'Probably, but I think it will work.'

***

Forcing one heavy eyelid open as he reached for the phone to cease its jarring ring, Rico eyed the glaring red numerals on the electronic clock and released his held breath in a disgusted sigh. Not even six. Even before the voice uttered a single word, he knew who was on the other end. He grabbed for the mobile phone and flipped it open then set it against the side of his face.

'Don't you ever sleep, Dad?'

'What the hell happened?'

'Good morning to you as well.' Rico struggled to a sitting position then swung his legs onto the floor as he brushed the sleep from his eyes. 'What happened was that your new man made such a racket he almost got himself caught! I was close enough to see how inept he was, close enough to have done the job myself and yet so well hidden and so quiet that no one, not even your precious Salvatore, knew I was there. Why can't you just let me get on with it? Your continual interference is stuffing things up,' Rico said in a tight voice then added in his mind, *because you have never trusted me, had enough faith in me to do anything. You always expected me to fail, you old bastard.*

'You've had three days and you've found out zilch.'

'Wrong. I know where Amanda is, I know what she looks like now, I know there is nothing hidden in her house and I am almost certain she hasn't even got the damn thing. You are barking up the wrong tree and I would have been able to confront her if you hadn't kept sending in your troops without consulting me. I would have had her last night if that idiot hadn't arrived on the scene, closely followed by a police car.'

Rico sank back onto the rumpled pillow and rubbed his aching brow. God, but he was sick of this: sick of the life his father had forced him into and the way he was treated like some useless mange-ridden dog. Why did he put up with this treatment? At least in gaol he was able to be his own man, to think for himself and act the way he wanted. Rico snorted. His bastard of a father still didn't know Rico had spent the time studying, earning a degree by correspondence, ridding his body of substances and becoming physically fit the natural way – by working out. The only son who his father regarded as a useless and brainless git had gained first class honours in a Bachelor of Business. It had been so nice to be so normal, earning the trust of fellow prisoners as well as the wardens. There were no continual put-downs, insults or complaints. For the first time in his life, Rico had earned the respect of his peers because his father hadn't been able to interfere.

Did he really want to continue this life on the wrong side of the law? He'd always hated what his father did. But being the only son, he'd been born to carry on the so-called *family business*. Hell, he had money of his own and plenty of it. He could be free to live a normal life by doing the same as Amanda had, change his identity and drop out of circulation. Hell, he had enough fake I.D's, most of which his father had no idea about. He had money offshore in secret accounts and with his background and dual citizenship he could even go to Italy to live without any trouble. But he would have to do it on the quiet, not tell anyone so his father couldn't track him down. But none of that would happen until he could convince Amanda to go with him.

'Rico!'

Rico started at the shouted word, bringing his mind back to his present problem. 'Yes, Dad.'

'Did you hear me or are you having it off with some broad?'

'What the hell? For Christ's sake give me some credit for having common sense.' He squeezed his eyes shut in frustration as the so familiar sensation of worthlessness his father had always instilled in him, welled to mammoth proportions. Never again, he thought as he realised his father was nothing but an out and out bully. 'Dad, I want a simple one word answer. Do you or do you not want me to confront Amanda to find out if she has the file?'

'Of course…'

'One word, Dad, yes or no.'

'Yes, but …'

'No buts!' Rico shouted. 'Give me twenty-four hours to act alone and I can guarantee I will have the answer but I want you to promise me there will be no more interference from Salvatore or anyone else in those twenty-four hours.' His words were greeted by a lengthy silence. Rico smiled. His father was probably in shock since Rico had never stood up to him before.

'Okay, you have my word, but the moment those twenty-four hours are up I'm sending in the troops.'

'Goodbye, Dad, I'll ring you in twenty-four hours and not before.' And elephants will fly before I believe you will keep your word you old bastard, he muttered under his breath as he slammed the phone shut then flopped back onto the pillow. He closed his eyes in the hope that he could go back to sleep but his mind began tumbling escape plans around and around. It took only a few minutes to realise he was never going to be able to relax so he rose, grabbed a clean set of clothes from his small suitcase and carried them into the en-suite bathroom of his hotel room. With a clear head, plans formulated.

Chapter Fifteen

From her position lying prostrate on the rear seat of James's car, Amy listened to the deliberately loud conversation between father and son. She already knew, word for word, what the two were going to say. Feeling totally ridiculous and ill at ease, she didn't like this plan one little bit and couldn't believe she'd let James talk her into it. The only bright side to the plans was that James had cancelled the proposed examination of her home with the police. She hadn't intended turning up in any case but hadn't disclosed that tiny fact. Now she didn't need to and James had the front door key plus a list of the belongings she wanted to keep. He was going to contact the letting agent, cancel her lease and pack her things. As far as she knew the house wasn't dirty unless Rico had been back and to pay a cleaning agency a couple of hundred dollars to make it spick and span for a final inspection was a small price to pay. She had no desire to return to a place that was no longer a home. It had been contaminated by filth, a stench she would never be able to stomach.

The boot slammed and the car shuddered in response. 'Are you ready, Dad? I can't miss my flight.' Jason sounded over-loud as he moved to the entrance of the already open garage door and stood just outside.

'Coming,' called James as he turned off the tap from watering the shrubs at the front of the house. 'You can drive,' he added, his fading voice indicating he had turned away.

Amy visualised the actions from the detailed discussions the three had had over breakfast. All her belongings were alongside Jason's backpack in the boot with not a skerrick of her presence remaining in the house. Everything of value was locked in James's safe and the foot-well next to her was stacked with piles of personal legal files and documents at which James didn't want any intruder sneaking a peek. James was hoping their little scam would lead Rico to breaking into his home in search for Amy during the couple of hours James would be away. The plainclothes police officers cruising around the area would be on the alert as soon as James left the area.

'I'll be back in a couple of hours, Cathy,' James called to the empty house, his voice sounding louder as he neared the car.

Two sets of approaching footsteps scraped on the driveway then both front car doors opened. The vehicle swayed one way then the other as each man slid into the seats and she smelt the now familiar scent of James's after-shave. It was an aroma that was beginning to give her a sense of not only pleasure, but also security. James meant safety.

'You ready, Amy?' James asked quietly as he latched his seatbelt.

'Yes,' Amy said as she heard the rattle and jingle of car keys then the engine turn over before humming into life. 'But I still don't like this.'

'It will work and it's only for a couple of days, three at the most.'

'Do you really believe Rico will fall for this?'

'What I believe is that he will be starting to become desperate. He needs to get you and the papers as quick as possible because he will have no doubt the authorities will be looking for him. He's already missed three appointments to report to the Sydney police. He was in breach of his parole conditions the moment he boarded the aircraft.'

Even though she was familiar with the route they were taking it felt strange trying to trace the movements of the car from her perspective of lying prostrate. The sensation of skewed directions felt really weird and the imbalance in her ear canals reflected in her stomach. 'Do you think he was watching?' she asked as she slid towards the piles of files when Jason swung around a corner. Using her hands braced on the seat in front of her head, she shoved her body back onto the seat. 'Careful, Jason, it's really hard to keep your balance lying like this.'

'Sorry,' called Jason as he slowed a tad.

'If he's as desperate as I think he is, he, or someone close to him, was somewhere around,' called James over his shoulder without turning his head.

Being as tall as he was, Amy had no difficulty in seeing James swing his head from side-to-side in the passenger seat diagonally opposite her head. She knew he was searching for any indication of a car following them or for signs of the yellow Porsche, a musty green hire car or a silvery blue sedan.

'Or his father,' she added.

'We're still not certain whether his father is here or still in Sydney. I'm waiting for confirmation. Rico could have just used his father's name or his father could even have ordered the car from the East. I do know his father is supposed to be sitting in court Tuesday morning so I have my doubts he would be here. Does Rico have any siblings?'

'Two married sisters. I liked them both until they defended Rico in the court case. Same with his mother. According to them, there was no way in this world their darling son and brother could possibly have lifted a finger to harm a woman, especially his adored wife. Adored my foot,' she added under her breath.

'Then how did they explain your injuries?' asked James.

'Must have been an intruder,' scoffed Amy imitating the accent of Rico's very Italian mother.

'On your wedding night? And where was Rico supposed to have been?'

'DNA proved we had… you know… sheesh, how embarrassing is this?' Amy felt a desperate need to curl up in a ball and pretend she was on some faraway island. Then she shot forwards when Jason stamped on the brakes and stopped suddenly. 'Far out,' she mumbled as she peeled her body from crushed files, dragged her left forearm from between the front seat and the paperwork then hoisted her body back onto the seat. 'Do you mind?' she yelled at Jason.

'Sorry,' called Jason as the car slid forwards again. 'A car pulled out in front of me.'

James peered into the back seat. 'Are you okay?'

'I'll live but lying like this in a moving vehicle does wonders for creating nausea. How much further have we got to go?' She dragged a small pile of files from the now messy heap and used them as a pillow to give her shoulders a bit of height in the hope that sitting a bit more upright would lessen the swirling of the contents of her stomach.

'We're approaching the Narrows Bridge,' said Jason.

'Wonderful, less than half-way,' jeered Amy. She thought about mentioning something about ruined paperwork when her stomach could no longer keep down her breakfast but then thought better of it. Instead she grabbed another handful of files and added them to her not so soft cushion, being careful to keep her head under the level of the window although since she could see truck drivers and passengers in buses, they must be able to see her. They must wonder why she was lying across the seat. She'd wonder if the positions were reversed. It took a few minutes of concerted effort to quell the nausea before she felt a little easier. They drove in relative silence, Amy listening to the occasional question from James about Jason noticing any trailing car in the rear vision mirrors. The relief was intense each time Jason replied in the negative.

It wasn't until Jason was pulling into the passenger alighting section outside the airport terminal that she heard James's mobile phone ring. He stepped out of the car at the same time as Jason. While Jason retrieved his bag from the boot, Amy strained to hear James's side of the phone conversation but he must have paused in front of the car for his voice became too mute to make out what he was saying.

'See you,' said Jason from the open boot. 'It was really nice getting to know you. I really wish you and Dad… I like you and you would be good for him.'

The boot slammed causing the car to rock before Amy was able to respond. Then from her position she saw father and son standing embraced outside her far window. Unlike a lot of youth Amy had met, Jason wasn't embarrassed about showing or receiving familial affection. It indicated his level of confidence and maturity. They patted each other on the back before pulling apart. Both men grinned at each other then Jason must have said something similar to James as what he'd said to her for James glanced in the window at her then shook his head as he looked back at Jason. Amy was surprised at the sudden stab of disappointment jabbing at her innards. Just as quickly, she dismissed the ludicrous notion. Even though James was the type of man she would ultimately like to have as a permanent partner, until she could settle in one spot and get rid of the crooks off her tail, there was no way she could even consider the possibility.

When Jason moved away from the car, he gave a last wave and she knew by his glance that it was to her but she felt sure no-one else would be aware the action wasn't a final farewell to the man moving around the rear of the vehicle towards the driver's seat.

The door opened and James eased into the seat, ducking his head as he settled. 'The police caught an intruder in my home but it wasn't Rico or his father. They are questioning him at the central lock-up but so far he has denied any link to Rico and they're sure the name he gave is fake.' James turned to look over his shoulder. 'I think it is safe enough for you to sit up. Do you want to come in the front?'

'We weren't followed?' asked Amy as she eased upright.

'I'm certain we weren't. Rico would have remained near home but now that he knows you weren't in the house he may head this way.'

Amy dropped back onto the seat. 'Then I shouldn't sit up.'

'Even though we mentioned the airport, we'll be long gone before he reaches here. We're going via a different route.'

Amy groaned, being well aware of where they were headed. Sitting back up, she opened the door and slid her feet out of the opening until they hit the ground. Having no legroom on the floor made her exit awkward and un-coordinated. She was thankful she was wearing slacks as she unfolded her body from the car because she knew she looked ungainly and a skirt would have ridden up around her waist leaving her indecently exposed. Within seconds she was sitting next to James and he pulled away from the kerb.

'Was there any damage to your belongings?' Amy asked as her eyes flicked around then into the side-driving mirror. Her nerves were itching to ping apart.

'No. The police watched the intruder enter through the window Jason left slightly ajar. They waited five minutes, giving him the opportunity to search through the house for you before going in after him. He was caught red-handed searching my wardrobe.'

Visions of her own escapade in the wardrobe flashed through her mind. 'Rico is desperate isn't he?' Amy turned towards James.

'I'd say so although there is something that has me mystified.' James glanced at her, smiled a sorry looking smile then turned his attention to the traffic.

'What's that?'

'Nowhere in the papers from that plastic file is Rico's name mentioned. There are plenty of other names, including his father's, with dates and specific actions along with amounts of money but Rico is never mentioned.'

'But the other papers – his name is there.'

'Yes but they are nowhere near as specific or damaging.'

'Then why is he looking for me?'

'Well the papers were in his cupboard so he must have known about them. Maybe his father sent him here. You were married to the man. Maybe his father thought you would talk to Rico.'

'Never going to happen. I could never trust him.' Somehow, Amy's arms had found their way around her body and were clinging tight. Dear Lord, would this tension ever ease off? She eased her grip and stretched her arms out before shaking the tension from tight muscles. Then she dropped her hands loosely into her lap.

'I'm kind of relieved he knows I'm no longer living with you because now you will be much safer. But will Rico know? This intruder, how will he be able to let Rico know?'

A snort escaped James's mouth. 'He was given his one phone call to call a lawyer. The police monitored the call. He spoke to Matteo who said, amongst other things, that he would send a lawyer.'

'And the other things?' asked Amy, feeling her tension return with a vengeance.

'Was there any indication of you being in the house was one question. The man said that neither you nor any of your belongings were in there. Rico will know we secreted you out. He also knows we came to the airport so I'm guessing he will head there.'

Amy groaned, hating this entire thing. Why couldn't Rico just leave her alone? Surely he already had all the retribution he could ever need. Leaving her for dead once was more than enough for one lifetime and she hadn't even done anything wrong to incur his wrath. Except for one thing.

James interrupted her thoughts. 'Why did Rico turn on you on your wedding night?'

Shock caused Amy to suck in her breath. It was as though James had been reading her mind with exactly what she was thinking. At the instant prickle of scratchiness in her eyeballs, she pressed her thumbnail into the palm of her hand as hard as she could in an endeavour to cause harsh pain to quell unbidden tears. She didn't do the tear thing any longer. No tears, no tears, no tears, she chanted in her head as a mantra until the need to weep dissipated. But it didn't ease the overwhelming sensation of distress and agony. Just the mention of that night and all her old anguish re-surfaced.

She turned her head to stare blindly out of the side window. Pictures, smells and remembered pain swirled. She heard herself mewl then clamped her lips tight before forcing her eyes to focus on something, anything so that her brain would concentrate on something real and in the present. Spying a cruise boat on the river heading towards the bridge they were crossing she forced her mind to imagine where it was going. Were they tourists visiting wineries in the Swan Valley? Was it a special event? Maybe a wedding party. Oh, damn, don't think about weddings. She squeezed her eyes shut and pressed her nail in harder.

'What the devil?'

Amy heard the muttered oath at the same time as her hand was grabbed and her fingers prized open. She forced her eyelids apart and glanced down. A stream of red liquid trickled down her palm.

'Amy? What happened?' James immediately released her hand then swung his head from side-to-side peering into driving mirrors. The tick, tick of the indicator was the only sound inside the car before it jolted over the kerbing and James steered the vehicle onto the dry brown verge. With the engine still running he reached over and grasped

Amy by the shoulders and swung her upper body around to face him.

'Talk to me,' he insisted as he lifted the console and withdrew a new packet of tissues, ripped the plastic with his nail before tearing a couple of white squares from the small plastic package and balled them into her palm.

'I don't want to talk about it,' Amy mumbled as she dropped her chin to her chest. Tortured was the only word she could think of as to how she felt. Then she heard a click and her seatbelt slacken before she was drawn across the console as warm arms cocooned her against a hard wall of muscle. The incredible tenderness of James's touch unravelled her stoicism. 'I think it was because he discovered I wasn't a virgin,' she managed to whisper before the floodgates opened.

'What?' James's voice elevated several octaves on the one short word as he drew away slightly, but he didn't release his hold. 'Did you ever claim you were?' He spoke more calmly against her ear as he settled her closer but there wasn't a lot of room and she was uncomfortable so she slid back as far as she could go which left her top half leant against James and her hip pressed uncomfortably against the hard console. She could tell by the tension quivering along his muscles that he was forcing the voice to remain gentle.

'No, he never asked.' Amy sniffed a very unladylike snuffle then searched around with one hand for the tissues. She felt them press into her hand. 'Thank you,' she mumbled as she yanked one from the packet and swiped at her wet face. She pulled back as far as James would allow her to go, which wasn't more than a few centimetres so she settled her head back on his shoulder. 'He knew I'd been in a couple of relationships. I was twenty-six, for heavens' sake. What did he expect? That I had been living in a nunnery? What did he think one did in a relationship? He sure as hell was no virgin. He often bragged about his conquests.' Feeling better now that the initial humiliation was out in the open, Amy pulled away from James and settled back into her seat, taking her time to clean up her ravaged face before continuing the conversation.

'So he just made assumptions and wasn't pleased when he found you had slept with a previous partner.' James sounded as though he was verbalising his thoughts aloud. Then he sat forwards, his forearms resting on the steering wheel and twisted around to face Amy. 'He never asked?'

Amy shook her head. 'It was never discussed but I had told him about my previous couple of boyfriends. He knew they were relatively long term relationships. He must have known I'd slept with both.'

'You mentioned earlier that Rico and you had never slept together before your wedding. Why? Whose idea was that?'

'His. He never made a move or suggested we sleep together.'

'Didn't you think that strange?'

'No, not really.' Another wave of embarrassment hit but then Amy figured she'd already told James most of the facts so another few minutes of humiliation weren't going to make a whole lot of difference and besides, she felt heaps better having the whole sorry saga out in the open. 'I'm not in the habit of jumping into bed with all and sundry. There were only the two guys I'd been dating previously and both those relationships lasted around two years. Rico and I had only been dating three months before we married so it wasn't a long-term relationship. I thought he was being rather chivalrous and sweet at the time. Boy, did I learn different. The first time we did… you know, was consensual.

Hell, it was our wedding night and I was really looking forward to… far out, this is so embarrassing. But when he discovered I wasn't a virgin he just lost it. And I mean really lost it. He went berserk for about half an hour. It was like something snapped inside him and he went absolutely crazy. He beat me, raped me, and… and… and…'

Staring directly ahead, Amy noticed how James's knuckles were white, clenched around the steering wheel as he sat ramrod straight. 'You want to tell me what else happened that night?' He slowly twisted his head to gain eye contact.

The contact was brief. Disconcerted by the topic under discussion, Amy yanked her head sideways to focus on the scenery through the side window. 'No, I never want to discuss it.'

A grey asbestos fence wasn't interesting enough to grab her attention. 'It brings back too many really bad memories. But,' she paused and breathed in and out several times; long calming breaths as she peered down a muddy coloured concrete driveway, hoping to find something unusual for her mind to rivet onto. 'I will leave you with a copy of my medical records if you promise to keep them private and not discuss them with me or anyone else. It's in my past and I want to keep it there.'

'What about the photos?' James began the process of pulling back into the stream of traffic to continue their journey.

Amy sighed in relief that they were moving. 'No photos. You can draw your own conclusions from the records. They will tell you all you need to know.' Amy leant forwards and pressed the knob to start the radio. Not happy with the raucous hard rock, she tried the CD and was pleasantly surprised to hear light classical symphonic sounds. She sat back and prayed James had received her not so subtle message that the discussion was closed while she forced her brain to concentrate on the music. She listened intently to every instrument, every pianissimo, fortissimo and glissando, while imagining she was in a concert hall studying the conductor as he led the strings, brasses, woodwinds and percussion. Closing her eyes, she moved onto the podium waving the baton in a slow three four rhythm, listening so intently for the slightest aberration of a single instrument that she was able to ignore James's attempts to intrude until they pulled up at their destination.

Then a new, different series of uneasy sensations swept through her. She didn't like this one little bit.

***

Having discovered the property he'd hidden in the previous night was vacant, Rico settled behind the slats of wood to observe the goings on at the lawyer's place. He leaned against the cool bricks of the house, using the wall as a shield from the sun, stretched out his legs and balanced the two litre plastic bottle of water by his hip. Having been woken before five, it was still early and being a Sunday he assumed most people would sleep in so he was prepared for a long wait.

The concrete under his backside was hard but smooth and cool. He wriggled until he felt comfortable then opened the plastic bag of food to inspect the contents. He'd grabbed what could be easily carried without making a total mess, from the dining room whilst downing a cup of coffee. The waitress hadn't minded since he'd already paid for breakfast and she'd accepted his explanation of wanting to breakfast by the river on such a glorious morning, making a joke of it by inviting her along to join him.

The aroma of fried bacon led his fingers to the hastily made scrambled egg and bacon sandwich. He un-wrapped the paper napkin, lifted the open package to his nose and breathed in, the scent immediately making saliva surge in his mouth. He bit into the toast, through the soft egg and tugged at the four rashers of bacon he'd piled into the sandwich. Even though it was only lukewarm, it tasted wonderful and went down quickly. He washed it down with a long swig of water before inspecting the remaining contents of the bag, two muffins and three apples. Save it for later, he thought as he bundled the plastic around and around to keep the contents fresh.

As he placed the bag to his other side, a furtive movement across the road caught his eye. He turned and knelt against the wood fence then peered through the gaps. 'I knew I couldn't trust you, you old bastard,' he said quietly as he followed the progress of Salvatore Zappacosta. By the man's size, shape and garb, Rico knew it was the same man. He smiled when a dark blue sedan cruised past and Salvatore froze against the wall of the house directly across the road from Rico. Police, which meant they were on the lookout for either Salvatore or him, or maybe both.

For the next hour, Rico watched, amused by the way Salvatore had to keep moving to avoid locals and the ever-present police car. Twice, the man had almost been caught and now he was squirming in full sun and probably sweating profusely under the black long-sleeved skivvy and dark jeans. Rico reached for the bottle of water and grinned as he held it in front of his eyes before slaking his thirst. Salvatore hadn't thought to bring sustenance – stupid man. And the get-up he was wearing was so damned out of place it was ludicrous that his father thought this man worthy of hiring. But then maybe Salvatore hadn't had a chance to change from his night prowl.

He saw Salvatore tense. Rico screwed the lid back on the bottle as he rose to his knees and positioned his body to seek out what had caused the tension. The lawyer was in the front garden. Rico watched the man water a few plants then raised to a squat as the garage door began to open. He heard the conversation between father and son. God, they looked so much alike. A twinge of jealousy niggled. How he had wanted a son with Amanda - followed a couple of years later by a daughter the image of her mother. He shook away the visions and concentrated back on the conversation.

'See you in a couple of hours, Cathy,' he heard the lawyer call. Cathy – so now she was calling herself Cathy.

As he watched the car vanish down the road, Rico settled back. Now was his chance to search the rest of her belongings, but first he had to get rid of Salvatore. But how? He pulled a knife from his pocket, pressed the lever and a long thin blade flicked out and glinted. Could he do it? Could he actually kill someone? As he pushed the tip of the blade against the concrete the metal flicked back into its casing. Rico pocketed the knife. There had to be a better way. Maybe call the cops again and have the man arrested.

He slid his phone from the pocket of his T-shirt and opened it out but paused when a marked police car crawled past. He followed the sounds as the car continued on around the corner and down the next road until he could hear it no more.

His eyes caught a movement. Salvatore was on the move. The dark figure slid over the fence into the lawyer's backyard. Rico shot upwards then immediately bent at the knees when his head rose over the top of the fence. What in hell's name was he supposed to do now?

He eased the gate open, crept to the edge of the house and peered up and down the road. Finding no sign of any human or car, Rico shot down the drive then across the road. He was about to clamber over the same fence when he heard an engine rev, followed by the squeal of tyres as though a car was taking off at speed. He turned tail and raced back across the road and was unlatching the gate when he heard the car turn into the road. Praying he hadn't been observed he slunk behind the fence and eased the gate closed then squatted on his haunches to peer between the slats.

The same police car pulled up silently at the property next door to the lawyer's. Rico released his breath in a whoosh then grinned. By the time the officers had snuck inside and returned with Salvatore handcuffed, Rico was sitting on his backside with his knees bent in front of him, fighting to contain laughter that was bubbling up, wanting release.

'Serves you right, old man, for lying to me,' Rico called as the police car drove away.

Just to make sure his strong suspicions were correct Rico waited a few minutes then was brazen in his approach to the house, striding to the front door and pressing a finger to the bell. Gut instinct told him Amanda wasn't home, but he searched the grounds, entered the already open window then searched the house, laughing raucously as he went. Not only had he been outsmarted, but so had his bastard of a father. 'One up to you, Amanda and I bet I know where you have gone.'

Chapter Sixteen

As Amy stepped from the car, the heat of the day hit with force after the cool of the air-conditioned space but it was nowhere near as hot as the previous few days. As she straightened, Amy swept her eyes over the house. The brightness from the late morning sun shimmered on pale cream cement render of an older style house that looked as though it had recently undergone an extensive renovation like similar properties in this outer city suburb. Mid, smoky-blue gutters and trim gave a classy contrast behind a well-manicured lawn amidst neat clipped mature shrubs. The lack of bright annual blooms in the garden beds hinted at the absence of a woman. Visions of purple petunias, white daisies and golden marigolds swept into Amy's mind: and maybe a bed of pink roses across the front window. Her musings halted when movement entered her peripheral vision. An automatic tensioning of her muscles caused her to wince when Jonathan Ward filled the frame of the side gateway she had walked through in the dark the previous night. There stood the reason she wasn't so keen on being here.

Wondering what insanity had caused her to agree to stay here, albeit with quite substantial pressure and logical reasoning from James, Amy straightened. He'd better not try to touch her again.

'I knew your face looked familiar.' Jonathon strode forwards with an outstretched hand. He studied her face. 'But I could have sworn you had blue eyes.'

Dropping her head Amy grinned to the ground then hesitated before taking the hand in the age-old handshake greeting. She didn't really feel the need to be over friendly but the man had agreed to hide her away over the next couple of days so she couldn't afford to be rude. Expecting a cold hardness, she was surprised to find his palm warm and soft but his grip was strong without being too overbearing.

'First, please allow me to apologise for my oafish behaviour last night. I could use the excuse that I'd had a few too many celebratory drinks, which I had, but it was my choice to down so many and it doesn't excuse my behaviour. I'm sorry.'

Taken aback by the humble and sincere apology, Amy's hand lingered a little too long in Jonathan's grasp. Becoming aware of the tightening tension of his hold, she tore her fingers away and took a step backwards, cannoning into James in the process. While concentrating on the man in front, she hadn't heard James approach from behind.

'Oops, sorry,' said Amy as she stepped sideways then turned to retrieve her belongings from the boot of the car. Realising she had been rude in not commenting on Jonathan's apology, she paused and turned. 'Apology accepted provided it doesn't happen again.'

'It won't. You have my word.' Jonathan passed her and tapped on the boot as an indication for James to open it. A click and the catch automatically released. Jonathan lifted the boot.

As Amy reached inside, she felt the brush of clothes from both sides, seconds before long arms reached in at the same time. 'We'll get your bags,' said James, the words so close to her ear she felt the warmth of his breath lick against her skin.

Not used to such chivalry after five years of fending for herself, Amy felt a surge of chagrin that her strong independence was being thwarted. Just as quickly she repressed the emotion before stepping back. These two were just being nice and it felt rather pleasant to have two men take care of the simple things and treat her like a lady. Even though she had known James for only a few days, she'd learnt that the gentlemanly behaviour was second nature with him. After last night, she hadn't expected the same from his brother.

'Is that everything?' asked James as he paused with one hand on the boot rim.

Checking the inside with a sweep of her eyes Amy nodded. 'Yes, there were only the three bags.' She followed the men inside until they stopped in the middle of a guest bedroom and placed her three bags in a neat row side-by-side. The décor was masculine plain but indicated the same renovation had taken place inside as well as out. She'd taken little notice of the décor in her brief foray into the house the night before but now she took her time to glance around. The same blue and cream colour scheme had been carried through but in this room there was a burgundy contrast. The furniture and fittings were elegant and modern but once again the feminine touch was missing.

A quick tour of the house ended with all three sitting around the kitchen table sipping strong aromatic filter coffee, which in no way eased the sense of awkwardness Amy felt. She didn't know what to say, or do and prayed someone would begin some sort of conversation.

'Your hair looks better blonde.'

The cup rattled on the saucer as Amy tightened her grip on the handle in shock from Jonathan's murmured statement. It was the last thing she expected to hear but it broke the maudlin silence.

'I agree,' said James. 'I saw it change from blonde, to bright red then to black all in the space of twenty-four hours. Each time I saw Amy it was as though an entirely different woman was standing in front of me, especially when the eyes changed colour at the same time.'

Hearing the hint of humour in James's voice, Amy cast a quick glance at both men then grinned at Jonathan's look of triumph. In that brief scan she noticed how both men had a similar smile. The left side of their mouths hitched slightly higher than the right and the corners of their eyes crinkled to create similar crease patterns. Now that she had the opportunity to study them side-by-side, she noticed the familial likeness and yet each man was different enough for an outsider to not realise they were brothers at first glance. Even though he was tall, Jonathan didn't have the same massive build as James. She wondered whether his childhood illness had stunted his growth to a certain extent.

There was an expectant hush and Amy figured they were waiting for her to say something. 'Even I have to look twice in the mirror to make sure it's me.' She lifted one hand to her hair. 'The black takes some getting used to.'

'I must go.' James pushed his chair back as he rose: the metal legs scraping on large ceramic tiles. He turned to Amy. 'Jon is going to drop you off at my office in the morning. We have appointments with Australian and British authorities to see what we can do about identity changes and papers. Take care.' He leant over and brushed his mouth against her cheek.

Amy was surprised to glimpse a strange look wash over Jonathan's face at what she took as nothing more than a friendly farewell peck. Jonathan looked jealous. When she caught his eye he quickly glanced away. Why the look? Was he jealous of his brother? If so, why?

'You have something for me?'

Amy's attention immediately swung to James. For a moment she had no idea what he meant.

'The medical records,' he said quietly. The whisper of a touch of his finger against her cheek softened the impact of his words. Somehow, she knew he was aware the very thought of the records would cause her angst.

'Of course, give me a minute.' Ignoring the questioning facial expression from Jonathan, Amy made her way back to the guest room she had been allotted and unstrapped the clips from her backpack. Upending the open bag onto the bed, she shook the bag gently until the contents slithered onto the geometrical patterned quilt. Knowing the thin file was at the bottom, Amy figured this was the easiest way to reach it and she needed to hang a few garments to allow the creases to fall out if she was meeting people from high places the next day. She hesitated before picking up the file. Was this the right thing to do? If she didn't allow James to read it, he would ask questions. Talking more about that night was not going to happen. Far better that he read the results for himself without her presence then he couldn't ask questions. But would he reveal the facts to others? He'd promised not to. Did she trust him? So far she had and he hadn't let her down, even going so far as to lie for her. She grabbed the blue file and bolted back to the kitchen before she could change her mind. She held it just out of his reach. 'You promise?' she asked.

'You have my word. I don't break promises unless it is a matter of life or death.' James didn't tug at the file but waited patiently for Amy to release her hold.

'Can I give you a warning about Rico? Just in case he turns up looking for me. He never uses firearms as a weapon. But he does use a knife. He prefers a longish, thin, double-sided blade. Sort of like one of those flick knives you see in American crime films.' Amy wasn't sure if James received the double meaning from her warning but maybe when he read about her injuries he would understand.

'Are you trying to tell me something?' With his other hand he chucked her under the chin in order that she lift her face to look at him.

Darn but he was good at reading her mind. 'Just a warning to take care. I feel really uncomfortable about you being out there alone. I'm scared. I know what he is like, what he can do.' An involuntary shiver passed down the length of her body. 'Can I ring you every couple of hours for my peace of mind? If you don't answer I'll call the police.'

James laughed. 'I appreciate your concern but I can look after myself and the police will still be looking for Rico. They'll be keeping an eye on your place after Forensics has been as well as mine. But thanks for the warning. I'll pass it on about the knife although I imagine they'll be expecting some sort of weapon.' He smiled at her, a gentle, comforting smile. 'Ring me by all means if it gives you some solace. But not after midnight, I do need a few hours sleep and that pleasure has been in short supply since meeting you. Take care.' He tapped the end of her nose and left.

'What was all that about?' asked Jonathan after waving his brother off then checking the front door was locked by jiggling and shoving at the door. That tiny action gave Amy a sense of relief and she felt a warm fuzzy sensation curl her insides when she realised Jonathan automatically went that extra length to ensure her safety.

'Nothing.' Amy wasn't about to relate the events of the past few days to anyone, least of all Jonathan. Even though he had agreed to protect her, she still didn't trust him.

'What's going on between you two?'

The tone of a definite innuendo had Amy bristle. 'Absolutely nothing apart from an amicable friendship based on your brother keeping me safe from that bastard. If you want to read anything else into it, then that's up to you, but you would be wrong on all counts.' Fired up, she turned to face Jonathan. 'And I'm not going to discuss any of it with you. I heard James tell you the basics when he rang you. You saw Rico threaten me so you know what I'm up against. Anything else is none of your darn business.' Furious, Amy spun away and headed towards her room seeking a sanctuary.

She heard Jonathan speed after her so was prepared when he grabbed her by the arm. 'I'm sorry. I didn't mean to upset you. I won't ask any more questions. It just appeared as though there was something more between you.'

Amy spun back around. 'Even if there was something more, it doesn't concern you.' She spied a flicker of something in his eyes and she instantly understood. 'You're jealous of your own brother! Why?'

'Hell no, it's just that he has everything: a fabulous marriage, two wonderful kids, a charmed life and now you. The first woman he goes out with is so damned perfect.'

Not expecting such praise from a man she barely knew, Amy felt many things at once: warmed by the compliment, remorse for her outburst and at the same time sorry for Jonathan. She was beginning to understand him better. 'I appreciate the compliment but believe me I'm nowhere near perfect. I probably have more hang-ups than you could ever imagine. And we aren't going out, as you call it. I was staying at his house so he brought me along to your party as a guest. It was probably more because he wasn't prepared to leave me at home by myself and he didn't know what else to do with me. At least here, with so many people around I was relatively safe.'

'He kissed you and touched you as though you meant something.'

Amy laughed. 'You are definitely jealous but the kiss was a dare from Jason and the touches were no more than him being the gentleman he is and showing consideration. And James doesn't have everything. He lost the love of his life way too soon under the most ghastly of circumstances and he is still grieving for Glenda. He's still hurting on the inside a great deal. Maybe you should talk to him about it, have a heart-to-heart, brother to brother. He's not ready to start dating again. And nor am I. In fact I often wonder if I ever will be ready.'

Eyeing the man standing leant up against the passage wall with his arms folded, it shocked her to recall a very similar stance from James. It was these little mannerisms that made the two brothers more alike than she had at first thought. 'In fact, I'm still terrified of men. I squealed last night because you scared me witless when you grabbed me, not because you kissed me. The sudden movement, the grabbing: that's why I screamed and that's why I insist it doesn't happen again.'

Jonathan straightened and swept his arm to indicate the kitchen in a silent invitation. 'Rico did this to you? Made you so afraid?'

'Yes, and I thought you weren't going to ask any questions.' Amy followed him then settled into the chair he pulled out for her.

'Okay, no questions about Rico, but how about I ask you to join me for lunch instead? I have oodles of food left over from last night. Cold barbecued sausages, a variety of salads plus Pavlova and cheesecake. If it doesn't get eaten I'll have to toss it.' His grin of conciliation had Amy grinning back.

'Sounds good, let me help.'

'No way, you are my guest. Allow me to show you that I can be just as much the gentleman as my brother. I understand you've had a rough few days so sit back and relax.'

By the time the afternoon had waned and the evening meal was almost over, Amy was flummoxed by Jonathan's behaviour. His over-the-top coddling was wearing thin to the extent Amy felt like putting her hands around his neck and throttling him. He was like a young puppy dog trailing after its mother. She'd been waited on, cosseted with cups of tea or coffee, asked a zillion times whether she was too hot or too cold with him adjusting the air-conditioner after each question even though she insisted she was fine. He'd trailed after her, plied her with questions to keep a conversation going, offered her TV programmes, DVD films and music to listen to. Now he was attending to her every need and to things she had no desire for, whilst sitting opposite her at the dining room table. He'd just adjusted the position of her water glass for the nth time and it was driving her crazy.

Unable to keep her mouth closed another second, Amy burst out with, 'Do you always treat your women friends with so much avid attention?'

'Of course, why?' He looked quite shocked at her comment.

'Oh, I was just wondering?' Now she felt ridiculous and regretted her outburst.

'You can't make a comment like that then dismiss it. What did you mean? You sounded as though I was doing something wrong. I thought women liked to be looked after.'

'They do but not so... so... far out, I feel as though I'm being stifled.' Not knowing where to look, Amy gave assiduous attention to her knife and fork, shuffling them from side-to-side on her plate then snapping her fingers back when they clattered, the sound seeming to echo around the room in the awkward silence.

'Stifled!' Jonathon's fork hit the floor as he straightened. Waves of tension flowed off him.

'I'm sorry. Stifled is probably not the best choice of word.' She dared to glance at him. At first she though he looked angry but then changed her mind to hurt. He looked downright hurt, as though she had offended him, and maybe she had. Somehow she had to make amends – explain what she meant a little better. But how to explain when she didn't really know what she meant?

'I don't know how to explain.' She pushed her plate to one side to avoid any more cutlery disasters. 'I class myself as an ordinary every day woman.' She grinned. 'Well one with a few too many emotional hang-ups but I work and socialise with quite a wide range of women. Yes, we like it when a man looks out for us. I know in this day and age that a lot of independent women scorn things like the door opening and the man moving to the outside of the pavement in protection mode, but I really like and appreciate those little things. But at the same time the women of today strive for and enjoy their independence. I like being able to think for myself, be responsible for my own life and to be able to do the things I enjoy without being told whether or not I can do them.' Knowing she was making a right royal hash of things, she picked up her glass a gulped down a mouthful of water. The moment she replaced it, Jonathan reached across the table and moved it slightly as though the placement wasn't exactly where it should be.

She pointed to the glass. 'That's what I meant by stifled.' She peered at him. 'Do you realise how many times you have moved my glass during this meal. Every single time I put it back down you moved it to where you wanted it.'

'I did?'

Amy laughed at the amazed look on his face. 'You did. And you've been hovering around me the entire afternoon as though I were made of porcelain china and would snap apart if left to my own devices for more than a few seconds. That is being stifled.' She sat back in her chair and folded her arms across her chest but was a little afraid of how he would take her outburst.

'I promised I would take care of you and I enjoy looking after a woman.' He imitated her actions by sitting back and crossing his arms.

'There is a huge difference between looking after and...'

'Stifling?' he finished for her, his brows rising.

'Yes.'

'I wasn't aware that I stifled.'

'You do.'

He grinned as though he were enjoying the verbal sparring. 'So tell me how I can un-stifle. Show me.' He unfolded his arms and spread them wide, resting his wrists on the table.

'Tell me something first. Answer my first question.'

'Which was?' He leant forwards.

'Do you always treat women this way – stifling them?'

A chuckle escaped his mouth before he clamped it shut. 'Without using the word starting with, 's', yes. Like I said before, I thought it was what women wanted. I was taught to take care of women.'

'There's a big difference between taking care and being overprotective. Maybe that's why you haven't been able to find a woman prepared to settle down with you.' When his eyes flared and his body tensed, Amy figured she had gone overboard.

'James mentioned that you had trouble keeping a woman for longer than a few months. Sheesh, I feel really bad.' She drew in a long shuddering breath. 'But maybe… hell, I've really put both feet in it haven't I?'

There was a lengthy pause during which Jonathan appeared to mull things over. 'Maybe yes, maybe no.' He sounded hesitant then really stared at her. 'Do you honestly think I stifle?'

Amy smiled. 'Yes, but maybe another word or phrase would be better. How can I explain? I think James had you wrong. He thinks you treat women as playthings put on this earth to kowtow to your every whim.' Noticing Jonathon tense Amy paused while thinking how to change tack. 'But he's wrong. I recognise you are as much a gentleman as your brother but I get the feeling you try too hard to impress. You said earlier that James had it all: the perfect marriage, perfect kids and life, which gives me the impression you want the same. But you want it so bad you try too darn hard. If you wanted to impress me, you would have to ease off the coddling. A lot,' she added after a pause.

'A lot,' Jonathan mused. 'In what way?' He reached over the table and grasped one of her hands. 'You are the first and only person to be so up front with me. I was beginning to believe there was something chronically wrong with me that women couldn't abide but I had no idea where I was going so wrong so often. I can't believe how well you have read me in so short a time. To be honest, yes, I want marriage and the family but I seem to frighten any potential partner away. So I'm interested in your theory.'

Amy tugged her hand away. 'I have no idea how to explain. Maybe I could use my parents as an example. Dad was a successful businessman with an astute mind. Mum was a more airy-fairy arty type. She was talented in almost every art or craft she tried. Where Dad liked everything to be just so Mum didn't mind clutter. They adored each other and so compromised. Dad's interest outside of work was astronomy. He built an observatory-type room in the attic, which was his bolthole. It was almost austere in neatness, the main feature being a large telescope. Mum had her own studio, which was clean but messy. The rest of the house was sort of in-between. I never heard either Mum or Dad put the other down. They accepted each other's quirks and never tried to change them. Both were comfortable in the love they had for each other. They trusted and adored each other and respected their differences. Dad supported Mum's artistic endeavours and willingly went to exhibitions and sales and never grumbled. Same with Mum. If there was some astronomical lecture going on, Mum gladly attended with Dad even though she barely understood the content.

They cared and fussed over each other and yet always gave space to be alone. From the little I've experienced today, you don't give space.'

Unsure about how her tirade was received, Amy stood and began collecting plates. Jonathan followed suit, sweeping around the table and taking the plates from her fingers. 'I'll see to these.'

Amy tugged them back. 'That's what I mean by overdoing things. Why can't you just let me help with the cleaning up? Right now I want to clean up after the meal because I enjoy sharing the workload. Why can't I?'

'Because you are my guest.' He took back the plates.

'If you were in the same situation as me, staying in my home, would you insist on helping me with the chores?'

'Of course! It's the right thing to do.'

'I rest my case, so let me assist with the chores.' She grabbed the two plates and immediately turned her back on him before heading for the kitchen and ignoring the clatter and ping as the cutlery hit the floor and rebounded several times. She lifted her eyes to the heavens; she and cutlery were not having the best of partnerships today.

Jonathan chuckled as he bent to retrieve the silverware. 'You've made your point. I quit stifling and give you space, but we'll share the load. You wash and I'll wipe. Then I'll allow you to put in your next call to James – all by yourself.'

***

It gladdened Rico's heart to hear Amanda laugh. After confirming his suspicions about where she planned to hide out, he'd spent the best part of the last hour peeking through various windows and listening to the conversation. He felt no hurry to confront her as all his father's cohorts were out of the picture and no one else knew where Amanda was.

Since he assumed the brother worked it meant Amanda would be alone on the morrow. They could talk at length, uninterrupted. He could give a full explanation about his life, what had caused him to snap and how he planned to escape from his father's overbearing clutches. Maybe, just maybe, she would forgive him his one transgression. Somehow he doubted it since that one incident had been of the worst kind but he was prepared to start over if Amanda gave him the slightest whiff of a chance. He still loved her, would always love her.

'Sleep peacefully, my love. You are safe for the night,' he mumbled as he turned away from the property to return to his hotel room for the night.

Chapter Seventeen

'Do you want to help with breakfast or would you like to prepare it all by yourself?'

Stunned by the remark, Amy paused in the archway as she entered the kitchen. With an all-knowing grin on his face, Jonathan was standing against the bench with a coffee mug in one hand. By the way steam rose and from the pungent but delicious aroma, Amy guessed the coffee was fresh. Surprised at the request, she felt hesitant about how to answer. 'Sure, but is this just because of what I said last night? I think I may have gone a bit overboard. I'm sorry if I overstepped the mark.'

'I've thought long and hard about what you said and have to admit maybe I can overdo the chivalry thing at times. Coffee?' He held up his mug as an invitation.

'Please.' Amy moved to lift a mug from the shelf but her hand brushed against his as he reached at the same time.

Jonathan immediately pulled back conceding defeat with a grin and holding his hand in a submissive gesture in the air. 'Do you really think it's the reason I can't... you know, keep a woman interested?'

'Jonathan...'

'Please call me *Jon*?' he begged by emphasising the first word. 'I hate my full name. It's such a mouthful.'

'As you wish. Jon,' she smiled as she stressed the diminutive. 'Without having ever met any of your female friends I can't be sure. All I can say is that I, personally, found the chivalry a bit - claustrophobic. But even saying that there are heaps of men out there who could learn a great deal from you. I've met quite a few who don't have a clue what the ladies like. Can I suggest you think about the reasons you were given by said females when you parted company?' She held her mug steady as Jon poured the dark liquid from the percolator then added a dash of milk. Amy was surprised he remembered how she liked her coffee.

'I've thought of little else during too many hours of insomnia. You could be right. Summarising most excuses into the most common theme goes something like, "I can't be myself," or "I can't breathe". What would you like for breakfast?'

'Toast will do me. I'm still trying to digest the mountain of food we ate last night.'

'Toast it is.' Jon paused and glanced at Amy with an enigmatic smile on his face. 'How about you make the toast while I set the table?' He grabbed a plastic bag containing sliced bread from the bench and held it out then pointed to an electric toaster already plugged in. It was obvious he'd been up a while and most doings for the light meal had already been taken from cupboards and set out but Amy understood that he was attempting to take a step back. She wondered how hard he found it to share the load: whether his fingers were itching to do the lot.

'You're a fast learner.' She grinned as she took the loaf from his hand. 'Tell me, was there one woman in particular you regretted parting company from?'

There was quite a long pause. Amy twisted her head and stared at Jon's back, which was all she could see as he searched the walk-in pantry for toast toppings. His back was ramrod-straight giving Amy the impression she had hit a raw nerve.

'Renee.'

There was another lengthy pause during which Amy didn't dare move lest she break his train of thought.

'She broke my heart six months ago.' His head appeared, the sadness in his eyes telling Amy that this Renee had meant a lot to him.

'What happened?'

'I asked her to marry me. She laughed then said that as much as she liked me, she could never live with me. I let her go.'

Amy was about to move over to him when the toaster popped. Instead she removed the hot, browned bread and slid the four slices onto two plates. 'Why didn't you fight for her if you felt so strongly about her?' She placed one plate in front of Jon and the other at her setting before easing into the seat.

'She wanted her freedom.' Jon sat opposite then handed Amy the butter.

'Did she actually say that or did she just intimate she couldn't live with you? Maybe she was hinting that you needed to change or maybe she wanted you to prove how you felt by chasing after her. If I felt that strongly about a man, I'd want him to fight a little to show he was serious. Did you love her?' Wanting to gauge Jon's reaction by reading his body language, Amy paused in the buttering of her toast.

'I still love her.' His heartfelt words sounded genuine.

'Enough to let her go because you thought she would be happier with someone else?' Amy smiled at his stunned expression then read the labels on the three jam pots, choosing orange marmalade. When she glanced up again, Jon was staring at his plate, his body as still as a marble statue. 'Jon?'

'You are too damned perceptive,' he mumbled into his chin as he gave assiduous attention to his toast, taking an inordinate amount to time to spread condiments then slice both pieces into four small squares.

The way he sounded and acted, gave Amy the distinct impression he was fighting for control. 'Why don't you call her, ask if you could have another go. If Renee felt the same way about you then she will be waiting. Then talk to her and find out exactly what it is she couldn't live with. Be open to her. Ask for the gory details about your shortcomings then lay your heart open. Women I know appreciate a man who is not afraid to discuss his emotions. I believe you are a nice man, Jonathan Ward but you try too damn hard to prove it.' As she ate, Amy kept glancing at Jon, who appeared to be chewing over her words as he ate but he wouldn't, or maybe couldn't look up. The man had a lot more sensitivity than she had at first thought and she knew he was hurting.

It wasn't until he had finished devouring his toast that he lifted his eyes. 'Do you really think she will be waiting?' His voice was quiet but held a hint of hope.

'If she has the same strong feelings for you, she'll give you another chance but you need to be honest with her and maybe ask her to help you be the man she wants. Perhaps ask her to tell you when you are overstepping the mark. Work out some simple word or action that she can give when she feels you are being overbearing. Make a game of it. Relationships need to be worked on continuously.' Amy scoffed loudly. 'Here's me telling you how to make things work and I would have to be the worst example on this earth. I made the biggest mistake of my life in my choice of husband and haven't had a decent relationship since.'

Jon reached across the table and grasped her hand. 'But you'd like to marry and have a family?'

A stab of pain jolted through her body. She felt what was left of her reproductive organs clench. 'Some things we can never have no matter how much we desire them,' she murmured as she grabbed her plate and knife then stood abruptly. She shook her head to dispel negative notions, her teeth nibbling at the inside of her cheek to create an overriding physical pain as she scrubbed the crumbs from the plate under a running tap. Then she rubbed it super dry with a tea towel as she fought to rein in seesawing emotions. Long fingers slid around her upper arm, stilling her. She couldn't suppress the jerk at the suddenness of the touch since she hadn't heard Jon approach.

'Amy, what's wrong?'

She released a long breath then drew in another, hissing the air between her teeth. 'Because of what Rico did to me that night, I can never have children of my own.'

'Oh, hell, Amy, I'm sorry.' He gently spun her around and drew her against his body, his arms swaddling her in an embrace.

All she could think of was how much alike the two brothers really were. It was either that or wallow in self-pity and she was as over wallowing as she was allowing tears to fall, although she had to admit she'd broken her own vow more than once in the past few days.

'The majority of men want their own family,' Amy mumbled against his chest. 'So it makes it almost impossible to have a serious relationship.' She squeezed her eyes tight and once again bit on the inside of her mouth. It was a habit she had developed as a means of controlling tears. Then she forced her muscles to relax and allowed herself to indulge in the pleasure of the warmth and comfort of a man's arms. If only she could find a really nice man who didn't want children. So far, the only men she'd come across who didn't have the desire for their own family were too selfish to want to share their lives. And here she was, being held by a man who was almost desperate for the happy marriage with offspring. She drew away, wriggling to ease his hold.

'Sorry,' she mumbled as she returned to the sink to find some menial chore to undertake in order to keep busy and painful memories at bay.

Moving up behind her, Jon said, 'you have nothing to be sorry about. I can't imagine how sad that knowledge makes you feel. But I'm betting the right man is out there for you. Not all men want the children. I know a couple who don't.'

To prevent the maudlin tears, Amy forced a laugh but knew the instant it was out that it sounded scornful. 'Yes, I've met a couple but they tend to be rather egotistical and selfish in nature. I don't want that either. I'd rather stay single than be tied to an egotist.' She wheeled away. 'Anyhow, enough talk about me, we have to go. You need to get to work and I've got a date with your brother.' She dropped her clean cutlery in the drawer and hurried from the room to gather together all she thought she would need.

Amy wouldn't allow Jon to bring up the subject again, interrupting every time he tried while travelling into the city, which was a tedious journey in the usual Monday morning crush of traffic snarls and hold-ups. Jon went out of his way to drop her off at James's office complex since his headquarters were on the other side of the central business district. She lingered as he pulled up alongside the curb. Reaching out, she placed her fingers on his hand. 'Ring Renee today. Have a long chat with her. Please?' She smiled as she slid from the car.

'I'll think about it,' Jon said as she pushed the door shut.

As he drove away, she willed him a mental message to make that phone call then turned and headed towards the front door of the office building.

It appeared the front receptionist was waiting for her for the moment Amy gave her name the young woman paged James without Amy having to give any reason for her visit. While waiting, she paced across the carpeted foyer, peering through the heavy glass doors for any sign of having being followed. So intent was she on searching faces of people passing that she didn't hear James approach. It wasn't until he placed a hand on her arm that she stopped suddenly, his touch causing that too frequent surge of adrenaline. 'Far out,' she hissed as she turned to face him.

'Sorry.' His grin belied his apology. 'I keep forgetting you don't appreciate sudden touches but I thought you were expecting me.'

'I was, but my mind was elsewhere. Are you aware that your brother is jealous of you?'

'Jon! Jealous! But why?'

Amy never thought she would be able to catch James off guard but the shocked look on his face was testament to the fact he was completely taken aback. 'Because you have everything he desires. The perfect marriage to the perfect wife with the perfect offspring equating to the perfect life.'

'Except I lost the perfect wife.' A wave of sadness swept across James's eyes before he masked the expression.

'Despite that, he's jealous and I have a feeling he has developed an inferiority complex and hence the reason he tries too hard to attract women. He needs your help. Where are we going?'

'To my office.' Settling a hand in the small of her back, James ushered Amy towards the elevator. 'And you've worked all this out in the space of less than twenty-four hours. I've known him all his life and I wouldn't have tagged him as being insecure.'

The doors opened and a slight increase in pressure in her back made Amy step forwards. 'I'm a woman.' She glanced up at the face alongside her. 'Didn't you know women were better on the emotional cues?'

'So they claim but what cues did you read in my brother?'

'He tries too hard to impress.' The doors opened again at the next floor and they stepped out together, walking side-by-side through a smaller reception area, the sole young receptionist appearing as though she was only there to field phone calls and direct clients to the correct office. 'He's not as bad as you made out. It's not that he thinks he is God's gift to women that he can't maintain a relationship, it's because he suffocates the atmosphere with being over-chivalrous. I couldn't breathe I was so well looked after. I felt like a thin strand of delicate glass that would shatter if Jon made one wrong move.'

'Please don't tell me he made another pass at you?' James led the way into his office and pulled out a chair.

Amy sank into the leather and swivelled around to face James as he sat on the other side of a large solid wood desk and moved aside a pile of files. Her breath jammed in her throat making it impossible to breathe when she recognised the top file: her medical records. James must have been studying them. She wasn't aware of the prolonged silence until James prodded her with a finger.

'Amy, did he make a pass?' James sounded imperious.

Becoming suddenly aware, Amy dragged her eyes away from the file and shook her head, not only in response to the question but as a means of tugging her mind away from the file's contents. How much had he read? Did he know all the gory details? 'No, of course not, he was the epitome of a gentleman.' She dared a peek at James, wondering if he had noticed what had grabbed her attention. 'He's in love with Renee, wanted to marry her.'

'Excuse me? He told you all this?' James leant forwards but he moved one hand onto *the* file then softened his voice. 'Yes, I've read it. The contents made me feel ill but I now understand your reaction to a couple of my comments. I'm sorry.'

Amy didn't need any more explanations. She knew exactly to what he was referring. A sigh escaped her lips as she flopped back into the seat. A knock at the door prevented any more conversation, for which she was more than thankful.

For the next three hours complicated discussions with a representative from both British and Australian Government authorities had Amy breathless with the speed in which she was granted temporary travel documents and a promise of permanent passports being posted within weeks. It took intense concentration to understand all the whys, wherefores and legal mumbo-jumbo with James explaining each and every detail patiently, ensuring Amy understood each facet before continuing with the next. Even though she had been through the process before, most of the paperwork had been carried out without her presence. Seeing her identity change before her eyes she was privy to the entire legal process, leaving her drained, both mentally and physically.

'So, Miss Catherine Heather Douglas, we will have the temporary travel documents ready by Wednesday. Official documents will be sent by registered mail within three weeks to wherever you happen to be. Just keep James informed of your whereabouts.' The Australian diplomat rose, his hand held out.

Amy shook the hand. 'So I can leave the country on Thursday?'

'Provided you end up in a British Commonwealth country until you have your official passport. Avoid Asia and the Americas – except for Canada of course.' The man smiled as he slid his paperwork into a briefcase.

'I feel so overwhelmed,' said Amy as she acknowledged the British Diplomat. 'Thank you, both.' She remained standing as James ushered the two men to the door. The only word she could think of to explain how she felt was completely numb with mush for a brain.

'Are you planning on travelling overseas?'

Before answering James, Amy sank back into the chair. 'Is there any reason why I can't?'

'No. In fact it would probably be the best thing for you to do right now. If you leave the country by the end of the week, Rico won't find you and you will be virtually untraceable travelling under your new name. Where would you like to go?'

This one was easy. She wanted to go back to her roots. 'Inverness - it's where I was born. I have family still living there: cousins, aunts and uncles from both sides of my family.'

At a loud rapping at the door, Amy swung around to see who was entering as James rose. Two men, dressed in suits, stepped into the room. Since neither was familiar to her, she assumed they were colleagues of James so she began gathering together her bits and pieces of paperwork and sliding them into a folder.

'Mrs Amanda Giovannazzo, is that the paperwork you have for us?'

Amy froze, the papers falling from her fingers then floating to the floor like huge snowflakes before puddling at her feet.

***

It took only a few minutes for Rico to break in once he discovered Amanda was not in the house where he had expected to find her. Worry that she had completely flown was the only reason he walked the half kilometre back to his car to collect his housebreaking kit. He needed certainty before beginning the search for her again. A quick amble through the house was all it took to ease his agitation. He paused in the open doorway of the guest room, staring at the neatly folded clothes on a chair before taking the two steps to reach them. Lifting the top garment, a blouse, he shook it out. It was the one she'd worn the previous day. He drew it to his face and sniffed in Amanda's essence, recognising the familiar rose-scented fragrance of the soap she always used: the same that had settled on his skin whilst using her house. It was why he didn't mind the feminine odour on his skin. It brought Amanda closer. Other memories, of happier times, flitted through his mind. Amanda at the beach, laughing as she ran towards the waves, screeching at the cold then high-tailing it back to the towel where she remained - refusing his pleas to enter the water despite his assurances that once you were in, the water wasn't so bad.

They'd dined out that evening – on the waterfront, then ambled arm-in-arm along the wet sand talking about the final plans for their wedding. He'd wanted to make love to her that night but didn't dare make the suggestion for fear of disappointing her. His libido wasn't always reliable – from the steroids, he'd been told later: too much later. They'd never warned him about the possible side effects of the steroids either - especially when you combined them with the little blue pills he'd taken to ensure a strong erection on their wedding night. Nobody told him about the possibility of the sudden uncontrollable rages – until it was too late.

He dropped the blouse back onto the pile. 'God, Amanda, I'm so sorry.'

Shaking his head to dispel the memories, he unzipped the backpack and upended it. If the papers were going to be anywhere, they would be here, with her belongings. Finding nothing, Rico ran his fingers over all the surfaces of the bag, searching small pockets both inside and out. He stuffed as much as he could back into the bag then gave the second, much smaller cloth bag a similar examination and found nothing, absolutely nothing.

'You don't have it do you, my love? But is Dad ever going to believe me?'

The only way he could be sure, was to ask her. Rico settled back on the bed and stretched out to wait, his mind a whirl on how best to approach the problem.

Chapter Eighteen

'We have a warrant for your arrest.'

At the second voice, Amy shuddered but James shot from his chair and planted his considerable body between her and the two strangers. At the same time Amy blurted, 'What?' and leapt to her feet. She took a step forwards, tripped over the leg of the swaying chair then staggered. James grasped her arm, giving her the stability to find her balance. Steady, she sank back into the chair. Unable to formulate words from the shock, she just sat there, stunned.

'Arrest for what and for whom?' It was obvious James was more quick witted than Amy for he sounded calm and in full control of his faculties, whereas her mind was still mush.

'Mrs Amanda Giovannazzo, for breaking, entering and theft.' The owner of first voice peered around James's shoulder. He was a squarish man with little neck and clean-shaven head. To Amy he looked like the typical rendition of a hoodlum and she bet he had a wide range of tattoos endowing his body under the clean-cut suit. When visions of multiple piercing in unmentionable places entered her brain, she shuddered.

'I can assure you that my fiancée is not called Amanda and I can also assure you, without a doubt that she is not married.'

The first shock had only begun to dissipate and her mind begun to come to grips with what had been said when James goes and stuns her again. She could do nothing better than gape at him as he twisted his head around and winked at her before turning back to face the two interlopers. James had handled the situation well but at what cost. He'd lied again, this time a whopper. Did they believe him or had she given the game away with her face, which she felt sure must read like an open book sporting the simplest of English? In an attempt to gather her shattered brain cells together so she could figure out what she could do or say, she slid from the chair and knelt on the floor and scooped the loose pages together into a higgledy pile then stuffed them into the folder.

'Show me the warrant, please?' she heard James say as she shoved the folder into her bag. A rustle followed his words then there was a hushed silence during which Amy assumed James read the paper, his legal knowledge dissecting every word. No way was she game to look up.

'Into what did this woman break and enter, and what is she supposed to have stolen? It doesn't say here.'

'She broke into her husband's house.' This was from the second stranger whom Amy assumed was a member of the police force since they were attempting to arrest her.

'How can a woman break into the house of her husband? Surely, if they are married, she has every right to enter her own house? And who the hell are you two?' James sounded as though he was fighting to suppress a temper that was on short fuse.

Amy slid back into the chair and grasped her bag against her chest as she tried to compose her racing heart while she listened. All she could see was James's back only half a metre from where she sat. It was as rigid as Jon's had been earlier. She could feel the suppressed energy radiating from James's body as though he was ready to strike. She felt sure, despite his casual tone of voice, he was as uptight as she.

'Senior Sergeant Peter Taylor and this is Sergeant John Letizia, New South Wales police. We were sent to bring back both Mr and Mrs Giovannazzo.'

Amy couldn't help the snort of derision that slipped out. James turned at the sound and held out one hand in invitation.

'Sweetheart, are you okay?'

'Just dandy,' Amy whispered for his ears only as she rose and slunk against his body, welcoming the security of his arm as it slipped around her shoulder and drew her in a tight embrace. If it wasn't for his grip, she felt sure she would slide to the floor like a wet tissue.

'I'm fine, just stunned at the wild accusation,' she said loud enough for all three men to hear. 'I can't believe these two thugs can come barging in here and accuse a total stranger of unbelievable charges.' She dared a glance at the two men. The second was much shorter and wiry. She started at the olive skin tone and dark hair, her mind immediately classing him as Italian, especially with the name Letizia. A rampage of thoughts raced through her mind. She'd bet her last dollar that these two were members of her ex-father-in-law's gang. She already knew the warrant was trumped up and she had a very strong suspicion about whose signature was on the bottom.

'We were told by our local counterparts that we would find Mrs Giovannazzo here. You are Amanda Giovannazzo aren't you?' The senior of the two stepped closer, holding out the warrant, but giving Amy a very close scrutiny, his eyes raking over every inch of her body. She knew it was a perverse reaction but she felt as though she were completely naked.

Amy shivered. 'I can assure you, I am not married, and no, my name is not Amanda.' Behind her back, Amy had her fingers crossed, but figured since she had legally changed her name, twice, she wasn't really lying. Inside, her innards felt like a tortuous tangle of tense nerves and surging adrenaline. Remaining upright on jellified legs was taking most of her concentration. If James released his hold she would slump to the floor in an unceremonious heap.

'You look like her,' said the same man.

'In what way does my fiancée look similar to this woman you are after?' James turned his body slightly towards the two men, thus shifting Amy in the opposite direction; she thought it was so they couldn't get a clear view. She had felt his muscles tension then quiver indicating he was no less on edge than she.

'Tall, slender.'

'Tall and slender!' James yelled. 'You base an identification merely on height and build. What about eye and hair colour and marked features?' He eased his hold then stepped even closer to the two men. 'One, you barged into my private office without identifying yourselves. Two, you made accusations about my fiancée without even attempting to verify her identity. Three, you can't arrest someone out of your jurisdiction and four, your warrant is invalid since you cannot arrest a woman for entering her own home and it does not specify, in detail, exactly what this Amanda was supposed to have stolen. Any judge here will laugh you out of court if you attempt to use this piece of paper to arrest someone in this state — if you ever find the woman first. Now I'd appreciate it if you leave. I have a lunch date with a client.' He moved forward, using his body to shepherd the two men from the room. Before stepping back he called for the receptionist at the central desk in the foyer to show the two gentlemen out.

Amy almost laughed out aloud at the word, gentlemen, but clamped her lips tight together to prevent the sound from escaping. When she tried to wriggle free, James tightened his hold, not releasing her until he was satisfied the two had gone and he had firmly shut the door. Then she was suddenly released and James turned his entire body around to face her.

'Fiancée?' Amy squawked, her hands moving to her hips.

'It was all I could think of in the spur of the moment and it worked.' His smile was sardonic then altered into a cheeky grin.

'A good job you had your left hand wrapped around me then.' Amy glanced at his ring finger then shot her eyes back up to his face. 'You've taken it off!'

'Last night. It was time and I have you to thank for giving me the courage to make the first move. But,' he slid two fingers into the space between the two top buttons of his shirt and withdrew a gold chain. Hanging from the chain was his wedding ring. 'This way it's out of sight but still close to my heart. I toyed with wearing Glenda's ring because it is smaller but this is the one she gave me.' For a brief moment pain washed through his eyes but disappeared again as he replaced the jewellery. 'If you *were* my fiancée, would you object to me wearing this?'

'I wouldn't because I understand your reason but maybe not all women would feel the same.' Feeling a wave of warmth and sympathy for James, Amy reached out and gently squeezed his forearm. 'You've taken a major step, congratulations. All we need to do now is find you a really nice lady who will understand that you will always hold Glenda in a corner of your heart. I believe you will find love again. Now, I'm going to find me an airline ticket.'

'You're really leaving?'

'I think it is about time I also started living and not be trapped in Rico's web. I can afford to take a year off and travel the world.'

'On the amount of cash you have sitting in my safe?'

'Actually no, I have enough money that I could live off the interest for the rest of my life.' She laughed at James's raised eyebrows. 'When Dad passed away, all his assets went to my sister and me. Fiona sold everything and banked my share in a trust account. When Mum and Dad first emigrated, they bought a house on the water in, what was then an affordable but seedier part of Sydney – Balmain. Over the past few years, the suburb has become more upmarket and properties eagerly sought after. It sold for almost three million dollars plus there were a few hundred thousand in cash after everything was sold. With my share and what I have saved in the deposit boxes, I can live quite comfortably.'

'I see. How about we eat first and then find you a plane ticket.' He grasped her arm to lead her out but Amy pulled back.

'I thought you had a luncheon engagement with a client.'

'I do, you are my client.'

'Not by choice,' Amy mumbled as she reached down to the floor by the seat she'd been ensconced in for the past few hours. 'I need my bag but can I leave some of my bits and pieces here?' She delved into her ever-present computer bag and withdrew her laptop and a few other bits and pieces and placed them on the desk. She added the messy pile of new personal papers. 'Can you look after these for me? I'll call in tomorrow to pick them up.'

'Of course, but I can drop them off tonight after work.'

'Umm…' How was she going to get out of this? She had places to go and didn't really want to explain to either James or his brother exactly where. And she didn't want them hanging around her either. 'I won't be home until about eight-thirty.'

James stopped in his tracks and turned from the door he'd just opened. 'Care to elaborate?'

'Not really since it is none of your business but I work out a couple of times a week at a gym. I missed Friday and have a regular session booked for tonight. I don't want to miss another night and I need to let them know I won't be attending any longer. Jon said he would drop me off,' she lied with her hidden fingers crossed once again.

'I don't really feel comfortable with you roaming around on your own. I can pick you up and drive you home.' James grasped her elbow and led the way in the opposite direction to which they had come earlier.

'Where are we going?' asked Amy as she hitched her much lighter bag onto her shoulder. It contained little except a wad of cash, her everyday personal bits and bobs and her gym clothes.

'I thought it would be better if we went out the back way. Those two goons might be waiting outside.'

'I'm glad you gave them the right title. My bet is that they are Giovanazzo gang members. Did you happen to notice who signed the warrant?'

'Ah, so you were thinking along the same lines as me. The scrawl was almost indecipherable but started with a G and had a couple of loops underneath that could be nothing but a double Z. Does that give you a hint?'

'Bastard,' Amy hissed. 'Would it hold up here in front of a judge?'

'I would make sure it didn't. Nobody can arrest you for breaking into your own home and you were married to him at the time. They also can't be non-specific about what was stolen. Papers, in general, won't cut it in a court of law. They need to outline exactly what each paper was.'

Amy chuckled. 'Even I don't know what was on the papers but I bet they wouldn't want to outline them specifically.' They reached the fire escape and headed down a floor of concrete steps, their footsteps echoing around the enclosed space.

'I'll give you a little hint as to what is included in the papers. The names of those two hoons are included in a list of about thirty-five people. Alongside each are dates and amounts of deposits made to each, plus their account details and for what they were paid. The deposits are quite substantial and what the payments were for are mind-blowing.'

'Really? I don't think I wanted to know those details. Are you serious?' She spun around to face him.

'Very serious and I guess I should inform you that I've made copies and handed one to our Commissioner who in turn made a copy and passed it onto the Federal Police. They are already investigating more thoroughly the activities of all the named people and planning a major bust. You have no idea how important and incriminating those papers are. The number of murders is mind-blowing and extortion amounts are in the millions. I must tell you that Rico is not implicated nearly as much as his father. I think that maybe Rico was simply a dogsbody teeing up things. I completely understand why Rico, or more so, his father, is so desperate to get the file back. Unfortunately neither knows that they are now in the hands of the authorities. My guess is that because none of them have been arrested before now, they think you are still holding the papers and have done nothing about them.'

They spilled out into a laneway at the rear of the building that led in one direction to the private car park for workers. Going the other way, they came out into the next major street.

A gusty wind was getting up, an easterly, Amy deduced, which meant another bout of hateful heat once the wind ceased. Sniffing, the air felt dry with a tinge of smoke containing a hint of eucalyptus. Bushfire somewhere. As she tugged down the corner of her blouse that had lifted with the wind, she searched the horizon for a pall of smoke and noticed a dark ball to the southeast. She prayed it wasn't the work of another firebug making the lives of fire fighters a misery. The thought brought her back to her own miseries. 'So you think he won't give up until he finds me?'

'No, that's why I don't feel comfortable with you wandering around by yourself.'

'How about I buy another wig and an outfit that hides my build somewhat? I'm thinking of some shapeless summer dress or a baggy top and slacks - something atypical for me. And I'll put in my dark brown contacts. '

'Might work but I want to see the changes before you take off alone.' After lifting one eyebrow in what was a determined message, James lifted one arm to the small of her back and guided her into a small eatery, finding them a seat at the back where he settled into the chair facing the street. Amy understood why without him having to say a word.

During the light lunch Amy made a couple of phone calls, the main one to her sister. She couldn't help but smile at Fiona's enthusiastic yelling for joy. It had been a while since they'd seen each other, keeping in contact with coded emails and letters. Anyone finding and reading their missives would think they were old school friends who had kept in contact over the years. Which wasn't exactly a lie since they did attend the same schools. Fifteen minutes after beginning the conversation, Amy closed up her mobile phone and knew she was grinning inanely. She couldn't help it.

'Fiona is going to take her family on holiday in a month's time. It appears she has this urgent desire to visit her birthplace and show it to her family,' Amy managed to get out before her joy rendered her speechless.

'I don't suppose she will also be catching up with her sister whilst on this holiday.' James grinned back having read the innuendo.

'You're a smart man, James Ward. I can't wait.' Amy whooped out aloud, drawing the attention of other patrons. 'God, I feel so alive, as if a monster iron anvil has been lifted off my shoulders. All I need to do now is find a spare seat on a flight to the U.K. and survive the next couple of days. I might get my hair permanently coloured instead of a wig.' Her hand automatically lifted to her hair and she ran her fingers through the jagged ebony tendrils.

'You can't. The photo we took of you this morning will be on your temporary travel documents. But with Jon or me with you at all times and you staying with Jon, you should be safe enough. Nobody really knows who you are.'

'I notice you didn't use any name for me with the Sydney cops.' Amy became thoughtful. 'What are we going to do about them? You do realise that if we ever catch Rico and he is handed over to those two, he will accidentally on purpose escape.'

'That's my job this afternoon. I'll be speaking with the Commissioner. But they have to catch him first. I still think he has gone underground.'

'Oh, he'll be around until he finds me. Of that I am certain.' Amy pushed her plate away and rose. She glanced at her watch. 'I'm off. I'm going to find a travel agent then I'll have a late afternoon snack and go to the gym.' She held up her hand when it looked as though James was going to protest. 'I promise I'll catch a taxi home. I'm not about to let Rico catch me when I'm so close to freedom.'

'You're not going anywhere alone until I approve of the wig and outfit. Do you have enough cash?'

'Yes, I kept back five thousand.' She patted the bag she had picked up from where she'd kept it held tight between her legs while they ate. 'But I don't know if they'll give me a ticket without identity papers.'

As they wove a path through the busy café, James said, 'you can buy and pay for a ticket online without showing papers so I can't see why not. As long as you have them at the airport for customs.'

***

'Tell me she's dead and you have the file!'

Rico winced at the domineering words as he sat up straight then swung his legs from the bed onto the floor. Stifling a yawn, he glanced at the clock radio on the bedside table. Christ! Was it that late? Hell, he'd slept way too long when he hadn't meant to sleep at all. Thank God for the phone call.

'I thought I asked you not to ring,' he whispered harshly as he crept to the door, listened then stuck his head around the corner. Had Amanda been, seen him and gone again?

'Well you didn't damn well ring me and the twenty-four hours are up. You've failed again haven't you, you useless excuse for a son.'

Rico squeezed his eyes shut. It shouldn't hurt. He shouldn't allow it to hurt. But damn the man, he never had anything positive to say. It was always failure, failure, failure: even when you did the right thing. He leant against the passage wall feeling the old anger and resentment rise up from his toes then engulf him. He jerked upright. No more, you old bastard. I refuse to let you control me one moment longer.

Rico crept down the passage, peering into each room as he passed. 'No I haven't failed but the trap is set. But if you don't get off this line – it will fail for I will be heard talking to you and you will be the one to stuff things up.'

'I've booked a flight for Saturday. Be at the airport with the papers!'

'And if she doesn't have them?' Rico paused at the lounge room window and searched the yard and street. There was a busy-ness in the atmosphere. People were starting to arrive home from work. Sprinklers were being turned on, mail collected and youngsters kicking ball across the road.

'She must have them. Who else would?'

Rico turned, examined the room to see if the plans he'd made in his head earlier, would work. 'Then why hasn't she used them, why haven't the cops arrived on everyone's doorstep? Why aren't we all in gaol? It just doesn't make sense. Besides, I've searched all her belongings, even the clothes she carries around with her. There are no files, no papers, nothing other than her personal everyday needs.' And no private papers, he suddenly realised. No bank details, passport, licence – nothing of a private nature. Which meant there was a secret cache somewhere. But where? Certainly not in this house, the lawyer's or her place. He'd looked, searched thoroughly.

At the sound of a car slowing he spun around, peered through the window then swore under his breath. The brother had stopped at the end of the drive to retrieve his mail.

'Dad, I've got to go. *Please* don't ring. I'll call you in the morning. The spider is about to catch his prey.'

To make sure he wouldn't be interrupted, Rico pressed the off button on his phone. It beeped once then there was silence.

Chapter Nineteen

Amy had fun trying on wigs of various colours, lengths and styles. Some looked downright ridiculous with both of them laughing at her image in a large mirror. She settled on a shoulder-length mass of brown waves. She'd never gone curly before and even though nondescript brown was the most common colour for hair, she'd never opted for the shade. Seeing how it changed her appearance, with a fringe masking her forehead and curls covering the side angles of her face, she wondered why. The change was dramatic, and even more so when she swapped hazel lenses for dark brown.

In the ladies' section of the same large department store, Amy took even longer searching for the right outfit. The discard pile of clothes she had tried on was huge but finally she was happy with a baggy pair of ecru linen slacks and an overlarge darker beige cotton shirt with three-quarter length sleeves and which came down to the top of her thigh. Brown was definitely not her colour, sapping her skin tone to such an extent her pallor took on a yellow hue but that was good, she decided. Before stepping out of the change booth to show James, she studied her outline in the floor length mirror. All her lean curves were hidden, making her look slightly frumpy and about two sizes larger than she was. Glamorous she wasn't but she definitely looked different. Gathering her own white slacks and pale pink blouse in one hand, she stepped from behind the curtain.

James's eyes boggled, causing her to laugh. 'What do you think?'

'If you were really my fiancée, I'd have to find some very diplomatic way of letting you know that I wouldn't be caught dead accompanying you on a date.' He smiled. 'It's perfect. The test will be if Jon recognises you when he picks you up.'

At the reminder of her little white lie, Amy dropped her head to avoid James spying any hint of a blush or look of guilt. Immediately she headed for the sales desk where she paid cash for the two items and asked for a plastic bag into which she shoved the clothes she'd worn earlier. She handed the bag to James. 'Can you please put this with my other things so I don't have to carry it around?'

They parted company at the entrance to a travel agency, James continuing onto his office while Amy entered. It took a while to find a spare seat at such short notice but by agreeing to pay the extra for business class, Amy finally held a one-way ticket in her hand. She was flying to the U.K. at 11a.m. on Thursday with a three-hour stopover in Singapore. Freedom was within her grasp and she certainly didn't mind travelling such a long distance in relative comfort. Besides, she figured, she'd more than earned the luxury and she could well afford the price.

With too much time to spare Amy wondered what she could do to fill in a couple of hours. She wandered aimlessly through arcades and shops, purchasing a few gifts for the young nephew and niece she would be seeing in person for the first time. She'd seen hundreds of digital images but fear for their safety had kept her away from her sister for five years. She had no doubt Fiona had been kept under covert surveillance by gang members, especially since Fiona had mentioned every time she felt suspicious of some car or person she'd spied hanging around too often. But Amy had always felt certain Fiona and her family would be safe until Amy made an appearance. She knew for sure that her father's place had been watched, but those in authority who had been instrumental in giving Amy her new identity had warned the entire family that it would happen. What she didn't know was whether the watchers were aware that they in turn were being observed. Michael Simpson had given her the details during their regular link-ups. The thought of Sergeant Simpson brought Amy's mind back to the present. She shuddered, knowing deep down that the man was dead. And even though Rico hadn't been free at the time, he would have been involved.

Deciding she had been in the city too long, Amy made her way to the nearest taxi rank. She still had an hour to fill in but figured the vicinity of the gym would be a little safer. She asked to be dropped off at a small delicatessen where she purchased an apple, a banana and a bottle of water then walked across the road to a shady park where she sank onto a wooden bench to eat the fruit she'd bought.

Within minutes a bronze-wing pigeon settled at her feet in the hope that some tiny morsel would drop onto the ground. As she chewed and savoured the crisp tart apple flesh, she was fascinated by the sheen of the iridescent greens on the bird's wings changing and flashing with every movement as the bird strutted around - its head bobbing with every step. Knowing the species were seedeaters she dug out the pips from the apple core and tossed them, along with small blobs of white flesh about a metre from her feet. The bird hopped a few steps away at her sudden movement then paused ready to take flight before changing its mind and bobbing over to inspect the bits. It picked up a seed then dropped it, moving to a speck of apple flesh and tasting that. It ate both, one after the other then cleaned up all that Amy had thrown. Amy smiled at the bird when it had finished and moved closer to her again, one eye peering up at her then back to the ground.

'Greedy little thing,' Amy said as she snapped off the end of the banana skin and peeled it downwards. She scooped up a tiny bit of flesh with her fingernail then balled it up between two fingers and dropped it at her feet.

'Mandy!' A male voice called from a distance startling Amy out of her reverie. As her heart began thumping the bronze-wing panicked and flew away, shedding down and dust as it flapped its wings in a mad frenzy. Unsure what to do, Amy bundled up her belongings and shoved them into her bag then stood, ready to imitate the bird and take flight but she wasn't sure from which direction the voice had come. Trying her best to act nonchalant she scanned the park in all directions, seeking out anyone nearing her. To her left a young couple wheeling a pram were chatting together while an elderly woman was doing as she had just been doing, sitting on a bench eating. Ahead of her she saw nothing and that worried her, but then why would anyone be hiding if they had called her name? She spun to her right. A teenage girl in school uniform had her back to Amy and appeared to be waiting.

'Mandy, wait up!' the same voice called but this time a little louder.

'I'm waiting,' whispered Amy, 'but where are you? And who are you?' The voice, she felt certain, was not one she recognised. She tried to attach it to Rico but it was too high and besides he had never called her Mandy, the diminutive not cultured enough for him. He had insisted she use her full name. It must be someone from her past, was the only conclusion she could draw as she kept turning this way and that seeking a man, any man heading her way. But who from her past would recognise her in this get-up? Inside, she was quivering mess, a continuous surge of adrenaline keeping her nerves stretched so tight she felt sure they would snap. She wanted to flee but until she knew which way to run she knew she couldn't take the chance.

The sound of footsteps running had Amy spin around on one foot as she shoved the strap of her computer bag over her head so that it wouldn't slip down when she sped away. At the sight of a male teenager pulling up next to the schoolgirl, Amy felt her innards slump in intense relief.

'I'll walk home with you,' she heard the lad say to the girl.

'Far out,' Amy muttered under her breath as she began to power walk in the direction of the gym. No more being stupid and staying out in the open. She prayed neither James nor Jon mentioned to each other about Jon picking her up and dropping her off at the gym. Either or both would be furious but no more furious than she was with herself. She was downright insane to think she was safe, even wearing a disguise.

The smell of stale sweat and a rush of cool air embraced Amy as she stepped into the small reception area of the gym. Even though she smiled at the familiar face on duty behind the desk, her smile went unacknowledged. Rather than be put out, she felt delighted at the lack of recognition as she walked past and entered the change-rooms. There she swapped one pair of baggy pants for another then discarded her top and slid her sleeves into an even looser garment. Wrapping the large open flaps around her upper torso she tied them in place with a long black woven belt that went around her waist twice before she took a great deal of care in knotting it just right.

After removing the wig and carefully laying it in her bag, Amy bypassed the large room containing a wide variety of exercise machines and entered a second, much smaller room. About six people dressed in identical clothes except for the colour of the belt, were sitting cross-legged on the floor. The silence, apart from an occasional deep exhalation, was in sharp contrast to the scrapes, whirrs and thuds of the twenty or so people working out in the gym. Here, people were in a state of deep concentration. Bowing to the man standing at the front, Amy murmured, 'Sensai,' then joined the group on the large canvas mat on the floor.

After ten minutes of deep contemplation, Amy went through a series of exercises stretching various muscles and tendons and practicing simple poses until the Sensai called them all to attention.

'You missed Friday,' he said in an aside to Amy.

'Yes, sorry, something important came up. I wasn't able to ring to let you know. And,' she paused, 'tonight will be my last night. I have to go away.'

The Sensai studied her for a moment. 'He's found you. We'll talk about it later.'

For the life of her, Amy could never understand how the Sensai could read her so well, but he always had. He knew exactly the reason she had spent five years studying and practising Karate with her rarely missing one of her regular three sessions every week. She'd never said at the very beginning why she was so determined to master the art but he'd guessed she'd been attacked and gradually over time had wheedled out of her quite a few of the facts. After that he'd encouraged her more and more, almost daring her at times through challenges to go the next step. He'd taught her all he knew and even though she knew it all, she kept up the practice, practice, practice, keeping her limbs agile, her skills honed and her awareness acute.

But despite the acuity of her senses, it despaired her just how many times she'd jolted at sudden movements over the past week. Was it because Rico had caught her unawares in a crowd? Would she have been caught out with less people around? Jon had scared the bejesus out of her by grabbing her when she should have sensed his presence. Was she losing her touch?

Determined to regain that pre-sense, she worked like the devil for the next hour during class, concentrating as hard as she could. When the session ended she waited until her classmates had left before approaching the Sensai. 'Can we combat for real?'

'He found you didn't he?'

'Yes, he's around and looking for me but I'm sure he doesn't know where I'm staying at the moment and I'm leaving the state on Thursday. But just in case, I need to practise.' There was no way she was going to tell anybody apart from James that she was leaving the country. If people didn't know then they couldn't be forced to tell.

'Combat for real, even though Karate isn't for attack, only for defence?' The Sensai's voice held a hint of anger.

'I know but to defend real life situations one needs to experience real life.'

'He will be armed?'

'He uses a knife. A long, thin double edged knife.'

'A knife you have experienced. Is he aware of your skills?'

Despite almost forcing her body to not reveal a reaction to the statement, she could tell the Sensai read the truth. 'I can't ever be sure but I've never revealed to anyone other than you and those in my class about the Karate. He's been in gaol until about two weeks ago.'

'Then how did he find you?'

'He, or someone associated with him, killed the man who gave me a new I.D. My guess is that he was tortured into giving details first.'

'He is a cruel and desperate man. If I agree to combat, you will be kind and take pity on me.' Only the slightest twitch at the corner of his mouth told Amy that the Sensai was joking. Even though she knew as much, he was far superior in his skills.

'I agree.' Before she had the words out the sensai attacked, catching her unawares with a sharp kick that caught her on the side of her arm before she was able to even think about going on the defensive. Within seconds she was flat on her back with him on top of her holding down every one of her limbs. Pain from the kick pinged along her nerves then stabbed. Even though she knew the kick had been restrained, she'd have a mighty bruise by morning. When he lifted his head he was grinning. The grin as well as the fact that he'd caught her unawares, made her mad. A determination she'd not ever felt before surged. Twisting her body as she bucked him off she then fought hard until she was able to get to her feet. With bent knees and arms set in a defensive stance she centred her balance and sidled around the mat playing cat and mouse, just waiting for the next attack. From the corner of her eye she noted that he had fisted his right hand as though grasping the hilt of a knife.

'Rico is left handed.'

Sensai immediately swapped hands and stabbed towards her chest. For the next fifteen minutes they fought hard, not holding back on the strength of kicks, hits and punches. Each one that connected with her body, and there were far more than she had envisioned, hurt like the devil. From the jarring when she managed to sneak through his tight defences, she figured he would be wearing a few bruises as well, but nowhere near as many as she.

'Enough!' The Sensai stood back and dropped his stance then bowed.

Showing her respect for his status, Amy bent at the waist ensuring her head went slightly lower.

'You fight very well. I think this Rico might be very sorry if he does find you. I'll miss you. Keep one eye on the left hand at all times and allow your sixth sense to feel his every movement before it comes. You must get into his mind, read the slightest twinge of every muscle. You are the master now, remember that.' With that, he turned away and headed towards the door. He never was a man for long conversations or idle chat.

'Thank you,' Amy called after him. He paused but didn't turn around. 'For everything,' she added.

He spoke without turning. 'You have been an excellent student, one of the best. Goodbyes are only for people who will never see each other again. When this is all over we will meet again. Be strong, be the master.' A brief glance over his shoulder contained a genuine heartfelt smile before he left the room.

Amy watched after him then limped back to the change rooms where she stripped off then stepped into a shower cubicle where she stood under the hottest water she could withstand to ease the soreness. Already she could see red welts darkening into bruises. Then she shut off the hot tap, letting out a yelp as the cold hit but without an icepack to rub on the sore spots, she guessed a cold shower was her best option. By the time she shut off the water completely, her teeth were chattering and her body was goose-fleshed. Not having a towel with her, she rubbed her body vigorously with the pants of her gi. Knowing she was going straight to Jon's home, she didn't bother with the new wig after dressing in the outfit she'd bought.

It was no more than fifty metres to a taxi stand where three empty taxis stood waiting to take patrons home from local eateries. She eased aching muscles into the back seat, gave directions then sank back into the seat with her eyes shut, willing her mind to relax and ignore the pain. She wasn't sure if she was plain dumb for insisting on combat or whether it had been the right thing to do. By the time the Sensai had withdrawn she was reading his every move and he had known that. But by catching her unawares to start with he had taught her a very valuable lesson. For the next few days she had to have every sense attuned to the slightest of moves from anyone.

After reaching their destination, Amy paid the fare then hoisted out her bag, the strong smell of over-ripe banana reminding her that she had stuffed the uneaten half into the front pocket. She didn't want to think about the mess she'd have to clean up as she strode down the concrete pathway to Jon's front door. As she stepped onto the front porch she remembered where the key Jon had given her was - in the front pocket. It took a few minutes of wiping sloppy banana flesh from the key against the damp gi pants before she slid the slippery key into the lock.

Amy pushed the front door open then swore under her breath. Right opposite her was Jon sitting in a chair, trussed up like the Christmas turkey. White tape was bound across his mouth to prevent him calling out a warning. An open cut on one brow was dripping blood down his face, one eye was puffed up and his cheek looked inflamed. What other injuries had he incurred?

'Welcome, my beautiful wife, come on in, Amanda.'

'And if I don't?' While speaking to a hidden Rico, Amy kept staring at Jon and pointed to the open door hoping Jon knew what she was asking with her frantic hand gestures. She spied the tiny acknowledgement with his eyeballs. They moved up and down then to the side towards the door. She prayed it meant Rico was behind the door.

'Then I'll kill your boyfriend.'

Chapter Twenty

With those words, Rico moved into view and immediately crossed the room to Jon and pressed a knife to his throat. Mesmerised by the glinting blade, Amy saw the crease of skin it made and then sucked in a deep breath as blood trickled. If she ran away that knife would penetrate and do a lot of damage. She knew exactly what type of damage and Rico would not leave witnesses. She shuddered at the thought then sucked in a breath for courage. She couldn't run. She had no choice but to face him. Now knowing where Rico was, she stepped into the room but immediately sidled across the wall into the corner furthest from the pair.

'You're going to kill him in any case.' She prayed her voice didn't indicate how scared she felt. It was all very well the Sensai drilling into her to stay calm, control your nerves, concentrate, and so easy to do those things on the mat but in real life when your opponent has a knife that looked about fifty metres long, pressed up against a friend's neck and drawing blood, making those nerves quit quivering was almost impossible.

'But not before he watches a real man show him just how you like it.' The knife eased away from Jon's throat but wavered in front of his face.

At the implied threat a surge of bile rose in Amy's throat, burning a trail up then down as she forced the acid back where it belonged. She knew what Rico meant - a repeat performance of what had almost ended her life. Stay calm, my foot! Concentrate Amy Masters. But what in heaven's name should she do? Logic began surfacing. First, she had to get him away from Jon.

'Well it certainly won't be you then for you wouldn't have a clue and you are nothing more than a sadistic creep. You're certainly no real man. Only cowards hurt a woman.' She smiled inwardly at the tensioning in Rico's body. Her remark had hit the target. 'So you intend raping me then.' She wanted him to admit his intention but the words sent a flash of remembrance through her mind. She shook her head to sweep it away.

'You're my wife so it won't be rape.'

Amy was stunned at the amount of emotion in his soft voice as he took a step towards her, inspected the knife then wiped the trace of Jon's blood on the thigh of his jeans.

A flash of something soft and deep flashed across his face before it was replaced by a smarmy grin meant to intimidate but all it did was increase the nausea in Amy's stomach. What really confused her was the way he said the words, so quiet and so full of passion. Did he still have feelings for her? No way. You couldn't care for someone and do what he'd done. How could she have been so blindly stupid to have not seen him for what he is? Unbelievable.

'In your dreams!' she scoffed as she stepped sideways away from him. Finding her balance she lifted her right leg then quickly reached down and slid off the ankle strap to her sandal then kicked the shoe from her foot. She heard the thud and scrape as it hit a wall and slid to the ground. 'We are not married and in the eyes of the law, never have been. The marriage was annulled, as you well know. The jury found you guilty of rape as well as attempted murder.' From the corner of her eye, she saw Jon's eyes flare to imitate large orbs. Poor man was going to get one hell of an education.

Rico took one step closer to her but it was one step away from Jon. Amy knew he was sizing her up. 'Oh, I've had plenty of dreams about how it should be,' he said, 'every damned night. But first I want the papers you stole from my office,' he added as his other foot inched forward.

Amy crossed her right leg over her left to step away, rebalanced and rid her other foot of the impeding shoe. Being able to bunch the muscles in her feet and feel the floor, she could move better and react faster on bare feet. 'I took nothing from your house that didn't belong to me. You rifled through my belongings and stole my passport and bank statements. I returned the compliment and rifled through your desk and took them back. I wanted nothing to do with you. I certainly didn't want any reminders of the cretin you are.'

Her insult hit home. A hiss of breath being drawn in through his teeth was the only indication. He stepped closer. 'Where did you find the keys?'

Taking another step away gave Amy a second to think and an idea came that might, just might, put him off. 'I didn't have to find them. They were in the lock of the top drawer of your desk. That, the cupboard door and the filing cabinet were hanging open.'

There was a heavy silence while Rico appeared to chew on her words. His eyes flared then screwed and for a second he glanced away, shook his head then waved the knife in the air as he sidled sideways a couple of quick steps. 'You are lying but the file of papers you took wasn't in the cabinet.'

Amy grinned then knew she shouldn't have when his eyes widened once again as though in triumph. But her grin had slipped out at the thought of him being so uncertain. 'You tipped my home upside down but you found no files, papers or anything else belonging to you because there weren't any to find. Maybe it was the two men that were in your house when I got there.'

Rico stopped dead. His entire body went rigid. 'What men?'

She knew she had startled him. His reaction was genuine. 'I didn't recognise either. They were coming down the stairs when I walked through the open front door. At first I thought someone from your family was there when I found the door open. Both men had a handful of files and looked like plain clothed detectives. You know, those cardboard envelope type files. Blue, green, yellow and red I think: at least five of each, maybe more. But then they said that your father had sent them.'

Rico swore, paused then said, 'You're lying.' But his tone indicated uncertainty.

'Why would I lie? I have nothing to gain. You've searched all my belongings. I have nothing of yours.' Since Rico remained still, Amy followed suit but every nerve in her body was well alert, just waiting for Rico to pounce. While she stood there she felt the aches and stings of her earlier encounter. The last thing she felt like doing was fighting for her life but there was no doubt in her mind that unless she did, she was dead before daybreak.

'What was in the chest?'

She grinned, knowing which chest he was talking about. 'My backpack and spare clothes.'

'Show me.'

Amy forced a laugh. 'You really think I don't know you've already searched through this house. Give me some credit for intelligence. You've been through my things and found nothing.'

He pointed to the bag she'd carried inside. It was still draped over her shoulder. Since it was always a part of her, she'd forgotten about it. Amy slid it from her shoulder and held it aloft in her left hand. 'You're welcome to look.'

'Toss it over.' He used his free hand to indicate by beckoning.

Now was her chance to get this charade over and done with. She had worked him away from Jon and Rico couldn't reach the other man easily without turning his back on her. She knew he wouldn't do that. With Jon tied up Amy was Rico's only target. 'Uh, uh - you want it - you come and get it.' She waved the bag to her side. He would have to use his left hand that was gripping the knife to grab it or cross his right hand over his body. Either would work as far as she was concerned. Either action would put him off balance and be awkward.

Instead, he opted for more talk. 'Empty the contents onto the floor.'

Amy smiled then wriggled the bag in invitation. 'There is only one way you are going to see what is inside,' she said as she took one small step towards him. This tiny action obviously disconcerted him for he frowned. She wondered what he was thinking. Did he know about the karate or was he simply surprised that she would dare to approach him? The old shy and uncertain Amanda would have been far to petrified to approach, even with such a tiny step. When an insidious grin crept from the corners of his mouth she thought she knew what he was thinking. He thought he had her: poor, weak little Amanda who is no match for big muscle-bound Rico.

It was only then that she noticed he'd lost the artificially enhanced muscled look he'd had before. She knew he'd been taking steroids for he'd used it as an excuse during the trial for attacking her. Claimed the steroids had caused him to snap. She smiled to herself. His outburst had incriminated him, for seconds earlier he had spent fifteen minutes denying harming her. Her lawyer had pounced on his unplanned confession.

With her thoughts centred on the trial, she almost missed the sudden movement. Rico lunged forwards waving the knife in his left hand. He grabbed for the bag with his right. As she dropped the bag Amy shot a high kick out, catching him on the forearm with force. She felt the bones in her arch jar against his ulna then heard a crack.

Rico squealed in pain as he jerked back then hissed, 'You little bitch,' as he swung the knife in an arc towards her chest.

It was obvious the intention was to do as much damage as he could with the first blow but Amy grabbed his wrist, curling both hands around and gripping tight at the same time as she bent at the waist, swung her hips into his abdomen then jerked as hard as she could, flipping him over her curled body. The suddenness of the impact caused him to release his hold on the knife and it went sailing through the air almost mimicking Rico's flight as his feet circled over Amy's crouched body and he landed with an almighty thud onto his side. Objects in cupboards and pictures hanging on the walls rattled at the impact.

Without releasing her grip, Amy followed through with the motion and swung around, twisting Rico's arm around in the shoulder joint. She knew it would hurt like hell, since she had experienced it herself when she'd been caught unawares in training. After hearing the breath whoosh from Rico as he landed, he screamed out the last of his air in agony.

'Nobody,' Amy yelled as she jerked the arm a little further, 'especially a psycho like you,' she slammed a foot into the side of his ribs, not caring if they snapped, 'is ever going to get the better of me again.' For good measure, she repeated her last action, ensuring it landed in the same spot. Glancing at his face, Rico's eyes were almost popping out of the sockets and his face was contorted with shock and pain. Guilt bit but then she dismissed it. He was the one that had come searching for her with an open flick knife. He was the one that had caused injury to Jon and then trussed him up. He was the one that started this confrontation. She was only defending Jon and herself and was being gentle compared to what he'd done and he needed to feel some of the terror and agony he'd inflicted.

Keeping the arm in a tight lock, Amy stepped around to straighten her body so she could get a good look at him. She had been waiting and working a long time for this retribution. It would never have come to this if he hadn't come looking for her but now that he had, she wanted to see every single reaction but at the same time she had to choose her words carefully lest she gave away hints that she knew about his shadier side. 'You didn't do your homework very well did you? Do you honestly think I would be dumb enough to let you attack me again?' This time she eased the tension in her foot by kicking at the side of his head. It wasn't all that hard. Nowhere near as hard as her nastier side wanted. But she wasn't a nasty person. She just wanted him to feel some of the fear and pain he'd dealt out to her.

Dragging him along by using his still twisted arm as a tow-rope, she moved toward the bag she had flung away as she had sent out her first kick. Rico screamed until she stopped. With one foot she looped the bag strap over her toe and pulled it closer then lifted it to her mouth. Rico arched his body in an attempt to free himself but instead he rolled onto his back when Amy jerked the arm as hard as she could.

'Do it again and you'll suffer,' Amy growled through clenched teeth as she released one hand from her hold and slid the zip to open the bag.

In an act of desperation, Rico bucked his body and swung one leg up in a wild kick. 'I just want to talk,' he panted out.

'Talk?' she yelled. 'Then why tie Jon up and harm him? Why threaten me with a weapon. Big mistake, Bucko,' said Amy. She aimed another kick to his side but he jerked away and the kick landed in his crotch. The yell of pain echoed around the room and bounced off the walls as Rico curled into as much of a ball as possible with one arm almost popping out of its socket.

Amy winced, knowing how much that would have hurt but it was his fault for moving. 'Next kick will be in the same spot, but harder. Now put both wrists together.' Amy had dropped the bag but bent to pull out her gi. With a sudden strong smell of banana she flung the still damp pants aside then dragged out the belt. When she realised Rico hadn't obeyed her instructions but had instead wrapped his other hand around one of her ankles, she had no choice but to stamp on the forearm that was on the floor then before he could even take a breath from the grunt, she aimed for his crotch again. It wasn't all that hard but water rushed to his eyes as he slid his free hand to cover the bruised part of his anatomy. His face had gone pale and looked clammy. His jaw moved like a guppy but no sound came out. He appeared to be beyond making any sound. Well, good, because she had been the same.

Despite knowing she should, Amy couldn't bring herself to have any sympathy for him. If she relented and let him go, he would kill her. She merely repeated her instruction. 'Put both hands together or I kick again. Same spot,' she added quietly when he looked about to ignore her. 'Here's how it is going to be - you obey then you don't get kicked. Easy. Even an ignoramus like you should be able to understand that simple notion.'

She smiled when he lifted his arm and placed one wrist against the other. Moisture had leaked from the corners of his eyes. She knew it was from agony but didn't care. 'Ooh, diddums, the big macho man is crying like a baby.' Then to make an even stronger impact, Amy held her karate belt in front of his eyes. 'See this? It's a black belt. Karate. I have two of them. You did teach me something way back then — not to let a punk like you ever hurt me again.' She began binding the woven fabric around his wrists, tying it in knots she had studied and practised. 'If you had done your research, you would have discovered that I have spent three nights a week for five years practising, practising, practising for when we met again.' Pulling the knot tight she then attached the other end to the leg of the chair Jon was trussed to. Jon's weight would prevent Rico from pulling free.

'Are you okay?' she asked Jon. He nodded then squealed when she ripped the tape from his mouth in one quick jerk. 'Sorry about that, but quick means the pain is short and I have a better use for the tape.' She knelt next to Rico and sealed his mouth, deliberately pressing the edges down hard.

'How does it feel, Sweetheart?' The last word was so cynical but Amy knew by the flare of his eyes that Rico understood. She had merely repeated his words to her, five years ago. She wondered if he realised what was coming next. In court he'd said that he couldn't remember exactly what he'd done: that he'd been in a daze. She still didn't know if it was the truth.

It took only a couple of minutes for her to withdraw the second black belt from her bag and tie his legs together. 'Now the interesting part,' Amy whispered harshly as she stood over him. Then she bent and unbuckled his belt, tugging hard to pull it from the keepers. He was still a muscle-bound brute but it looked as though he had spent his time in jail working out. His build looked to be all naturally gained.

Not satisfied with just the belt, she poked the brass button of his jeans through the hole then tugged on the zipper until it came down. A muffled sound came from Rico but Amy just twisted her head and stared at him. His face told the story. He was scared witless, which delighted Amy. She'd been scared witless. She'd been beyond utterly terrified. 'I see you understand.'

Moving to his feet, she removed his shoes and socks then grasped the hems of his jean legs and lifted his legs in the air before giving one almighty heave. The jeans came down, dragging his underwear with them and she left them wrinkled at his trussed ankles.

'What in heaven's name are you doing?' Jon called. He sounded frantic.

Amy paused as she glanced at Jon. 'Nothing more than he did to me.' She turned to Rico. 'Turn over.'

Rico swung his head from side to side then struggled to free his binds but refused to turn over. So Amy lifted a foot as though she were going to subject his crotch to another onslaught. Rico jerked his body until he was lying on his stomach.

Amy paused, wondering whether or not she could really go through with this. She should call the police and maybe James. Instead she grasped the buckle and lifted the belt high then whipped it through the air, wincing in remembered pain as the leather slashed across Rico's ankles, the end hissing against the polished floorboards and missing the flesh. It wasn't hard but the whip sound was sharp and loud.

'One,' Amy counted out aloud. She heard Jon swear but ignored him as she swung the belt again, this time leaving a red welt slightly higher on the calf. Rico's body jerked. 'Two.'

A muffled whimper came from Rico as number three hit. This time Amy had got the distance right and the end connected with flesh but not hard enough to cut through. Ignoring Jon's yells to stop she repeated the action, each whip landing slightly higher up the body, leaving red welts until she called out, 'Thirteen.' The last lash was across the shoulders but from the hips up his shirt had given him a certain amount of protection, which was far more protection than she'd had and he'd used the buckle end to flay her skin.

Finished, Amy stood back, breathing deeply and studied the result. She hadn't used half as much force as he had, the marks barely red and the skin not even broken compared to the mashed flesh he had left behind. But she was happy with the result even though she wasn't done with him yet. She fed the belt back through the loops then shoved her arms under Rico's body and turned him back over. Her skin crawled at the feel of his flesh but she forced the sensation from her mind.

Rico's face was awash with tears and looked agonized. 'Do you remember what comes next?' asked Amy. The muffled groan sounded like a plea as wild eyes rolled around his sockets. Amy strode across the room and searched for the knife, finding it behind a sofa. She grasped it by using the corner of her gi top to prevent fingerprints. As she moved back to Rico she waved the implement in front of his eyes. She hesitated then waved it again. Damn it but he needed to feel the fear so he understood just how much he had hurt her. 'Not the same one but just as long and just as sharp which means it will do just as much damage. Say goodbye to your manhood.'

'What the hell?' Jon yelled. 'You can't do that to a man?'

Amy spun around. 'The only man in this room is you. That,' she pointed towards Rico, 'is nothing but a psychopathic, imbecilic excuse for a human being. I gave you a hint about what he did to me - well he used a knife similar to this.' Amy spat the words out as she lifted the knife up high. 'You have no idea how much he hurt me, no idea how I almost bled to death, no idea the pain I went through, no idea the terror I went through. Now, you tell me he doesn't deserve the same.' She felt all her old anger, pain and humiliation surge and could feel herself shaking.

'You'll go to gaol, Amy,' Jon pleaded.

'Do you think I care?' Amy screeched. 'You, of all people must know what it is like to feel so hopeless because you can't have what you so much want deep in your heart. You want marriage and a family as desperately as I. You understand the emotional void, the pain, the need.' She felt tears well but fought them back as she turned away and knelt by Rico's hips and placed the edge of the knife on his flaccid manhood.

'You destroyed me, you slimy bastard.' She ran the knife up and down. She was careful not to penetrate the skin but the intent was on making him feel the sharp edge and believe she was cutting. The point of the knife pressed in. Rico was rigid appearing to be too afraid to move.

'Amy, don't,' Jon yelled seconds before the front door flew open with a resounding bang as it bounced off the wall.

'What the hell?'

'James stop her, you can't let her,' called Jon.

'From where I'm standing it seems Amy is the one with the weapon and she looks as mad as an angry tiger snake.'

With his voice growing louder as he spoke Amy knew he was nearing her so she stilled, holding the knifepoint steady and maintaining the pressure - yet she knew she wouldn't go ahead. She couldn't go ahead. It wasn't in her to cause the same damage Rico had. Somehow she felt a surge of relief that James had arrived.

'You don't want to do that, Amy.' James knelt beside her.

'I need him to understand what terror feels like.' she replied slowly, pausing between each word. In one sense she wanted to really hurt him but then again she would never lower herself to mete out the same level of brutality that Rico had but it gave her a tiny bit of comfort to know that Rico had felt some level of fear. Maybe now he understood.

James laid a hand on hers and wrapped his fingers around her clenched fist but didn't force her hand away. 'But you won't because the scumbag isn't worth it. You told me that when you had the opportunity to put a carving knife through his ribs but didn't. He's not worth going to gaol for and you are a much better person than he could ever hope to be. Give me the knife.'

The gentleness of both his voice and touch eased Amy's anger. She lifted her hand and passed the hilt of the knife into James's much bigger palm. 'He said he was going to rape me in front of Jon.'

Swapping the knife to his other hand, James slid his arm around Amy's shoulder then eased her to a standing position, tightening his hold when Amy stumbled. Her legs felt boneless. A tremor started up around her knees then wound around and around all the way up her body. In some vague mist she heard James ask his brother, 'Is this true?'

'Yes, then I'm sure he was going to kill us both, even though he told me he only wanted to talk to Amy. How about getting me out of here?' was all Amy heard Jon say before a grey mist washed over her eyes and she felt as though she was falling. Somewhere in the background she felt her legs being lifted from the ground then she was flying. She heard a rumble against her ear then lucidity began clearing her senses and she heard the same voice say, 'She's in shock.'

Next thing Amy was aware of was lying on the couch with something cold against her forehead. As her eyes focussed, James came into view.

'You fainted,' he said with a tender smile on his face. 'Are you okay? I think my brother is a little fed up with being bound to a chair.'

'I'm fine.' Amy waved him away then watched as James released Jon from his bonds. Jon staggered as he stood then shook his limbs as though to get the blood flowing again. It was only then that Amy noticed a large patch of blood on Jon's shirt.

'Oh, God, he stabbed you!' she called as she attempted to stand. Another wave of dizziness forced her back onto the sofa.

Chapter Twenty-One

'It's only a flesh wound. He caught me on the side when I tackled him. I think it might be a good idea to call the police.'

'Already done,' interrupted James. 'I heard the commotion from outside, took a peek through the window then called them. They should be here very soon. Let's get a look at that wound.' James lifted his brother's shirt. The action must have yanked the crust from the already forming scab for fresh blood began running from a vicious looking gash. The moment Amy saw it she pushed up from the sofa, ignored the new wave of giddiness and stalked over to Rico.

'You cold-blooded bastard,' she hissed moments before she lifted her leg and stomped on his crotch, not caring a damn how much damage she did and ignoring his yells of agony. The only reason she ceased kicking was because she was grabbed around the waist and dragged back across the room then dumped onto the sofa.

'Enough, Amy!' James yelled then softened his voice. 'Jon is going to be all right. It looks nasty but he was correct, it is only a flesh wound and probably won't even need stitches. Now calm down.' To ensure she did just that, he pressed both hands onto her shoulders keeping her pinned in the seat.

Breathing hard and feeling furious, Amy stared into his face. She knew she shouldn't have reacted so viciously but when visions of Rico's attack on her flashed through her memory, something inside her snapped. 'Rico had no right to harm Jon,' Amy panted. 'Jon had nothing to do with this. I warned you that he would hurt everyone who helped me, which reminds me,' she took a last shuddering breath then closed her eyes and willed her racing heart to calm, taking time to ease her breathing.

'Reminds you of what?'

Amy forced her eyes open. 'I think I know where he buried Sally and probably Sergeant Simpson. I need a map book of New South Wales, the environs of Sydney in particular.'

'How?' Was all James managed to get out before Amy continued.

'Something I remembered from the emails he sent me when he was in gaol.' Amy pointed to the contortioned body on the floor noticing that the tape over Rico's mouth had half peeled away, which was why she'd heard him scream out. She felt suddenly nauseous that she had acted in anger. Rico's eyes were closed and he looked very still. 'Is he dead?' Amy asked. 'God, I hope so.'

James jerked around then sprang to his feet. 'I hope not,' he mumbled as he rushed over to Rico, squatted on his haunches then felt for a pulse and put the side of his face near Rico's nose to feel for breath. As he rose he glanced at Rico's genital area before turning to look at Amy.

'He's alive but passed out - probably from excruciating pain. You've done a fair bit of damage. Even my eyes were watering from the pain you inflicted.'

'And mine,' said Jon as he joined James and inspected the damage. 'Good grief! The poor bastard.'

Before Amy had a chance to get up to see for her self, two uniformed police officers rushed through the still open door with guns drawn.

For Amy, the next few hours were a mind-numbing whirl of activity and questions with James taking charge and preventing her from saying anything that might incriminate her. He'd led Jon with leading questions intimating Rico the culprit in everything. The fact that Rico was half naked was put down to his preparing to rape Amy. His scrotal injuries were explained away as Amy's petrified defence as she fought him off. Much to her chagrin, James relayed some of the gory details of injuries from five years ago to give credence and explanations as to why Amy reacted in such a frenzied manner.

By the time the paramedics had tended Jon's injuries by cleansing and taping, taken Rico away for surgery on his mashed manhood and the police had completed their painstaking investigations, Amy felt completely exhausted. Much of the time she had remained sitting on the sofa, James daring her with one of his domineering supercilious glares whenever she made to get up. Every time she had opened her mouth to offer opinions into the discussions he had said just one word 'Amy!' but with such an intonation that Amy had simply shut her mouth and dropped her eyes. He could be such an intimidating bully she kept thinking while at the same time praying he was on her side if this ever went to court and she had to defend herself against charges of assault occasioning bodily harm: for she was as guilty as hell about causing bodily harm. She'd peeked at Rico's prostrate form as she passed him on the way to the toilet after pleading desperation and James had accompanied her all the way. Rico's private parts were a mass of dark blue split skin surrounded by dark red encrustations. Amy knew she should have felt remorse but instead she had grinned at the sight and deep inside she felt vindicated. His injuries were nothing compared to what he had done to her and most important – he had felt the fear.

The only stumbling block had been when Rico had been turned over and there had been a deathly silence as those near him had stared at his back. Even though she had fought madly to prevent it, she knew James had noticed her rising blush when he'd lifted his eyes to look at her. He at least understood the meaning of the thirteen stripes. An equalling telling silence had ensued when a paramedic asked what had happened to cause the welts. James and Jon had simply shrugged their shoulders in ignorance and Amy had followed suit, releasing a held breath when nothing else was said. Everyone had assumed that her own bruises, that were now glaringly obvious, had come from Rico. Amy said nothing: that way she wasn't telling lies - let them assume what they liked. She'd worry about consequences for her actions if or when, Rico complained. By then she hoped to be out of the country with a new identity.

At the sound of the door closing on the last departing humans, Amy forced open eyes that had a strong inclination to stay shut. She felt both emotional and physical exhaustion and was aware of every single one of her smarting and aching bruises. Both Jon and James were staring at her.

'How are you feeling?' Jon asked.

'Like I'm underneath the iron tracks of an enormous army tank and it is running backwards and forwards over my body. Right now I just want to sink into oblivion. What time is it?'

James peered at the watch on his wrist. 'Almost two.'

Amy shot upright, groaning at the protesting muscles. 'In the morning?' she squeaked.

'I think we could all do with some sleep,' said Jon. 'I'm going to have a quick shower to clean off this gunge.' He pointed to the dark stains on the shirt hanging loose over grey suit trousers that had a similar, almost black blotch.

'I feel so bad about you getting hurt.' Amy rose and lifted the shirt to peer at the plastered skin.

'It was my fault. Rico didn't go for me.' Jon tugged the corner of his shirt back and let it drop. 'In fact he assured me he didn't want to hurt me, and wouldn't if I agreed to be tied up.'

Stepping forward, Amy brushed the pad of her forefinger over the swellings on his face. 'Then how did you get these?'

'I didn't say I gave in gracefully.' His grin was sheepish. 'I didn't trust the man's word. Later, he claimed he only wanted to talk to you, Amy. He needed to clear the air with you and warn you about his father.'

'Pardon!' Amy fell back onto the sofa, unable to believe what she had heard.

'Hell, I was tied up for two hours waiting for you to come home. We had quite a long chat. He's still in love with you.'

'What?' The word exploded from Amy's mouth then she twisted to stare at James when he echoed the sound a split second after.

Searching for a chair, Jon was about to sit in the one he'd been tied to, changed his mind and crossed the room to settle in a single lounge chair. He groaned as he sat.

'The way Rico spoke about you I believed him when he said you were the love of his life. He was almost in tears when he detailed your wedding night. It appears his father got him hooked on steroids to make him look more masculine but the drugs interfered with his libido.'

As James perched next to Amy he gave her a knowing glance. She understood what his raised eyebrow meant. Maybe this was the reason Rico had never pushed the physical aspect of their relationship. There was a twinge of guilt as she turned back to Jon.

'He took two of those male sex enhancing pills during the reception to ensure he could have an erection and it appears they reacted with the steroids. He snapped into an uncontrollable rage and says he went berserk. When he realised what he'd done he went to get his car out of the parking lot to take you to hospital but when he rushed back to the room you had disappeared. He searched for you for several days.'

Amy felt faint. She flopped back against the leather, her mind feeling as though it was spinning in a giant spin drier. Images of her coming around, staggering to the bathroom to wash away flowing blood then holding a towel pressed against her genital area while she stumbled along the corridor banging on doors until someone let her in, skittered through her brain. 'I don't believe this.' She glanced at James. 'Could it be true?'

'Possible. Steroids can do that. I've heard of the rages. Was he on steroids?'

'I didn't know then, but it was a claim at the trial. I didn't believe him then but seeing him now, with more natural muscle build, I'd guess it was true. Looking back, his build then was too bulky to be natural but I knew no better. Why would I even think things like that?' She swept a hand across her eyes as though to clear her mind. 'But why now; why was he searching for me?'

'He wanted to talk to you, explain what happened. Says he doesn't regret the time in gaol because he deserved it for hurting you. But he wanted to clear things with you. And to warn you about his father, who apparently wants you dead and Rico was supposed to carry out the deed. It seems his father thinks you have some vital paper work.'

James laughed: a deprecating snort. 'Vital is a good word but vitally incriminating is much better. Rico's father is one nasty mobster.'

'You had the file?' asked Jon in disbelief.

'Amy didn't know she had it. It was in another file into which Amy stored some papers. There's something else that has me confused. Amy, you said that Rico sent you threatening emails from gaol.'

Amy sat forward. 'Yes.'

'Inmates don't have access to email.'

'But… they had his name at the bottom.'

'Typed. Anyone can type a name.'

'You think someone else sent them?' Unable to sit still a moment longer, Amy rose and then began prowling to ease the agitation building up inside her. Could she have been so wrong? Had Rico intended taking her to hospital? Then why was he searching for her so avidly at all the emergency departments?

'His father, maybe,' said Jon, bringing Amy's thoughts back to the present.

'More probable than Rico,' said James, 'especially if Amy was the cause of his son going to gaol. Then there is Sally Bowers.'

Amy paused mid-stride and swung around to face James. 'Sally?'

'You said she disappeared one week after Rico was sent to gaol. If he was incarcerated then he couldn't have been responsible for her disappearance. Couldn't have killed or buried her.'

'Is this Sally a lawyer?' asked Jon.

Amy twisted a half circle and stared at him. What did he know about Sally? 'Yes.'

'According to Rico, his father had her killed, and some Sergeant. I don't recall Rico giving me a name.'

'Far out,' said Amy as she plopped back into the seat.

'Which reminds me,' said James, 'You think you know where they might be buried.'

'Maybe, maybe not, but something jolted a memory tonight. Rico took me to a forested area north of Sydney once. It was a place he loved exploring as a child. I think they lived nearby when he was growing up. His father had built a cabin in some clearing. They might even have owned the land or even still do. I'm not sure. But I think I can locate it on a map. Forestville I think it was. Forest – wood, they mean the same so it could have been a hint in that rhyme I was sent.'

James stood then held out a hand to Amy. 'Let's worry about that after we've had a few hours sleep. You look ready to collapse.'

'I feel numb with exhaustion and confusion but doubt my mind will rest long enough for me to sleep. You must be just as tired.'

James pulled her upright. 'I am.' He turned to his brother. 'Is there somewhere I can crash for a few hours? I'd rather stay here in case Giovannazzo senior has any cronies on Amy's tail.'

'That's all I need to know,' whispered Amy, her voice dripping with sarcasm.

'Which reminds me,' said Jon, 'according to Rico, the guy arrested breaking into your place is a hired killer Rico's father has used on more than one occasion.'

There was a heavy silence during which Amy could do no more than gape at Jon. 'He was going to kill me?' she finally squeaked after finding her breath.

'But he didn't,' said James as he swung an arm around her shoulders and gave a gentle squeeze. 'We were ahead of him and now you are going to bed. Jon and I are both here to protect you for tonight. Rico is in hospital under guard, his father is still in Sydney, his hired gun is being held and the two officers sent over are under constant surveillance. Local police are keeping an eye on both your and my places, which tells me Rico was the only one who knew you were here. It's my guess it was him, who followed us the other night while the hired gun was watching my place, waiting for us to return. It would explain the two entirely different number plates and car colours.' James chucked Amy under the chin. 'I have a feeling Rico was telling Jon the truth and was protecting you. Maybe he still does care for you.'

'Why didn't he tell me?' At the mystified looks on both men Amy added, 'You know, earlier tonight, or when he grabbed me at work.'

'You hardly gave him a chance this evening,' said Jon as he stood the other side of her. 'You gagged him.' Amy couldn't miss the broad wink Jon bestowed upon James. 'I'd be careful of our Amy. She's lethal with her feet. Double black belt in karate.'

Before she could say a thing, Jon headed for the bathroom, laughing then calling over his shoulder a moment before he shut the door. 'The bed is made up in the other spare room. See you both in the morning.'

'Black belts, eh?' mused James as he feigned escaping from her reach by zigzagging backwards down the passage with his arms jousting until he disappeared into the room next to hers, leaving Amy standing in the passage, her mind swirling.

Chapter Twenty-Two

Amy hadn't expected to sleep but when she glanced at her watch upon waking the next morning and saw how late it was, she figured her body had been more exhausted than her brain. A quick shower cleared away remaining fuzziness but she lingered over towelling her body dry, inspecting the range of bruises inflicted by the Sensai. When she'd said no holds barred, she hadn't expected him to take her at her word so literally. While she dressed and completed her ablutions she forced her body to undertake stretching and limbering exercises, wincing at knotted muscles where impact had left blue smudges.

The murmur of voices as she tossed her nightclothes on the unmade bed surprised Amy. She had presumed both men would have already spent a couple of hours at work. Then she wondered if maybe the police were back asking more questions. But there were only James and Jon hunched over something on the table when she stepped into the kitchen. Both men glanced up.

'Morning, sleepyhead,' said James as he rose from his chair and pulled out another for her.

'Morning. What are you two doing here? Aren't you supposed to be at work?'

'We both took the day off. Coffee?' asked Jon as he also rose. His injured face looked worse; the bruises were at their height and the cuts an angry red. Without waiting for her response, he poured dark liquid into a mug, placed it in front of Amy and moved a carton of milk within her reach then settled back into his chair, winking as he indicated for her to add her own milk.

James slid a book in front of her eyes as Amy lifted the mug. His finger pointed to a spot. Glancing down, Amy saw it was a map.

'Forestville. Is this the place?'

Amy studied the page then nodded. 'I think so, yes.'

'Good, I've already rung the Inspector they've put in charge of this investigation. If the Federal Sergeant is buried there, the ground will be freshly disturbed. First they're going to search land ownership records to see if they can nail down the exact position.'

A tingle of unease crept along Amy's nerve endings. 'What investigation?'

'Ah,' was all James said as he dragged the book back then slammed it shut.

'Such a small word,' said Amy as she caught James's eye, 'but coming from you it has such a huge meaning. What investigation?'

James took his time about sitting by grasping the chair, carefully lifting it and resetting it on all four legs before slowly lowering his body. It was obvious he was stalling. Amy was about to say something to break the agonising silence when James glanced at her. 'As soon as I handed all your papers to the Commissioner, he set the ball rolling. Officers from several states have been working non-stop investigating and gathering information. This is enormous and is going to cause an almighty ruckus right across the country. It appears a lot of the people on that list have been suspects for many years but they've never been able to prove anything. That file has been the key to unravelling an entire network of underworld dealings.'

Completely taken aback, Amy could do nothing other than stare as the impact of James's words hit.

'No wonder they were after Amy.'

Amy swung her head to look at Jon then found her voice. 'But why now? Why wait five years?'

'Maybe they didn't know the file was missing until Rico got out of gaol. I mean, nothing has happened. The police haven't been asking questions and since quite a few of the listed names work in legal entities, probably as snoops, and there haven't been any rumblings of investigation, they didn't suspect the file was missing. But I'm speculating,' said James. 'Let's go out for lunch then we've been asked to spend a couple of hours at Police Headquarters.'

The last was said so quietly the hairs on the back of Amy's neck rose. She searched James's face for a clue, any clue as to why they were needed at the headquarters. Then she remembered Rico. Had he made a complaint? Was she about to be arrested?

'Rico?' she managed to force out.

'Is being kept under sedation. He was operated on to repair the damage. He lost one testicle, has severe bruising to the other and maybe can't have children. But they won't know about his fertility until they can run tests later on down the track. But I suspect he'll be going back to gaol for quite some time so his ability to reproduce is going to be immaterial.'

She didn't know why she suddenly felt guilty, but remorse swamped Amy. 'I feel guilty. Am I going to be arrested?' She dared a peek at James.

'No, Rico has said nothing since he's still comatose and if what Jon said last night is true and Rico still has feelings for you, I don't think he will. No, today is just tying up loose ends about your past and about these past few days.'

Amy brushed her hand through her hair. 'Few days! It feels like forever.' She counted on her fingers. 'This is the sixth day.' She glanced at both men. 'I can't believe I only met you two six days ago. I know you both better than I know the people I've been working with for the past five years.' She shook her head in disbelief. 'Amazing.'

'It's been quite a week,' said James as he patted Amy's clenched hand then pushed his chair back. 'You must be starving, let's go and eat.'

The rest of the day passed in a blur of activity. There were questions after questions and much embarrassment as Amy related her past dealings with the Giovannazzo family. After a take-away evening meal eaten in Jon's lounge-room, Amy gathered together her belongings and returned home with James.

Before Jon shut her in the passenger side of James's car, he squatted at her side. 'Are you still leaving on Thursday?'

'Yes, if the police say I can go.'

'Then how about you both join me for a farewell dinner tomorrow night?' His face reddened. 'There's someone I want you to meet before you go.' He lifted his shuttered eyelids and a soft smile spread across his face.

'You rang Renee?' Amy squealed then flung her arms around Jon's neck almost knocking him onto his backside.

Jon laughed as he struggled to maintain his balance. 'You were right. She's agreed to give me another chance. I told her all you said and she laughed then yelled, "alleluia".'

Amy swung her legs out of the car then wrapped her arms around Jon's neck again before planting a kiss on his cheek. 'I'm so happy for you and I'd love to meet her. If James won't come to dinner then I'll come by myself. Wow!' Amy felt overjoyed as she folded her body back into the car and slung the seatbelt into place.

'We'll both be there. Ring me tomorrow with a time and place,' interrupted James as he leant across the steering wheel and peered out. 'I'm proud of you, Jon and not just for the Renee thing. You put your life on the line last night for Amy. And I'm going to make sure Amy gets on her flight.' James started up the engine.

'Thank you,' mumbled Jon as he stood and slammed the door shut. There was a hitch in his voice giving Amy the impression he was overwhelmed by his brother's accolade.

She waited until they were driving away before speaking. 'Jon was touched by what you said. I think it meant a lot to him.'

'I meant it.'

'I think he knows that. He looks up to you.' She couldn't help the grin she knew was plastered across her face. 'I'm so happy for him. I hope it works out.' She poked James in the ribs. 'All we have to do now is find the right woman for you.'

James laughed. 'And the right man for you.' Then he sobered and took his eyes off the road, glancing in Amy's direction.

'What?' She didn't know what it was but there was something about that glance, about the ensuing silence that niggled away.

'I want to make a suggestion.'

There was a lengthy pause, sending more vibes of unease along Amy's nerves. 'For heaven's sake, spill it out.'

'I take the entire month of May off for my annual holidays. This year I have plans to travel. Angie and I are going to meet in Paris for a week to catch up. I miss having her around.'

'That's wonderful.' But Amy knew there was more coming by the tension emanating from James. She wasn't sure she was going to like this so threw in a question. 'I'm surprised you felt comfortable about her travelling alone. She's only what – seventeen?'

'Eighteen. Her birthday is early January. But she's a very mature eighteen and she is travelling with two girlfriends. She wasn't even a teenager when her mother first became ill. Angie grew up and matured very quickly. She and Jason carried out a lot of the chores when Glenda was too ill to do anything. They both washed, ironed, cleaned, shopped, and cooked. You name it they did it. Plus Angie took on a lot of the caring for her mother's more intimate needs when I wasn't home. The kids did much more than kids their age should have to but they never begrudged a moment. I tried to get in-home and nursing help but the kids fought it, saying they wanted the family to stay a family.'

'You must be proud of them.'

'Immensely. What I would have had to pay helpers, I put into bank accounts for Angie and Jas for them to spend or save, as they wanted. Angie chose to save for this year off plus she knows I'll fund any shortfall but she's a frugal girl so I doubt I'll have to. Jason has invested his money for the future. He thought about travelling but wanted to get his degree first. Angie emails me almost every day.'

'But you must worry about her.'

'Yes and no. She's a sensible person as are her two friends but she's my daughter. I worry as any normal parent worries. So far they haven't had any close calls or found themselves in scary situations. They are sticking to Europe and staying away from any touchy areas. I trust them.'

'I'm looking forward to be able to do the same.' Amy sighed. The thought of being able to explore the world without having to constantly look over her shoulder was only just really hitting home. 'Do you think I will be free of the mafia?'

James glanced at her then pulled up at a red light. 'If all goes to plan, yes, although I'm not sure we should call them Mafia. Criminal – definitely, and probably family-run but the Mafia isn't as strong as it used to be.'

Amy stared back. How come James can say so little and yet his few words have so many meanings? 'What plans?'

'Ah!'

'Whenever you use that word I now know that it means heaps. Please explain?' She had to wait while James eased through the intersection and was free of traffic congestion.

'I've been told that the authorities in each state are planning a co-ordinated mass arrest of all the people named on those papers you've had hidden away for five years.'

'When? And I didn't know I had the flipping papers.'

'As soon as they've located each person.'

'But will I be needed to testify?'

'You won't be here and Amy Masters won't exist. That's why you were grilled so thoroughly today.'

Amy twisted her body around. 'You knew all this. Did you plan today?'

The grin on James's face gave him away. 'I made a few suggestions.'

'Bastard,' Amy muttered under her breath causing James to laugh.

'It frees you to travel, which is what I wanted to talk to you about.' When James pulled into the parking area of a children's playground and turned off the engine, a sensation of unease snaked down Amy's spine.

'Am I going to like this?'

James twisted his upper body around to face her. 'Maybe, maybe not but I hope so. I was wondering if, after spending a week with Angie, I could catch up with you.'

As her heart began shooting out a surge of adrenaline, Amy wondered what it took for a healthy heart to go into arrest. 'Catch up as in…?'

'Catch up as in spend the remainder of my time exploring wherever you happen to be – with you.' He frowned. 'Hell, I don't know how to explain this but you've touched me here.' When he thumped the left side of his chest Amy felt shocked. Did he have feelings for her above friendship?

'I just thought that maybe we could spend a few weeks together getting to know each other a bit better without all this,' He waved his hand around in all directions, 'this turmoil of the past week. See how we connect under normal circumstances. Hell, Amy, I like you – a lot.'

She smiled at the sudden rising pinkness of his neck. She placed a hand on his forearm and gave it a squeeze. 'I like you too. Since… you know… I've never been able to trust a man but I trust you and that's saying something. So yes, I'd love to explore with you.' Feeling an acute embarrassment, she added, 'I can't believe I just said that. Can we go?'

James released a shout of laughter as he started the engine again.

Chapter Twenty-Three

Even though she felt weary, Amy also felt excited as she carefully swiped the angled end of a coral lip-gloss across her upper lip. Smacking her lips together to evenly spread the colour across her mouth, she stood back from the mirror to study her reflection. She cocked her head from side-to-side to see as much of her hair as possible. Visiting the hairdresser had been just one of the places she'd been during the day. Her layered black hair now had a professional touch especially since she'd had her hair blown dry to give it a bit more body for this special night. Wearing a new blue two-piece flowing outfit she decided to not wear any contact lenses. The deep blue slinky fabric was not only easy to pack without wrinkling but it deepened the colour of her eyes. She felt good. Better than she'd felt in a long time.

As she slid her feet into a pair of low-heeled slinky sandals, she cast her mind back. When was the last time she'd felt this carefree and happy? The day she married Rico. Far out, why did that name creep into her mind? Tonight was a happy night. Forcing Rico's picture away, Amy grabbed another new purchase - a small evening bag and slid the tube of gloss inside. She glanced around the room at the neat piles all ready to be crammed into a brand spanking new suitcase. After collecting her new travelling papers, her quick shopping spree had been productive but now that she didn't have the need to be ready to flee, she'd allowed James to talk her into taking with her more than she'd intended.

She paused at the doorway and took a final peek at her dress. James had insisted she purchase something pretty and feminine for tonight saying she'd need at least one really nice outfit whilst overseas. She'd argued the point insisting practical was better for travel. He'd argued back intimating that when he took her to fancy places so they could get to know one another better, he'd be wearing a suit to impress her. She'd hidden her face to hide her blush but took the hint and was happy with the result. But would James like it?

The wolf whistle as she entered the lounge gave her an immediate answer. She paused at the threshold of the room and glanced up. Amy had seen him in a suit before but this lighter grey with a charcoal shirt open at the neck gave James a different aura. Gone was the crusty lawyer and in his place stood one heck of a good-looking man. He looked finer, taller.

'You look amazing,' James said as he crossed the room.

'So do you.' Feeling suddenly shy, Amy didn't know what to do so she just stood there.

'You chose well.' He must have sensed her unease for he simply slid a hand behind her back and gently ushered her towards the garage, switching off lights and locking doors as he went.

Amy felt relieved and even more so as they drove in relative silence listening to light classical music from the CD player, with only an occasional exchange of idle chitchat. But even so she was acutely aware of the man beside her. His revelation the day before caused her to see him in a different light – a potential romantic interest. She'd been exploring her feelings for James all day. Yes, she liked him, probably more than she wanted to admit. She trusted him and felt that was the most important thing – well for her it was. But did she feel this new awareness just because of circumstances and because James happened to be in the right place at the right time? Would her feelings change during the following couple of months? Maybe she should socialise between now and May, meet a few men, go out on dates. Her cousins in Scotland would surely introduce her to a few people.

'What are you thinking?'

Amy jolted upright at the sudden intrusion on her thoughts. 'Pardon?'

'You were sighing then smiling then sighing some more. I wondered what you were thinking about.' James pulled into the parking lot of a well-known South Perth restaurant.

Amy straightened and looked around. She hadn't even been aware of them crossing the river. 'Sorry, I was just thinking about things in general. It's been quite a week.'

She knew by his soft chuckle that he didn't believe a word but there was no way she was going to reveal her true thoughts. No way was she ready for that type of conversation.

'Have you met Renee before?' she asked as a way of diverting more personal questions.

James rounded the front of the car then opened Amy's door. 'Yes, she's a lovely lady. I'd always thought she and Jon were a good match and was surprised when they parted company but I had no idea why. Jon never gave the real reason.'

'He loves her and she must have feelings for him if she's agreed to try again. I hope so.' Amy noticed she was acutely aware of James's hand in the small of her back as he guided her inside. Never before had a man shown her such chivalry, not even… far out, she had to stop allowing Rico into her mind, especially when she was with another man and considering him as a potential romantic interest. Now where did that thought come from? Romance? Maybe the ten weeks apart was an excellent idea to give them both an opportunity to see how they felt once they were on opposite sides of the world.

As they were shown to their table, Jon stood, blocking off Amy's view of Renee. 'James, you remember Renee, Amy this is Renee.'

As Jon stepped aside, Amy was taken by a vivacious smile under a mop of tight dark brown curls. Since Renee was seated, Amy couldn't make out her height but she appeared to be curvaceous, her female assets hidden under a demure dress in a swirl of soft greens.

'Renee, I'm very happy to meet you.' Amy nodded to the woman since there was no offer of a hand. At a nudge in her side, she glanced at James who was holding out the chair opposite Renee. Amy sank into the lush seat, murmuring her thanks as James eased the chair back in as she sat.

Conversation was stilted and polite until after meal orders were taken. Amy wasn't sure who was feeling the most uptight. It wasn't until she caught Jon in the act of reaching over to settle Renee's glass a little closer to her plate that Amy dared quit being so formal. She kicked Jon under the table then indicated with a nod of her head in the direction of the glass.

Jon's responsive laughter broke the atmosphere. 'Sorry, I have to quit stifling.' He grinned at his partner as he slapped his own hand in admonition.

Renee caught Amy's eye. 'Jon related your conversation. You are a smart lady.'

'You should have told him what he was doing that upset you.'

'I know, but I didn't know how. I didn't want to hurt his feelings.'

Amy felt relieved when Jon swept his arm around Renee's shoulders and gave her a hug. 'No more being afraid to say what you are thinking. I'm a big boy. I can handle anything you throw at me.' He lifted Renee's hand and planted a kiss on the back.

Then Amy felt her own hand being squeezed. She peeked at James from the corner of her eye and caught his small nod, reading it as approval but was more than thankful when her hand was immediately released. James wasn't pushing things.

After that, the evening was perfect in Amy's eyes. Once everyone felt comfortable, the conversation was bright with Renee's bubbly personality coming to the fore. Amy could see why Jon was taken with her. They'd just ordered coffee when Renee stood and excused herself. Wanting to talk to her, Amy followed suit, running a couple of steps to catch her up. 'Renee?'

Renee paused and waited. 'I can never thank you enough,' she said as they continued on together.

'He loves you.'

Renee stopped and stood still just inside the restroom door. 'Then why did he suggest we split up?'

Amy eased past Renee, then continued into a cubicle and shut the door. 'Because you said you couldn't live with him,' she called over the partition. 'He let you go because he thought you would be happier with someone else.'

'That doesn't make sense,' Renee called back.

'Yes it does. He loved you enough to want your happiness over his. You being happy was the most important thing to him.' There was a deathly silence followed by a tearing of paper and the blowing of a nose.

'I'll kill him! Six months of misery! The stupid fool!'

Amy grinned at the sudden outburst from Renee. It told her what she wanted to know. Renee loved Jon as much as he loved her. The moment the toilet flushed, Amy heard the door swing open and rebound off the wall. The tap turned on too hard was followed by a hushed curse. Renee sounded mad. Amy joined her.

'That stupid man!' Renee said to her image in the mirror as she wiped down the splashes of water with a paper towel then caught Amy's grinning reflection.

'I'm so glad you love him,' said Amy. 'He's a good honest man and is dying for a family he can love. If he's anything like his brother he will never let you down.'

Amy couldn't help grinning at the astonished expression on Renee's face. 'Go out there and tell him how you feel about him.'

'You think?' Renee looked hesitant.

'From what I can gather, you're not the only one who has been miserable for the past six months.'

'Really!'

Amy laughed. 'Yes, really! Now go.' Amy followed but kept pace. She didn't want to miss this for anything.

Renee barged out of the small room and stormed down the passage then kept up the rapid pace until she neared their table. 'Jonathan Ward,' she called, 'you are an imbecile.'

Amy laughed as the entire restaurant turned to watch the impending fracas. Poor Jon looked very afraid.

'You have given me six months of absolute misery, for what?' The voice hadn't dropped a single decibel.

Amy stopped walking a couple of metres from the table, amused at the dawning realisation on Jon's face.

'I love you, you great oaf!' Renee finally blurted out moments before she burst into tears.

Then Amy felt the rush of her own tears as Jon shot upwards and swept his arms around Renee then settled his chin on her head as they swayed to and from in a tight embrace. His eyes were closed but he had the biggest smile Amy had ever seen.

When they got to the kissing stage and the patrons erupted into applause, Amy slunk back into her seat and raised her eyebrows at James.

He laughed then leaned close. 'I think it's time we left these two alone. What did you say to her?'

Amy picked up her bag and stood as James pulled her chair out. 'Nothing but the truth after I figured out she was in love with him.' She pulled free from where James had a grip on her elbow and tapped Jon on the shoulder. 'Maybe you two should go home. We're leaving you in peace.'

Jon grabbed her as she turned to leave. Then she felt her breath whoosh from her lungs and her mouth stuffed with shirt when he grasped her against his body. 'Thank you, Amy.'

'Just don't stuff it up and make sure you send me a wedding invitation via James.' She laughed as she peeled away and headed for the door.

She waited outside while James paid the bill and he'd only just stepped outside when he paused and reached into his shirt pocket and withdrew his mobile phone. She'd not heard it ring but he opened it up and began speaking. When she heard him say, 'Rico!' she ceased walking and turned to face James, her heart thundering. She wanted to follow as James walked away but it appeared obvious the conversation was to be private with James turning his back on her. Instead she headed towards the car and waited by the closed door. By the time James closed his phone she was on tenterhooks.

'That was Rico. He wants to see me.' James opened her door.

'Why?' Amy slid into the seat then waited until James climbed in the other side. Somehow her heart had shot into her throat causing her breath to stutter.

'He says he wants to give me some information to ensure his father is sent to gaol.'

'Excuse me?' Amy was staggered by the information.

'He also asked if I thought you'd agree to talk to him.'

Amy shook her head. 'No way.' She turned to face James. 'What did you tell him?'

'I said I'd ask. Why don't you think about it?'

While they drove home that was all she could think about. And for most of the night while she packed then while she repacked at sun-up. Sleep had been scant but she figured it was a good thing. She'd be able to sleep on the plane. Amy was still tossing her options around in her head while she showered and dressed. It wasn't until she sat at the table after preparing breakfast that she came to a final decision. The moment James joined her she said, 'I don't want to see him. I loved him for three months, hated him for twelve months then was terrified of him for the next four years. To me the past is past. Today is a new chapter of my life. I'm free of torment, free to let go the past and build a future as a new person. I can't mar that by visiting him. Are you going to see him?'

'Yes. He says he has information. If it means bringing an end to his father's regime then I feel it important to hear him out.'

'Then tell him I'm sorry about the other night. I didn't mean to cause so much damage. But I was scared.'

'Amy.' She felt his hand on her forearm. 'Don't torment yourself. You had a right to be so scared. I think he understands that. He said he wasn't going to press charges against you.'

Amy shot her glance up. 'He did?'

James smiled. 'He still cares for you.'

'I don't want to hear that. Let's eat. I've got a plane to catch.'

Amy was thankful James didn't pursue the conversation. Even at the airport he didn't mention Rico. Towards the time she had to go through customs she began to feel awkward. She didn't know how to say goodbye. As the final boarding call was announced she grabbed her carry-on bag and mumbled a farewell as she headed towards the gate.

A hand landed on her shoulder at the same time she heard her name. She stopped and waited, too afraid to turn around. James spun her around to face him, his hands on her upper arms to prevent her from moving.

'What's the matter?' James asked.

'Nothing.' Everything, she thought. Her emotions felt as though they were being flung around in a force five cyclone.

'Nothing, my foot, you're scared. Probably as scared as me.'

Her eyes lifted. James was scared?

'This awakening of emotions is as new to me as it is to you. All I know is that if you were staying, I'd be asking you out on a regular basis to see if what I feel for you is real: to find out if it develops into something more. Are we still catching up in May?'

'Of course.' Of that, Amy was certain.

'Good, I can't wait. But let me assure you there will be no strings attached. I want to spend time with you to see what happens. I'll never pressure you to turn our friendship into something you don't want. At the very least, I have a feeling we'll be good friends for life. If on the other hand our feelings develop into something more, well, we'll just let it evolve. Now give me a hug.'

Amy flung her arms around his waist. His words had eased her emotional conflict and she wanted the feel of his embrace lodged in her memory bank.

'May I kiss you goodbye?'

She paused, lifted her head then nodded. 'I'd like that.'

He placed his hands either side of her face, searched her eyes for a moment then settled his mouth over hers in a sweet kiss. The gentleness of his embrace touched something in her heart.

'Have fun, Amy. You deserve it. You have four weeks to catch up with your Scottish relatives then four weeks with your sister and then only another week before we catch up. And keep in contact – at least once a week otherwise I'm going to be forced to use your key to raid your bank deposit boxes and call the police.' There was a grin on his face as he gave her a final squeeze then released her.

'I'd forgotten all about those. It makes little difference now.'

'It will be an added security to keep the copies hidden away until this whole mess is cleaned up and you are back. And you will be back.' He kissed her again, this time with a different slant. It was deeper, longer, turning her insides to mush.

Fighting down a huge swell of emotions, Amy walked to the door then turned and waved. James hadn't moved but was watching her. She blew him a kiss then entered her new life, her lips still tingling and her heart beating far harder than it should. But this time, for once, it wasn't from fear.

<h1 style="text-align:center">Chapter Twenty-Four</h1>

'I swear, Dad, Amanda is gone.'

'Did you get the file?'

'She didn't have it. She said there were two suits in my house when she went to collect her belongings. They carried out a heap of files. Were they your men?'

'Don't be so damned stupid, of course not. How the hell was I supposed to know where you kept the papers? You didn't fall for her little scam did you?'

'Dad, she did not have the papers.' Rico emphasised each word.

'Where is she?'

'I told you, she's gone. She'll never be found.'

'Gone as in dead?'

'Isn't that what you wanted?'

'You don't have the gumption. You're nothing but a yellow livered fool. You don't have the balls for being a real man.' Wincing at his father's last statement, Rico immediately thought about the empty scrotum on his left side. He'd laughed when they told him they could make it look real by inserting a prothesis similar to what they used in breast enlargements.

When he heard his father yelling, Rico centred his concentration back on the phone.

'What the hell? Who are you? Get out?'

Rico stared at the phone. Who was his father talking to? He slid it back over his ear.

'You can't arrest me - I'm a judge. Let go, you fool or I'll have your job.'

Rico couldn't suppress the grin that broke out across his face at the sound of a scuffle amidst verbose swearing from his father as he heard a long list of charges being read out. Realisation hit. There was only one way the authorities could have known even half of the facts.

'You clever bitch, Amanda! Oh, God, you are so good.' He burst out laughing holding a hand to his lower abdomen to ease the pain. As he sobered he wiped tears from his eyes. 'You are so good, sweetheart. He's finally been caught.' Rico grinned then sniggered, fighting back the laughter because it hurt his injuries so much.

At a sudden knock at the door, he eased his body upright and wiped the smile from his face. This was probably the police coming to arrest him as well. Although his name wasn't anywhere on that file. He'd made sure of that. But arrest him they would. He was after all his father's son. But no way could he go back to gaol. He'd be a dead man after a bout of torture. His father would ensure his painful demise because his father would have no doubts about where the information came from.

'Come in,' he called far more confidently than he felt.

With his heart lodged somewhere in his throat, he watched the door ease open then relaxed his tense muscles when he saw the lawyer enter. Adrenaline flowed as he looked past the huge man. When no one else came in, disappointment hit. 'Amanda's not coming is she?' His innards twisted into a tight knot. The one thing he wanted most in the world, the one thing that kept him going was the hope that Amanda would give him a second chance.

'Sorry,' said James. 'She said to apologise for your injuries, she didn't mean to go so far.'

'I deserved it. Why didn't she come?'

James moved to the side of the bed and pulled out the only chair in the private room. 'She wants to keep the past in the past. She said she loved you for three months but that turned to hatred and fear; something she can't let go. She wants to start a new life as from today.'

Rico forced a smile. 'She's gone away again. That's good. My father believes I killed her so he won't ever look for her again so she'll be safe. But I've never killed anyone in my life. I could never do it. That's why I have information for you. I want my father and his cronies put away for life.' He reached over and pulled out the drawer to his bedside table.

'You almost killed Amy.'

'I know and it is my biggest regret. I didn't mean to. I loved her. Still do. She was the best thing that ever happened to me.'

'Then why?'

'Something in me snapped. I honestly don't remember what happened. All I can recall is coming out of a stupor and seeing Amanda. He brushed a hand across his eyes and down his face in an attempt to wash away the agony. 'Oh, God, I couldn't believe the mess. Then she disappeared.' Rico buried his head in his hands. A wave of nausea trembled through his gut. 'I searched everywhere for her, especially all the hospitals for I knew she needed medical attention.'

'So it wasn't because she wasn't a virgin.'

His head jerked up. 'Hell no! I knew she'd had a physical relationship with her previous two partners. Did she really think that?'

James nodded.

'Hell, I'm sorry. Please make sure she knows the truth. You do know where she is, don't you?'

James shrugged his shoulders, not committing one way or the other.

'I don't want you to tell me. Look, the only way I can think of to make amends is to give you these. I've been awake most of the night writing down as many details as I can. Offshore accounts, names, events, places and how my father was involved in each. He was the boss. Everything that happened was because my father ordered it. And there's this.' Rico shuffled through the papers and handed three folded papers to James. 'This is my final will. I want Amanda to have everything.'

'Your will?' James hesitated, the papers held between the two men.

'I need you to witness it. You're a lawyer so you should know the ropes.'

'We need two people, but why now?' James paused as though thinking. 'You're not planning anything – you know – untoward?'

Rico shook his head in negation. 'No, of course not, it's just in case. I was on the phone to my father a few minutes ago and heard him being arrested. When this stuff comes to

light in court my father will know where it came from. If
he or any of his henchmen are put in the same gaol as me,
I'm a dead man. I'm just ensuring Amanda gets my assets if
that happens.'

'We can offer you a certain amount of protection for
this information,' said James as he waved the wad of papers
in the air.

'You get back to me on any offer but in the meantime
I've asked my doctor to be the other witness. Let's get that
done first.' Rico pressed the call button then pointed to the
papers. 'Read that while we wait.'

James was only halfway through when a nurse entered.
While she fetched the doctor he scanned the remaining page
then looked up at Rico. 'You know Amy won't accept this.'

'I hope she does. Look, the Australian accounts are
legitimate money I made through investments. The offshore
accounts are, shall we say, not so legitimate but see if you
can talk Amanda into using the money for some charitable
organization if she refuses to keep it: maybe cancer research
or something to do with children. Try to explain to her
how much I hate the life I was born into but when you
are the only son of a family criminal gang boss, you either
obey instructions or you die.' He glanced at James. 'Did
you know they were going to arrest my father?'

'I knew. There are a couple of officers on guard outside
to make sure you don't escape before they arrest you.' James
waved a hand in the direction of the door. 'But from what
I've heard, you'll be in here for several days yet.'

Rico expected as much but he'd already taken steps to
ensure he wasn't going to be arrested. 'Amanda had the file
didn't she?'

'Yes, but she didn't know she had it. She gave me some
paperwork to read, her medical file, and I found it caught

up amongst her papers. Apparently she reached into a box in a cupboard in your office for a cardboard file and just shoved her paperwork in without looking. She still isn't even aware of what the file contained.'

Rico burst out laughing again then winced as his sore injuries made their presence felt. 'I knew something like that had happened. If she'd known then she would have handed the papers to the police. God, this is so funny. My father gets his comeuppance through sheer fate. Look, there's something you need to know. When I met Amanda I knew I didn't want to involve her in my father's life. I was the money man and record keeper of my father's outfit. I wasn't an action man involved in the skulduggery.'

'But you knew what was going on.'

'Hell, yes. But I didn't have much choice. No choice, in fact. I hate what my father stood for, hated the life and quite frankly hated him. It didn't matter so much when I was a single man but Amanda? Well she changed everything. I can't tell you how much I love that woman. That file she had, well that was a doctored copy of the records my father had. He knew I had a copy but I had altered my copy. He didn't know and still doesn't. I'd given it more detail and my name wasn't anywhere on it. I had intended sending my copy to the authorities while I was away on my honeymoon. I wanted a new life with Amanda without the seedy background. I wanted my father and his cohorts put away. I knew he would go down for a great deal of time. I was hoping it would all happen while I was away and then I could talk Amanda into staying away when the shit hit the fan. I had the money to set up anywhere she wanted until it was safe for me to come home.'

At that moment the doctor entered. James guided both men through the legalities of signing the will, getting Rico to add a couple of sentences here and there to ensure the document couldn't be challenged.

Once the door closed on the doctor's back, James scanned the other papers Rico had written out. His brows rose several times before he folded the sheets into three and slid them inside his coat pocket. 'I'll make sure these go to the right people. I'm glad you signed each page. How about I countersign each before I leave?'

'Is that necessary?' Rico leant back against the pillows, willing the man to hurry. Now that he knew he'd lost the love of his life for good, he wanted to begin Plan B.

'It won't take me a minute.'

Rico fought to control the agonizing pain rolling through his body as he watched James open out the papers and sign each one before he replaced them into his pocket. 'Is there anything else?' James stood and replaced the chair.

'Take care of Amanda for me.'

'I…'

'I know you care about her. I can see it in your eyes whenever her name is mentioned and I watched the way you cared for her at the barbecue. She deserves a good man like you.'

'I barely know her. We only met a week ago.'

'And I fell in love with her the first day I met her. She was my only love. I truly wish she had come today but tell her I understand. I just wanted to see her one last time, to explain, apologise and beg her forgiveness. I appreciate your time… and apologise to your brother. My intention was not to harm him. But…'

'He fought back.' James interrupted.

'Yes, but I realise he was only trying to protect Amanda. Thank you for coming but now I want to phone my mother and two sisters. I'd rather break the news to them as gently as I can. I don't think they are yet aware of my father's arrest. But then again maybe they are since both my brothers-in-law work for the bastard.'

James nodded then left. The moment he had gone, Rico removed a handful of pills he'd stolen during the night, from under his pillow and downed them, one by one, washing each down with copious water to ensure they dissolved quickly. He had no life without Amanda and no way was he going back to gaol. It had been much easier than he'd thought to break into the pharmacy on this floor and he'd ensured that he took only one pill from as many packets as he figured were strong enough to be lethal if taken in quantity. Some names he recognised while others he had a vague idea of their potency only from the poison's rating printed on the outside of each package. In combination, he prayed they worked effectively and rapidly.

To fill in the time for them to take effect, he phoned his mother who obviously hadn't yet heard of his father's arrest. He spoke at length until a heavy drowsiness dragged his eyes shut. An incredible pain gripped his innards. 'I love you, Mama,' he said before hanging up. Not wanting his body to eject the strong medication, he swallowed down the rising acid then closed his eyes and pictured Amanda during the glorious three months of their courtship as he waited for the pills to take him from the life he hated.

www.ingramcontent.com/pod-product-compliance
Lightning Source LLC
Chambersburg PA
CBHW061010120726
47910CB00006B/1849